The Beach House: Coming Home

Also by Georgia Bockoven

The Beach House:
Coming Home

GEORGIA
BOCKOVEN

WILLIAM MORROW
An Imprint of HarperCollins*Publishers*

HarperCollins
PUBLISHERS
— Since 1817 —

P.S.™ is a trademark of HarperCollins Publishers.

HarperCollins books may be purchased for educational, business, or sales promotional use. For information, please email the Special Markets Department at SPsales@harpercollins.com.

FIRST EDITION

Designed by Diahann Sturge
Title page illustration © Makkuro GL/Shutterstock, Inc.
Chapter opener illustration © EngravingFactory/Shutterstock, Inc.

Library of Congress Cataloging-in-Publication Data has been applied for.

ISBN 978-0-06-238898-8

17 18 19 20 21   LSC   10 9 8 7 6 5 4 3

For John—my best friend, the love of my life

After you've given your baby to strangers,
what do you say when someone asks
if you have children?

The Beach House:
Coming Home

Prologue

El Niño teased the California coast, promising weeks of rain, but delivering just enough to keep hope alive. For months the desperately dry earth had absorbed what little moisture could be absorbed from fog while creeks and rivers and reservoirs all but disappeared.

And then in the spring, as if she were wagging her finger in anger and frustration over the carbon that was suffocating her, Mother Nature delivered a series of storms and earthquakes no one could have predicted, not even the men and women who did such things for a living. Fierce wind and pounding rain hit the entire Monterey Bay area with breathtaking force, ripping shingles and tiles from roofs and turning them into missiles that hit the unwary with the force of a baseball bat.

As the flooding increased, neighborhoods turned into islands where residents counted on the kindness of strangers to see them through.

The earthquakes hit in a series so subtle they were felt only by people who worked the night shifts. For the observant, clues were everywhere the morning after. Vases and ceramic dogs and candlesticks shifted positions on shiny surfaces leaving thin outlines of dust. Paintings and photographs hung crooked.

In the Santa Lucia Mountains, lying east across the Salinas Valley, pines and cypress and ancient oaks had struggled for over three years to pull sustenance from soil where moisture had not reached deeper than two inches. Finally, losing their battle during the powerful storm and the nightly earthquakes, the oldest and most fragile trees cracked and fell where they stood or simply lost their tenuous hold on hillsides and tumbled into ravines.

At the beach house a hidden leak developed in the valley of the roof that separated the kitchen from the living room. Months of almost daily downpours went by and the leak remained undetected until, on a sunshine-filled morning, Grace, the young caretaker who lived next door, arrived to find the kitchen ravaged. Water-laden cupboards and granite tile fell off the wall as nails and saturated Sheetrock gave way. Slowly, a storm at a time, and an earthquake at a time, the entire back corner of the house readied itself for collapse.

Julia Lawson, the absentee owner whose love for the beach house ranked just below her love for her family, had finally put aside the kitchen design magazines she'd purchased before the remodel when her cell rang.

She listened as Grace tearfully described the damage, then reassured her that none of what happened was her fault. Even before she called her contractor, Jeremy Richmond, she made plans to fly from Virginia to Santa Cruz the next morning.

Because he'd worked on the remodel of the house before the leak, he felt compelled to handle the repairs himself, which meant shuffling an already impossibly tight work schedule.

Julia didn't share the fact that she was secretly thrilled to have an opportunity to right a wrong she felt she'd done to the house during the first renovation. She still didn't understand what had convinced her that duplicating her kitchen in Virginia was a good idea.

How could she not see that her century-old beach house was not a stainless steel and granite type of house. It was a memory. Of home. Of love. Of dreams past and present. Of family, even when that memory had nothing to do with reality, it was a part of the tapestry that made the house special.

Before she'd changed everything with her top-of-the-line appliances and sparkling countertops, it had been effortless to close her eyes and hear the sounds of mothers and daughters and sisters preparing a holiday meal. She could smell the chocolate chip cookies Joe and Maggie baked every summer to share with neighbors who stopped by on their way to the beach. And she could hear the sizzle of the vegetables on the grill that Ken prepared after their weekly visits to the farmer's market.

Ken . . .

When he died almost ten years ago, she wasn't yet thirty. She'd looked into her future and struggled to find ways to go on alone. She could immerse herself in Ken's software company or she could join other local entrepreneurs in philanthropic causes. She didn't have to look long or hard to find possibilities to feel fulfilled. She could be happy, or so she told herself, as long as she found a way to be happy alone.

What she didn't know, what she didn't discover until Ken died, was a coincidental magic that was as much a part of the beach house as morning fog. For her, it started the first time she stayed at the house without Ken. Waiting until the last minute to prepare for the summer renters, a long-standing tradition started by the couple who sold the house to Ken and continued through more than a decade of stories that unfolded month by month from June through August.

Julia finally summoned the courage to make the drive to the coast, arriving at sunset. Instead of going inside, she headed for the beach, facing her fears while trying to decide if it was time to sell the house and say a final good-bye.

The house had other plans. It greeted her arrival with a broken faucet that sent her to the cottage next door to ask for help from her longtime friend, Andrew. Instead she found a doctor who'd given up his practice to move to Santa Cruz for the summer to write medical thrillers.

For someone who'd believed finding a soul mate was a one-time thing, Julia fought falling in love with Eric. She lost. For anyone able to recognize the whispered voice of magic or the true meaning of karma, they would have no trouble hearing the beach house let out a contented sigh. For that one summer, its work was done.

A decade later the storm damage that set up the hurried trip west from her home in Virginia was only supposed to last as long as it took to go shopping with Jeremy. Once she'd chosen the new cabinets and tile and appliances, she'd be on her way east again. As often happened when she was at the beach house, she found reasons to stay. A couple of days turned into a week, and then two. Despite a longing to be with her husband and children again, she didn't want their reunion to be in Virginia. She wanted them with her in California. And not just for a summer.

While she waited for deliveries, she weeded and prepared the soil for the flower gardens. This year there would be pink bleeding hearts spilling over buttercup-yellow and crimson begonias. For the year-round resident, Anna's hummingbirds, fuchsias were a given. Penstemon, in a half dozen colors, were planted for the bees and butterflies. Tucked in wherever she could find room would be nasturtiums and poppies and whatever she found in bloom during her excursion to her favorite nursery. There was never any rhyme or reason or order to her design, just love, both given and received.

As she worked, without conscious thought, she held conversations with the people she'd loved and lost in her years at the beach house.

She told Ken she was happy, knowing it was all he'd ever wanted for her.

She told Joe and Maggie how deeply they were missed and that not a day went by she didn't purposefully say their names out loud, believing with all her heart that as long as she lived, they would live through her. As always, she told them yet another story about their beloved cat, Josi, who had moved to Virginia to live with her and Eric but had never stopped looking longingly for them to return. Josi had lived a long life, loved and cared for, tolerating the birth of two babies who had to be taught a cat's tail was not a leash. Josi left them on a stormy night, curled into Eric's side, purring her special expression of love for him with every breath until the last.

They scattered her ashes in the garden at the beach house where they knew she would find the people who had loved her first. With Josi, cats became an integral part of the folklore, appearing whenever there was a heart in need of healing or a connection that needed to be repaired.

After the new appliances were chosen and the deliveries completed, Julia rose with the sun and went for one final walk on the beach before flying back to Virginia. She sat on the log that had washed ashore decades earlier and was as much a fixture in the cove as the cliffs. A lone western gull joined her, sidestepping in her direction until it was barely an arm's distance away. It stopped and stood perfectly still as if transfixed at the broad ocean expanse.

A dozen brown pelicans surfed the updraft of a line of breaking waves while immediately below a pod of common dolphins skimmed the water on their way to feed in the deeper waters of Monterey Bay.

She looked at her watch and saw that it was time to leave for the airport. On the way back to the stairs, she found a plastic shovel, the kind that kids used to fill buckets with wet sand when they built castles.

She felt a sudden, almost overwhelming fear that her children would never know what it was like to build those castles, or see humpback whales lunge feeding. They wouldn't see rafts of otters gathered in kelp bed shelters, or an ocean alive with hundreds of dolphins. How could you love something you didn't know?

Julia turned the house keys over to Jeremy and left for the San José airport comforted by her newfound determination that she and Eric would finally have the conversation they had put off too long.

Chapter One

June

A squeaky meow snapped Melinda Campbell out of her mental drift. She shifted her position in the backseat of the cab and glanced at the purposely unnamed kitten in the pet carrier on the seat beside her. As kittens went, this one ranked near the bottom on the cuteness scale. According to everything she'd found online, at four weeks old most cat babies still had flat features and small ears. This one sported bat-like ears so large they almost touched. Her dull black fur stuck out in haphazard tufts, and her walk was more lumbering hippo than stealthy predator, the result of frostbitten paws still a week shy of being healed.

The cabdriver settled in his seat and lowered the flag on an old-fashioned taxi meter. "Don't worry," he said with a broad smile when he saw her give him a questioning look. "It's not functional. I just like the retro look and it's a great conversation starter." He chuckled. "My daughter says I was born in the wrong decade and that if she ever finds a time machine, she's going to send me back somewhere I'd fit in."

"I come from a city with a lot of cabs," Melinda said. "And I've never seen anything like it." It was the best she could do to hold up her end of the conversation.

"This your first time to the Monterey Bay area?"

"First time anywhere in California," she answered.

He shifted in his seat to make eye contact. "Look—if I'm out of bounds, just tell me, but I wouldn't feel right if I didn't say something. Are you aware that it's over forty miles from Monterey to Santa Cruz?" He handed her a laminated sheet of paper showing mileage and charges. "It would be cheaper to rent a car for an entire week than it's going to be to pay for this one trip."

"Someone else made the arrangements. Since he lives here, I assume he knows how far it is."

"Then he must have known San José airport would have been closer and cheaper." The driver shook his head and shrugged. "To each his own."

She shoved her hands under her legs to keep them still. Two days ago she would have sworn it was impossible for someone to shake as badly as she had been shaking for the past forty-eight hours. She would have been wrong. But then she'd never had so much riding on an outcome and had never been as scared or anxious as she was now.

The driver put the address she'd given him into his GPS. "You picked a good time to visit," he said. "We've been going through a drought. It finally broke a year ago and everything is green again."

"We've had floods."

"Texas?"

"Minnesota. But I've missed most of it. I've been working in Juneau, Alaska, for the past six months."

"No kidding. I always wanted to go to Alaska."

A tiny paw darted out of the carrier and tapped Melinda's leg. She untucked her hand from under her leg and put two fingers through the carrier door. The kitten rubbed her head against one and then the other.

Little more than skin and bones when Melinda found her digging through the trash at the back of her condo, the kitten hadn't impressed the people at the emergency vet clinic enough for them to make any but a cursory effort to care for her. At three to four weeks old, she was far too young to be on her own and, with so many strikes against her, including potential medical bills, unlikely to be accepted by any of the shelters. With a matter-of-fact casualness, the vet had dismissed any possibility the kitten could be saved, insisting that as emaciated and dehydrated as she was, she wouldn't have lasted another night on her own. He didn't hesitate telling Melinda that it would be a kindness to end the suffering of a cat no one would adopt anyway.

Unnoticed, while the kitten's fate was being so easily and casually discussed, she worked her way across the metal exam table, fighting to keep her balance on the slippery surface. When she reached Melinda she gave her a look that said—*you don't believe that crap, do you?*

The one sure way to get Melinda to do something was to tell her she couldn't. With a resigned sigh, she tucked the kitten between her shoulder and chin as if she were a cell phone, and tried to forget the fleas she'd seen earlier. Armed with a sheet of instructions for the care and feeding of newborn kittens, Melinda headed for her car, making a stop at the pet store for supplies before heading home.

After the kitten had stoically tolerated a flea bath and comb-out, and consumed an entire bottle of kitten formula, Melinda introduced her to the litter box. By the time she had settled on a pillow on the sofa, her head was nodding like a bobblehead doll.

Melinda made herself a cup of coffee, put two oatmeal cookies on a napkin and returned to settle on the opposite end of the sofa. The kitten crawled off her pillow, fighting for balance as she gingerly made her way across the cushions separating her and Melinda. Once there, she crawled onto Melinda's lap, made two complete circles, dropped and turned into a tiny, vibrating ball. Melinda didn't have to look to know the kitten was fast asleep.

"What happened to you?" she said softly. "Why were you out there all alone?" She gently freed a claw that had caught on her sweater. "Where is your mother?"

The question brought a lump to her throat. Mothers and babies were lost to each other all the time. No one knew that better than Melinda.

Dipping into her reservoir of determination, Melinda picked up the phone. Mentally acknowledging that she was on a fool's errand, she single-mindedly worked her way through the short list of animal rescue organizations she'd found online. It didn't take long to discover Juneau, Alaska, was a dog town. Cats need not apply.

She laid her phone on the end table and propped her feet on the ottoman. Okay, so she'd take the kitten back to Minneapolis with her. Half the people she knew at the home office owned cats, some more than one. How hard would it be to find someone who was willing to take in a cat that came with a free year's supply of food and medical care as an enticement?

With her job at Juneau DockSide Shipping ending that coming Friday and everything nonessential packed and waiting to be picked up, how much trouble could it be to have a half-pound kitten added to the mix?

The cabdriver stopped at a red light and glanced in the rearview mirror. "That a cat you have in there?"

"Not yet, but she's working on it."

He took off his cap and ran his hand through his hair. "What are her options?"

Melinda laughed for the first time in days. "It's a kitten. She had a rough beginning, and I was told she's about half the size she should be."

"We've had a few of those at our house, too. My youngest daughter is some kind of magnet when it comes to stray animals." He bore to the right and merged onto the highway. "First thing my wife says when Elana shows up with one of her strays is that she can keep it until it's healthy but it's not staying."

"And?"

"She's a bigger pushover than Elana. When it comes time to give them away, she can't do it."

It was on the tip of Melinda's tongue to ask him if he'd take her kitten, but an unanticipated sense of loss kept her from forming the words. He said them for her.

"Are you looking for someone to take the kitten off your hands?"

"No . . . *yes*," she admitted. "At least I was." She looked at the tiny paw reaching out to her. "I travel. All the time, for months at a time. And when I am home, I'm hardly ever at home."

"I can see where that could be a problem."

The fear that had propelled her the past three days wasn't an ordinary kind of fear, it was the kind that made her so sick to her stomach she couldn't eat. And it had nothing to do with a scrawny, heart-stealing ball of fluff.

At times she struggled to draw in a breath, the way a person carrying a hundred extra pounds did after climbing a dozen flights of stairs. She was mentally exhausted but sleep had become an enemy, one that brought dreams more closely resembling nightmares.

Melinda's resolve to keep her emotional distance from the kitten hadn't lasted through their first night together at the condo. An hour after going to bed, she woke to find the kitten softly snoring on the pillow beside her. Somehow she had found a way to scale a box spring and mattress on a platform frame. It must have seemed the equivalent of a kitten Mount Everest.

Her heart melted completely when the kitten woke and they locked gazes. She was completely undone when a paw reached out and patted her cheek.

Now Melinda gently took that same paw between her thumb and finger. "It's not you," she said in what was rapidly becoming a mantra. "It's just really rotten timing."

She rolled to her side until she was nose to nose with the kitten. "I promise I'll find you a great home. One where they can see what a beautiful cat you're going to be"—a tear slid down her cheek—"if you ever grow into those enormous ears."

Said with foolish confidence. She should know better.

Chapter Two

Hang in there," Melinda said as she shifted position to move the carrier to her lap. "The worst is behind us." Melinda turned her focus to the travelogue the driver had started in Monterey and kept up through miles of farm country, adding a sprinkling of history along with stories of the rich and famous who called the region home.

"This is Moss Landing," he said as they neared two towering stacks that marked a natural gas power plant on the edge of a harbor. "If you don't come back for any other reason, you have to make time to see the otters. At last count there was a hundred or so living in the harbor and slough area."

He went on to talk about an unprecedented anchovy bloom that had happened in the Bay that past year. Humpback whales had arrived in larger numbers than anyone could remember seeing—ever. Dolphins and sea lions, orcas and even blue whales arrived with them. Pelicans churned the water into a froth when thousands dived to catch fish trying to escape the larger predators patrolling below the surface. The oceanographic ships that work in the Bay measured the bloom at a hundred and fifty to two hundred feet thick.

Melinda nodded and smiled and decided against telling him she likely wouldn't be there long enough to see or do anything he'd suggested.

Ten minutes later they arrived at the beach house, where she would stay as long as she was in Santa Cruz. Everything had happened so fast Melinda still didn't understand what had prompted the call. There had been no promises on Jeremy's part, only, *We'll see how it goes when you get here.*

Normally she would have challenged anyone who called and insisted she disregard caution and rational thinking. In exchange she would get something she'd desperately wanted all her adult life—to see her daughter again. She had no reason to trust him. But how could she not when the stakes were so high?

Drawing a line in the sand would leave nothing but a target for the next wave. So here she was, a couple of thousand miles from home, too sick to her stomach to eat, too filled with fear to sleep.

The driver stopped in front of a brick walkway lined with flowers planted in dozens of sizes, shapes, and colors. There was a wonderful appeal to the disorder that reminded Melinda of a Monet painting. Bees and butterflies sorted through the blossoms. A hummingbird stopped to hover in front of her as she got out of the car. The porch held two tall lapis blue pots on either side of the front door with lace leaf miniature weeping Japanese maples draped over the sides.

"It's so much more than I expected," she said, more to herself than the driver. Her gaze swept the details of the house itself, at the functioning gray shutters and solar panels built into the roofing material. Somehow the house managed to maintain its charm and look its age without looking tired.

"The contractor they hired is famous around here for restoring old homes. It's almost as if he can talk to the houses and they tell him what they need."

She longed to ask him if he knew Jeremy, or more importantly, Jeremy's daughter. Instead she headed for the porch where, as promised, she found the house and car rental keys under the mat. The driver followed her inside.

"You want me to leave the suitcases here or put them in the bedroom?"

"Here is fine."

Melinda paid him, then followed him back outside. "Hopefully I'll be here long enough to see some of the places you suggested."

He handed her a business card. "Let me know if you'd like any suggestions for restaurants or the best whale-watching boat out of Monterey or"—he grinned—"if you need help finding someone to adopt your cat."

She glanced down at the card and smiled at the logo—a

cab that looked as if it had been drawn by a ten-year-old. "I will. Thank you."

"*De nada*," he shouted over his shoulder as he got in the cab.

She watched him drive away, the bright yellow cab disappearing at the first turn in the narrow, eucalyptus-lined road.

Before Melinda went back inside she stopped to look at the cottage next door. Something about the way it sat perched on a rocky outcropping, surrounded by a haphazard assortment of orange and red and yellow nasturtiums, appealed to her. She loved the weathered rear deck and could see that it offered an expansive view of the ocean.

Although the cottage was nothing like the house her father had built for her mother in Eastern Kentucky, they had a commonality that came through in the whimsy of how they'd been put together. Each broke design rules, ignoring architectural dictates for the placement of doors and windows, relying instead on the main entrance tucked under an arching portico at the back of the house.

Feeling guilty that the kitten was still caged, Melinda went back inside. The kitten stood on point at the cage door, seeking confirmation they'd reached the end of their journey. When Melinda lowered herself to her haunches and opened the door, the kitten made a loud, excited meow, stuck her head out, and sniffed.

"It's okay. I promise."

She looked at Melinda before tentatively venturing out, one paw at a time until her entire bony body was free to explore.

"So, what do you think?" Melinda asked.

The kitten answered with a squeaky purr.

"Really? You haven't been here five minutes and you approve already?" This time the answer was more howl than meow. "Okay, okay, I hear you." She picked up the kitten and carried her to the bathroom where she set up the litter box. After a quick look at the four bedrooms, she chose the one at the back of the house with the sliding glass door and small, private deck facing the ocean.

Finally, they headed for the kitchen, where Melinda unpacked the ingredients and prepared the repugnant-looking gruel the vet had prescribed as the next step in the feeding routine. After the gruel came a half bottle of kitten milk, consumed from a bottle with a nipple so long it looked as if it would choke her.

The meal ended with paw licking and cheek cleaning and attempts to groom herself, some successful, some sweet failures when she lost her balance and toppled over.

Melinda considered creating a nest for the kitten on the chair by the window and going for a walk on the beach. The kitten had other ideas. She sat on the sofa and patiently waited, her gaze following Melinda's every move, in need of nurturing almost as much as Melinda needed to give it.

The walk on the beach could wait. She had two weeks. Hopefully more.

Chapter Three

Melinda tucked the kitten under her chin and settled on the end cushion of the navy blue sofa that faced the fireplace. Nautical design needlepoint and crewel pillows lined one side of the raised hearth, adding bright colors to the neutral palette on the walls and furniture. Either an owner with a passion for needlework or a designer with an unlimited budget had created the understated look. In all of her gypsy years of short-term assignments with Wyndham and Parker Security Systems, she'd stayed in some nice places, but they had all felt like rentals. The beach house was different.

Here, there were floor-to-ceiling walnut bookshelves flanking the fireplace. "My father would think he'd died and gone to heaven if he could see these riches," she told the kitten. A sad smile followed. "Which, it so happens, he did. Die, that is. I hope God knew heaven wouldn't be heaven for him without books."

She squinted, trying to read titles, discovering everything from Carl Sagan and Margaret Atwood to Stephen King and Jane Austen. There were what looked like textbooks on philosophy and several volumes on the comparative study of the world's major religions.

Two shelves were low enough to be easily perused by children and were filled with books Melinda remembered her father reading to her as a child. He'd guided her into a love of literature with wit and joy, sharing memories of how he'd sneaked *Animal Farm* and *Lord of the Flies* into bed to read with a flashlight and how he'd avidly consumed every Tarzan book written by Edgar Rice Burroughs. He still had his original Tarzan paperbacks when he died, their pages yellow and brittle. Melinda sneaked them into his paper casket before it was put in the crematory, a secret she shared with the attendant, but no one else, not even her mother.

Her father believed a love of books was the greatest gift he could give her, insisting there was no better way to hitch a ride on a magic dragon or learn about love and giving from an apple tree or to simply escape a world that no longer brought pleasure, only pain and frustration.

These were the moments, the lessons, the sharing that made her ache with longing when she thought of what she had missed with her own daughter.

Caught in a web of memories, Melinda drifted home to Kentucky while she waited for the phone to ring.

Melinda was twelve years old the first time she saw Daniel Clausen without half the school hanging around. He scared the bejesus out of her as she meandered through what she considered her private section of the hemlock forest between the school and her house. It was too late to purposely ignore him the way she did when they ran into each other in the hallways at school. But there was still time to prop her hands on her hips and glare at him. It was the only way she knew to show how little she cared that he was the son of the richest man in Walker County while, thanks to the corporation that owned the mine where her father had worked, she was the daughter of one of the poorest.

Of the hundred or so kids at Oakley Middle School, he was the last person she expected to come across in woods so contaminated by coal runoff not even squirrels survived there anymore.

She glanced around. "Where's Skeeter?"

"Home by now, I'd guess." He got up from the rock where he'd been sitting and made his way down the hill toward her.

"I thought you never went anywhere without him." What was Daniel Clausen doing in her woods? On her trail? This was her private shortcut home. He had no business being here. She turned and headed for the

creek. *Maybe if she ignored him he'd go away and leave her alone.*

He caught up to her as she neared the log that spanned the creek. "Do you always walk home this way?"

She hiked the straps to her backpack higher on her shoulders. It seemed the books her father ordered from the mobile library got heavier every week, all of them oversize hardbounds without a paperback in the bunch. Along with her homework, the load was too heavy to waste time standing around shooting the breeze with the likes of Daniel Clausen.

Convinced he was there to give her a hard time, Melinda said, "No, sometimes I walk like this." She ignored the log and crossed the creek where it had run dry, moving with an exaggerated limp. When she reached the other side, she glanced back. The hurt in his eyes made her flinch. Daniel might act as if he was better than the rest of them, but to his credit he wasn't one of the bullies that roamed the school like junkyard dogs, chained too long and kicked too many times and looking to make everyone else's life as miserable as their own.

She came back. "I was just funnin' with you."

He shrugged. "It's okay. I shouldn't have come."

"You were actually waiting for me?" Again, she shifted the backpack that refused to stay in place on her narrow shoulders. "Why?"

"I figured you'd found a new way home. I like trying new things."

The curtain drew back from the window that had kept her from seeing what he was really saying. Despite his background and the fact that nearly every girl in eighth grade had a crush on him, the school bullies had found a new target. Not even being the richest kid in the school or having a father as mean as one of those junkyard dogs could protect him.

"This is a good one 'cause it's longer and everyone thinks the best way is the shortest way," she said. *"I don't ever see anyone back here."*

"Why do you care about something like that?" The unspoken part of the question was something she'd heard since sixth grade—no one messed with the prettiest girl in school unless it was to steal a kiss or even more—whatever would give some guy bragging rights.

She turned and crossed the creek, stepping on the stones she'd put there last fall before the rains came. *"It gives me time to think."*

Her willingness to continue the conversation was all the encouragement he needed. He followed her, hopping from one stone to the next. *"About what?"*

"Whatever I want."

"I like being alone, too," he said with a forced laugh. *"Good thing, huh?"*

"What about Skeeter?"

"What about him?"

"I thought you were friends."

"Not even close. He hung around because he got it in his head that I could protect him. When he realized I couldn't, he moved on to Willard."

Daniel Clausen was born in Walker County, but moved to Nashville with his mother when his parents divorced. He was shipped back to his father a couple of years later when she remarried, and with the exception of a couple of holidays, had lived there since.

He was no more a part of the community than the outsiders who drove through town in their fancy trucks and vans looking for antiques the locals considered junk. "If you don't tell anyone else about my trail, I guess it would be okay if you use it once in a while."

He pointed to her backpack. "You want me to carry that?"

"Why would I?"

He threw his hands wide. "You're as easy to rile as my sister used to be."

Melinda moved around the moss-covered foundation of one of the early settler homes that dotted her forest. "I just don't want you thinking you're better or stronger than me."

"I am. Not better, just stronger."

"What a jerk."

He laughed. "Now you really sound like my sister. Or at least how I remember her. It's been a long time . . ."

"How come you don't talk about her?" she asked, filling in the awkward silence. There was no use pretending Daniel wasn't the one person at school that everyone talked about. The quieter he was, the more he stuck to himself, the more curious everyone was. What they didn't know for fact, they made up.

"Abby doesn't live with us anymore. She ran off her first day of high school and no one has heard from her since. Or if they have, they didn't tell me." He kicked a stone as if it was a football and stopped to see how far it would go. "One day when she has a job and an apartment, she's coming back for me."

Melinda could see that it had cost him to tell her. His sister coming back for him was his dream, not Abby's.

"My brother doesn't live with us anymore, either," Daniel said. "Two years ago he just up and left and we never heard from him again. I guess he figured if Abby could get away with it, he could, too. My mom thinks he joined the army. She had my uncle do some checking but he couldn't find anything."

"What do you think happened to him?" She'd heard rumors about Abby, the kind told in whispers and half grins. The ugliness of the stories were beyond Melinda's comprehension and she rejected them out of hand.

Several minutes passed before he answered. "He used to talk about jumping out of a plane without a parachute, but he always laughed when he said it. But it was never his usual laugh, the kind that made him snort. *It was more the kind that was sad, not happy. I asked him about it after he and my father had one of their fights. He didn't say anything, just grabbed me and gave me a noogie. He left that night and I never saw him again."*

Daniel stopped to remove a twig caught in his shoelace. He looked up at Melinda. "Go on," he said with a dismissive wave. "I can find my way from here."

Startled by his sudden mood change, she took a step backward. She searched for but couldn't find the words to erase the impact of his revelations. She'd stumbled into his world too soon and there was no way back. "I don't mind—"

"I do."

With her father's voice echoing in the background of her mind, telling her to let people give their stories in their own time, she had sense enough not to press Daniel. "I'll leave a trail up to where I turn off for my house. Your place is 'bout a quarter mile farther down the holler, right after that test hole they blasted in the side of Hangman's Hill last year. Look for a piece of yellow paper with a rock on it." She moved to leave and then turned back. "Probably would be best to take the papers with you. That way no one can find them and start wondering how they got there and figure we're up to something."

He nodded without looking at her.

Melinda walked away from Daniel at her usual

pace, but after reaching the top of the hill where she could no longer be seen, she broke into a run, the backpack slapping her like a jockey's whip as it bounced against her coat. She was overcome with a peculiar need to be with her father, to curl into his side where he sat nested on the end of the sofa, listening to his deep Kentucky drawl as he planted seeds of longing in her receptive mind. There were times when they had to wait for the coughing spells to end, but they happened so often now that she hardly noticed.

He was her magic carpet ride to worlds a million miles from home. How did living on an island in a house built on stilts make a person different from one who lived on the top floor of a building in a city where you had to wear a mask to protect you from the outside air? These were the kinds of questions her father asked when they finished one of his books. He insisted there were no right or wrong answers, only her opinions and, most important, a mind open to change when the time came for her to explore the world on her own.

Tonight she would be the one asking questions. She would do her homework, and make their dinner, perhaps even open a jar of the spiced peaches her mother had put up two years ago, before she told him about the curious boy she had met on the way home.

Everything she thought she knew about Daniel was wrong. All it had taken was a long talk and short walk through the woods to let her see that. He wasn't the

stuck-up, spoiled rich kid who believed himself superior
to the boys in bib overalls and hand-me-down boots.
She wanted her father to tell her it was all right to be
Daniel's friend, that it didn't matter that he was the
son of the most hated man in Walker County.

Would she do anything different if she could go back? Would she sacrifice more? Could she? The answer was always the same. She wouldn't because she couldn't.

She ran her hand across the kitten's back, seeking comfort in the simple gesture. The kitten stretched and rolled to her side to look at Melinda.

"I'm scared," she said aloud, almost as if she expected the kitten to answer. "No—it's more than scared. I'm terrified."

For almost thirteen years she'd held on to the dream of seeing her daughter again. At her most desperate, she'd combed over the papers she'd signed relinquishing custody, looking for something she might have missed, even knowing there was no way she would act on it should she find something.

The rules that governed adoption in Mississippi were clear and precise. There was no legal age to protect her. Melinda could have been thirteen years old instead of sixteen when she gave birth to her daughter and it wouldn't have mattered. Once the papers were signed, the biological mother and father, the grandparents, and the siblings lost all familial rights. Forever. No exceptions. No loopholes. Melinda could put her name on a state registry, but her daughter would have to wait until she was twenty-one to gain access.

For twelve years, every time the phone rang and it was a number Melinda didn't recognize, her heart leaped to her throat. When mail arrived with return addresses in states where she didn't know anyone, her hands shook as she tore open the envelope. And then now, after finally convincing herself to let the dream die, the call came.

What happened that made Jeremy and Tess change their minds about letting her see the daughter she'd given away?

Melinda had openly questioned him. He'd sidestepped answering. When she asked how he'd found her, he didn't answer that either. Which made her suspicious, and inclined to believe someone, somehow, had found out about the adoption and was working a scam. Still, more powerful than the skepticism was a desire to believe the stranger on the other end of the line. Only that thin thread of hope kept her from hanging up on him.

He went from cryptic to reluctantly cooperative when she told him she was going to hang up unless he gave her a reason to believe he was who he said he was. Only then did he supply the details about the adoption that she needed in order to be convinced. He told Melinda he and Tess were three days late getting to the hospital because of a series of tornadoes that hit central Mississippi, knocking out electricity and blocking roads with tangled trees.

Instead of immediately losing her baby to the adoptive parents, Melinda was left to care for her while the staff handled the influx of patients with broken bones, twisted backs, and head wounds.

Fully aware her heart was being honed to an easily broken edge, for three days she held her baby, memorizing the curves of her cheeks, the feathery softness of her hair, the tiny, starburst mole at the back of her knee. Over and over again, she told her about her father and her grandparents and how deeply she was loved. She sang nursery rhymes, and told her Humpty Dumpty could have been put together again if they'd used Gorilla Glue.

She bit her lip when tears squeezed her throat. She smiled even when it hurt.

When the adoptive parents arrived and the nurse came to get her baby, a pain went through Melinda that made it impossible to form the words to say good-bye. She insisted she would be the one to put her daughter in her new father's arms. He looked at her in fear and fleeting sorrow, turned his back and walked away. She went to the window to watch them drive away, staring at the empty road long after they were gone.

And now, with a simple phone call, the one thing she'd believed impossible had happened in the middle of her favorite TV show as if it was a day like every other day. It didn't matter that she had doubts or was consumed with questions—she'd been given the chance to see her daughter and she would walk across burning coals to make it happen.

She agreed to the meeting and to his terms. He gave her his phone number. Her hands shook so badly she dropped the pen and had to write it twice before it was legible.

She had four days to complete the wrap-up in Juneau, a

job that usually took a week. Six months was enough time to settle into a location and make leaving more complicated. There were new friends to visit one last time even knowing they likely would never see each other again, meetings with the client both social and business, a dinner with the senators assigned to a committee to look into the security of the state computer systems, a health certificate from a vet for the kitten, and, finally, changing the airline tickets Jeremy had sent in an overnight package to first class so she could take the kitten on board with her.

Every day every breath was an effort, none more so than when she called the home office and told her boss she was taking time off. It wasn't a question, it was a statement, something they weren't used to from her. Usually she was as pliant as a willow in spring, easily bent in any direction the company required. She traveled without complaint, taking assignments that lasted anywhere from a month to a year, some with less than a week turnaround time. Her life was the company, her family an album of faded photographs.

She tried to focus on the positive, but couldn't open the door to her heart, no matter how slight, without Jeremy's last words closing it again.

He had ended the conversation with a forceful reminder that in no way was he making an overture to include her in their lives permanently.

It was just a meeting.

Nothing more.

She listened, but she didn't hear.

Chapter Four

Despite it being a glorious, sun-drenched day, Melinda spent the entire time indoors. She moved from the sofa to the chair in front of the sliding glass door, her phone in her hip pocket, the kitten on her lap.

She stared unseeing at the activity in the cove, only peripherally noticing children constructing sand castles, seagulls begging for scraps from picnic baskets, and brightly colored beach towels and folding chairs with their occupants focused on magazines and paperback books and electronic devices. The kitten alternated positions from curled into a tight ball to stretched full length along Melinda's leg.

The cell didn't ring.

The overnight package Jeremy sent included information

about the beach house and the rental car along with a stream-of-consciousness list of emergency contacts, stores, and when he would call to set up a meeting.

Her world revolved around computers so it was only natural that as soon as she knew Jeremy's full name, she'd investigate. She found basic information, mostly from trade magazines that featured articles about his construction company and how it had grown from a one-man operation to a business noted for employing the finest craftsmen in Northern California. She also found a couple of archived pieces in the *Santa Cruz Sentinel* about his tenure on the board of directors for a local charity that worked to purchase and restore wildlife habitat. Oddly, nothing she'd read had included anything about his immediate family, no daughter and no wife.

She glanced at her phone, checking the time and making sure she hadn't accidentally silenced it. She'd skipped breakfast and missed lunch and should have been hungry, but she was so sick to her stomach with apprehension that just the thought of trying to swallow even a bowl of cereal made her gag.

The kitten stretched, circled, and settled again, then thought better of it and took off down the hall toward the bathroom. The only cats Melinda had been exposed to growing up were barn cats. They were never fed or sheltered beyond opening a door to the root cellar or providing access to the barn. They earned their keep by controlling rodents. Their own numbers were controlled by foxes or coyotes or hunting dogs trained to go after them for sport.

Which made cats in Eastern Kentucky where she'd grown up wary of humans. The humans reciprocated with beliefs passed from one generation to the next that cats were harbingers of evil.

Especially black cats. They had an unsavory history that went back centuries and likely as not involved women and witchcraft.

Melinda looked up to see her supposedly evil kitten bounding toward her with what could only be described as a smile. She meowed in greeting and climbed up Melinda's outstretched leg, making it to her lap in two surprisingly well-executed leaps. She circled and settled in, giving her still-tender paws a quick cleaning before dropping her head and falling asleep.

Five minutes later the doorbell rang. Her immediate reaction was a feeling of panic. Jeremy said he would call first. She'd counted on that time, however short, to mentally prepare for their meeting.

Moving the kitten to the flannel jacket she'd put on the sofa earlier, she quickly checked her hair to make sure it hadn't done something weird when she switched from the sweater she'd put on in Juneau to the only warm-weather clothing she'd taken to Alaska—a camisole and crochet tank.

A hard swallow helped control the stomach spasms that accompanied every step. Why couldn't she be like all the other females she knew and just cry when life made her the target in a game of emotional dodgeball?

She took a deep breath, forced a smile and opened the

door. The smile disappeared as soon as she saw she'd been wrong about Jeremy calling first.

A tall, lean man Melinda had imprinted in her memory but only vaguely truly remembered blinked and took a step backward. Melinda couldn't tell if he was surprised or disappointed. Either way, she was clearly not the woman he'd expected. He removed his frayed baseball cap and stuffed it in his back pocket, regaining his composure. "You've changed," he said.

"That's what happens when you grow up," she said, her voice dripping sarcasm. *Don't do that*, she mentally warned herself. Jeremy held the power. She would gain nothing by alienating him.

"Of course. I guess I had trouble picturing what a difference nearly thirteen years would make."

"Some days I think the changes are for the better," she said in a gentler tone. "Others, I'm not so sure." In person Jeremy looked the part of someone who spent his life outdoors—lanky but muscled with sun-streaked brown hair on the long side of easily groomed. His beard was a day or two beyond the popular bedroom look still favored by *GQ* models, and lightly sprinkled with either blond or gray, she couldn't tell which in the bright sunlight. Dark brown eyes flashed a mixed message somewhere between weary and wary. She wouldn't be surprised if it was both.

His physical appearance invited speculation, a little like a fill-in-the-questionnaire-on-how-to-create-the-perfect-father-for-your-daughter. Physically, she wouldn't change much, other than make him a little less tired-looking. For the rest, the most important attributes, she would have checked off a sense of humor, a sprinkling of mischief, and an innate tenderness. She'd thought a lot about the man she wanted her daughter to call Dad and those were the traits that always came out on top.

"I'm going to assume you're Jeremy Richmond?" she said when he didn't supply the information himself.

"I figured you'd already guessed that." He gave her a knowing smile. "But then the photograph of me at the Builders' Award Dinner isn't the best and we didn't spend a lot of time together at the hospital."

"No, we didn't. And," she added, "you're right about the photograph. It wasn't helpful at all." Of course he would figure out that the first thing she would do after learning his name was look for him online. Fighting an inclination to say something flippant, Melinda reminded herself she had nothing to gain and everything to lose. Her mother used to tell her that devils danced on the tip of her tongue, especially when she was scared or angry. At the moment she was a long way from being angry, and scared didn't begin to describe the terror gripping her stomach.

Jeremy rocked backward, looked down at his boots and then up again at Melinda. "Would it be all right if I came in?"

"Sorry, of course." She opened the door wider, moving to give him room to enter without making physical contact. She took a minute to look outside, focusing on his truck. No one was inside, not his wife . . . not anyone. Disappointment settled over her shoulders like a coarse wool blanket.

She closed the door and turned to face him. What now?

"As I recall the day we met, you looked like hell," he said, taking them back to their only meeting. "As if you'd been crying for a long time. And you looked young. Way too young to have a baby."

"I've never cried well. People don't feel sorry for me, they look for ways to escape." Again, she tried to smile. "As fast as they can."

"I remember everything about that day. To me it was more like you were dealing with a broken heart," he said with breath-stealing kindness. "How fast I left had nothing to do with how you looked. From the minute I saw my little girl, even though I knew it wasn't possible legally, I was terrified you might change your mind."

With those few words, she was back at the rural hospital where she'd given birth, sharing a room with a woman nearing the last stages of dementia who comforted herself by reciting Shakespeare's sonnets. "Whether or not to give my baby up for adoption wasn't a choice, it was a necessity."

"No matter the reason, for me, all logic vanished the minute I saw you coming down the hallway to put your baby in my arms. I didn't know that it was possible to fall in love that fast."

They had this in common. What he could not know was that she could still feel the weight of her daughter in her arms and how lost she'd been when that weight disappeared.

"You've changed, too," she said, taking the conversation back to sheltered ground. Should she extend her hand? Was there a protocol for formally meeting the adoptive father of your daughter? She waited for him to give her a clue.

Jeremy ran his hand over his stubble, stopping to scratch his chin. "A little more gray I suppose, and a few new wrinkles."

He shifted from one booted foot to the other. They were work boots, the kind with steel toes and shanks that had creases across the top from years of sitting on his haunches to work on something low. His jeans had holes, but they were the earned kind, denim worn through where his tool belt rode against his hips.

She made a fluttering hand movement, a gesture she'd inherited from her mother that belied her effort to appear in control. She was losing the confidence battle. "Just curious—is this your house?" She'd seen nothing to indicate anyone actually lived there except for a kitchen full of food. "I know you did the remodel, but wondered how you arranged for me to stay here."

"I wish it was mine," he said. "I've tried to talk the owner into selling it to me, but she's not ready to let go. Too many memories."

Melinda understood about houses and memories. Even after all this time, selling her parents' home still seemed like a betrayal.

"Would you like something to drink?" *What?* All of a sudden she'd transitioned into the role of hostess? "As you undoubtedly know, there's juice and soda in the refrigerator, but I'm not sure what's in the cupboards. Coffee maybe? Or tea?"

She made that stupid fluttering gesture again. "I'm assuming I have you to thank for the supplies?"

"Not me—a friend of mine. She lives in the cottage next door. When I got tied up . . ." He visibly struggled with how to finish. "With something I wasn't expecting, she pitched in." Jeremy glanced around the room, his gaze stopping on the unpacked suitcases.

Melinda cringed at the message the suitcases communicated—she wasn't planning to be there long enough to make an effort to unpack. "So your friend knows who I am and why I'm here?"

"There's not much Cheryl doesn't know. She's been a god-send the past couple of years." He looked up, staring at the crown molding above the fireplace, his eyes narrowed in concentration. "I count on her a lot more than I should, especially with her and her husband, Andrew, planning to move to Botswana next year."

"Why Botswana?" she asked, not because she cared, but because she couldn't come up with anything else to say.

"Their youngest daughter is on assignment with *National Geographic*."

"That's impressive." Their conversation had turned surreal. They were acting like two people killing time at a bus stop with no more in common than the need to get from one side of town to the other.

Jeremy hesitated before answering a question Melinda hadn't asked. "She's on a decade-long study photographing the loss of elephants through poaching and trophy hunting by assholes like that dentist who killed Cecil the Lion a couple of years ago."

Melinda had lived her entire life in an environment where hunting was part of the culture. She knew men who could not have fed their families after the mines closed without the deer and elk they brought down each fall and winter. But she also knew men and women who killed for nothing more than bragging rights, and they turned her stomach.

"When are they leaving?" Melinda felt an unreasonable flash of jealousy that she wasn't the woman her daughter turned to when she needed a friend. She made a dismissive gesture to stop him answering. "Never mind. It's not important."

He answered anyway. "They're hoping to have the details worked out by the end of the year. Telling them good-bye is going to be even harder on Shiloh than me."

"Shiloh?" Melinda repeated, confused at the introduction of someone new.

"My daughter?"

Melinda caught her breath in surprise both at the name and that she hadn't thought to ask until now. In her mind her daughter had always been Danielle, named for her father, a gift he'd never received because he'd died before he knew she existed. "You named her after a Civil War battlefield?"

"It's a family name, one that's been passed down for more generations than anyone can remember."

She wasn't sure how she felt about the name but it wasn't as if she had any real choice. "You haven't said anything about Tess. How does she feel about Shiloh looking for me?"

Jeremy made a face. "It doesn't matter how she feels."

Melinda waited for him to finish, to at least offer some kind of explanation. As she waited, the perfect family portrait she carried in her mind the way a man carried a wallet in his pocket faded to a barely discernible image, as if it had been left in the sun too long. "Why?"

"It's not something I want to talk about any more than it's something you need to know." The verbal door slammed with a resounding bang.

Jeremy strode over to the sliding glass door and stared outside. "You found everything okay?"

She wasn't sure what he meant by "everything," but answered, "Yes. Thank you."

He turned to look at her. "There's a couple of bikes and beach umbrellas in the garage. Help yourself to anything you find while you're here."

He had to be kidding.

"Sorry," he said. "That was a stupid thing to say."

"That's okay. I've been known to say stupid things, too." What in the hell was going on? Why didn't he simply tell her when and where she would meet Shiloh?

"What do you do with your time off when you're in Minneapolis?"

Another inane question. "Why do you ask? Is it important?"

What possible difference did it make whether she had hobbies or lovers or a passion for old movies?

"Not important. Just something Shiloh might want to know."

His questioning didn't make sense when Shiloh could ask whatever she wanted to know as soon as they were together. Melinda stiffened. Unless that wasn't his intention. A bubble of heat burst in her chest sending tendrils into her neck and along her arms. She either confronted him or went along with the hope she'd read too much into his odd behavior. "When I'm in Minneapolis I do volunteer work at one of the local hospitals."

"What do you do there?"

She sighed, resigned to answering whether she wanted to or not. "I cuddle babies. At the hospital where I volunteer, a lot of the babies are born drug addicted and don't have family support. There isn't enough hospital staff to give them the human contact they need." She shrugged. "That's where the volunteers come in."

Jeremy ran his hands across his face as if it were possible to erase his obvious fatigue. "This isn't working. We need to talk."

Chapter Five

Finally. What she'd been waiting for turned into a stomach-turning uneasiness. Melinda sat on the arm of the chair at the window facing the cove. She folded her hands and clasped them tight to hide how badly they were shaking. Fear inched along her spine.

Jeremy moved to the bookshelf and ran his finger along the spines of a row of children's literature. His back to Melinda, he said, "I'm sorry. I know it isn't fair and it's sure as hell not what you came all this way to hear, but I've changed my mind about letting you see Shiloh, at least for now." He turned to look at her. "It's not a good time for her—for either of us. Right now we both need to concentrate on other things."

He'd made it sound like a canceled invitation to a birthday party.

Puzzled by her lack of a reaction, he added, "Do you understand what I'm saying?"

Melinda struggled to come up with an answer. She already had an entire box of bandages taped to her heart, futile attempts to heal the number of times it had been broken. She'd survived those wounds because she couldn't do anything about them. This was different. "What happened? Why did you change your mind?"

"The details aren't important."

"They're important to me." She couldn't keep the tremor from her voice. Was it something she'd said? The way she looked? Had she somehow given him the impression she wasn't good enough or smart enough to be in Danielle's—no, in *Shiloh's* life?

As if he could read her mind, he said, "It isn't you. A lot has changed around here in the past couple of days. I had no idea this was brewing when I called."

It took everything she could summon to control the urge to shout that she wasn't some stranger who'd appeared out of his past, someone he could invite to stay or ask to leave on a whim. Despite his warning from that first phone call that she was not being invited into their lives permanently, that her time with Shiloh at the beach house wouldn't be repeated until Shiloh was twenty-one and able to decide for herself. Like it or not, the bottle had been uncorked and rubbed and the genie was out. There was no going back.

"What could possibly have—"

"For one, Shiloh is in the hospital."

Melinda swallowed, hard. There was an edge to her voice when she said, "And you waited until now to tell me?"

He gave her a look that spoke volumes. Intuitively, she reasoned out his thought process. He'd never wanted her there and the only reason he cared whether she stayed was how Shiloh would react if she left. If he could find another way to get rid of her without consequence, he'd do it in a heartbeat.

Jeremy headed for the kitchen. When she followed, he said, "You know, it's not as if I owe you an explanation."

Her hands planted on her hips, she glared at him. "Can you really be so obtuse?"

"Don't go there," he warned. "I deal with Shiloh's illness on a daily basis. This isn't her first time in the hospital and it's not my first time at the rodeo when it comes to dealing with self-centered women."

"I'm going to let that pass because you don't have a clue what kind of woman I am, but the minute you picked up the phone and called to tell me I could see Shiloh, you opened a door I've been standing outside for almost thirteen years. There's no way in hell that I'm letting you close it now." She was beyond angry at his cavalier treatment. "There hasn't been a night I've gone to bed without thinking about the little girl I held in my arms for three days before you showed up and took her away. There isn't one night I don't lie awake wondering if you and Tess tell her often enough that you love her, if she feels loved—if you've ever told her that I loved her, too."

"About Tess . . ." Instead of saying anything more, he went into the kitchen, took a glass out of the cupboard, and filled it with tap water. "Never mind. It's not important."

She stood in the doorway and took several deep breaths before she trusted herself to ask, "You said Shiloh was in the hospital. What's wrong with her?"

"She has systemic lupus erythmatosus."

"In simple English. I recognize the lupus part, but none of the rest."

"Childhood lupus. She was diagnosed when she was four years old."

Not the best news, but not the worst either. Melinda knew lupus the way she knew black lung disease and breast cancer—personally. She didn't need Jeremy to tell her that her daughter had not lived an easy life, but it didn't mean she wouldn't live a good life. There were worse things that happened to children. She'd seen them at the hospital and knew that with luck and a top-tiered and intuitive medical staff, lupus could be fought. "Did she have a flare-up of an old problem?" Melinda asked. "Or is it something new?"

An eyebrow raised in question. He stalled answering by slowly draining his glass. "New. Or that's the way it appears right now. It's the first time her kidneys have been involved. Her doctor is running tests to make sure there isn't something else going on."

"Would it be all right if I talked to her doctor?"

Jeremy let out a laugh that was a long way from humor. "I'm going to assume you're joking. No way am I giving you permission to get any information from Shiloh's doctor."

"Why?" she asked, more to hear his answer than because she believed she could change his mind.

"First, I don't know you. And second, when Shiloh convinced me to let her see you—and believe me, it took a hell of a lot of convincing—she didn't want me to say anything about the lupus. She was afraid you wouldn't come, or if you did, it would be because you felt sorry for her. It's important that when she does meet you for the first time, it's on her own terms."

Melinda almost smiled. Jeremy might wish she would take her suitcase and slip away in the night, but he'd already accepted that wasn't going to happen—unless he could figure out a way to scare her into leaving. One way or another, he was going to have to deal with her.

"There had to be something that triggered Shiloh's sudden need to find me," she said.

"It wasn't all that sudden," he said. "She's been talking about looking for you for months now. For some screwy reason she goes through periods where she gets it in her head she's not going to make it to twenty-one. She insists if she doesn't do something to see you right now she'll never get to see you. What you need to understand is that when Shiloh sets her mind to something, it's like being caught in an avalanche."

"And yet you changed your mind. Why?"

Jeremy crossed the room to the French door that opened onto a flagstone patio edged in a low-growing boxwood hedge. "She maneuvered me into a corner where it was harder to say no than to give in."

"Pretty impressive for a twelve-year-old."

"Almost thirteen and going on twenty." He ran the tip of his finger over a mitered corner on the French door. "It's what can happen when you're a kid with an illness that keeps you housebound for months at a time. Eventually all your best friends have medical degrees and are more inclined to talk about what it takes to get into medical school than who got slimed at the latest award shows. When she was home, she spent her free time reading college course books that our neighbor couldn't bear to turn in to the used bookstore."

Jeremy turned to look at Melinda before adding, "Shiloh is conversant in subjects ranging from marine biology to forensic science to economics."

There was no way for him to know he'd just given her a gift. "My father would be thrilled to hear that he and his grand-daughter shared something so important to both of them. Thank you for telling me."

"I figured it had to come from someone. The only reading I've done since becoming a father are trade journals and the books Shiloh and I read together."

She liked that Jeremy was proud of Shiloh's accomplishments, but wondered what her life was like away from him. When she was in remission did she have girlfriends and sleepovers? Did she read teen magazines that decreed fashion trends with the control of a dictator? Did Jeremy know how to help her create a wardrobe that not only accommodated her need to avoid ultraviolet light but let her look like a normal twelve-year-old?

Did he recognize what it felt like for Shiloh to be three and a half weeks away from entering her teen years? It was a birthday more important than turning sixteen and only slightly less important than turning twenty-one.

How was it that Jeremy didn't recognize why Shiloh would want her mother there to help her celebrate?

Chapter Six

So what did she do?" Melinda asked.

He blinked, staring at her as if he'd already forgotten what they were talking about.

"To convince you to look for me," Melinda prompted. She pulled out the bar stool from under the soapstone counter and sat down. She needed to find out everything she could about Jeremy if she had any hope of turning this around. Either that or camp outside his house until he relented and let her see Shiloh. With his business firmly rooted in Monterey, moving out of state to get away was out of the question.

Jeremy plucked an orange out of the fruit bowl, starting it at the stem end and removing the peeling in one continuous motion. He separated the whole fruit into halves and offered one to her. She shook her head knowing even bringing a small section close to her mouth would make her gag.

He put the orange aside. "It's hard to describe how determined Shiloh can be when she's made up her mind she wants something. A perfect example is the mess we're in right now."

"Meaning?" She knew he was talking about her and resented being referred to as a mess.

"If this meeting between the two of you is going to happen, it should happen at a less chaotic time."

She wished she could tell him she would do anything, she would go through anything to see Shiloh, whatever the circumstances.

Melinda came forward and put her elbows on the counter. "How did she pull it off?"

"Shiloh was at the hospital for some tests when a new volunteer for Teri's Best Friend stopped by to talk to her. She'd seen Shiloh's name on a list of potential gift recipients and thought it would be a good time to start the process."

"I've never heard of Teri's Best Friend. What is it?"

"One of the charities that grants wishes for kids with chronic, life-threatening illnesses."

Melinda's eyes flared. "Life threatening? She really is dying?"

"She latched onto this dying idea when she started going through the hormone thing."

"What hormone thing?"

He held up his hand to stop her. "We'll get to that in a minute. First, the dying thing. What Shiloh learned during the interview is that she didn't need to be dying for her wish to be granted. To be eligible, all she needed was a chronic, debilitating medical condition. From there it was a matter of talking to the right people at the charity. They knew her request might be tricky, but I'm convinced that's what intrigued them. They were the new kids on the block, charity wise, and needed publicity to get operating capital."

"No one realized they needed to let you in on what was going on?"

"There were two things working against them. It was a new charity run by good-hearted people who'd recently lost their daughter and had no real idea what they were doing—"

"And?"

"And Shiloh managed to convince them I would be thrilled to find her biological mother. As I understand it, she strongly hinted that finding her other family could make a difference should she ever need an organ transplant."

"You must have been upset when you found out."

"Not so much upset as disturbed. Her stunt made me realize how serious she was about finding you." He crossed the room, opened the refrigerator, and looked inside as if it held something magical. After several seconds it started beeping, announcing the door was ajar. He grabbed a bottle of peach tea and held it up to Melinda.

She shook her head, wondering if his grazing was normal or an indication that he, too, was nervous.

"Of course having a couple of lawyers on the board of directors didn't hurt. Instead of automatically dismissing the idea, they looked at it as a challenge. They were completely caught up in the process when someone on the board finally thought to ask how I felt about what they were doing."

"And that's when they found out you had no idea what was going on?"

"That's when all hell broke loose."

"I assume there were consequences?" Melinda sat back up and stretched.

"I'm looking at it." He took a long swallow of the tea. "I figured she had to be desperate to do something that involved one lie after another. Shiloh is stubborn, she's never been purposefully deceitful."

"So you gave in."

He glared at her. "What would you have done?"

"Exactly what you did. Only I wouldn't have changed my mind at the last minute. What's the point when Shiloh already knows who I am and how to find me?"

"Obviously this has all happened so fast I haven't had the time to think it through."

Melinda couldn't help but smile at his admission. "You still haven't told me why. What triggered Shiloh's need to find me? And why now?"

"There's a hell of a lot I don't want to tell you, but it's not because I'm hiding anything. Pure and simple, it's none of your business. Maybe it would be different if I actually wanted you here, but I don't. Shiloh and I are a family. There's nothing you can add that either of us need."

Shiloh and I? What about Tess? For an instant she wondered if Jeremy was trying to hurt her on purpose or if she was simply collateral damage in his battle with Shiloh. She was an obvious, even an understandable target for his frustration. But if she had any hope of bringing him around, somehow she had to hang on and control her temper until Jeremy understood she wasn't the enemy.

The only way she could do that was to give him enough time to get to know her, to really know her. Trust was the coin of the realm they occupied and right now her purse was empty.

JEREMY TOOK ANOTHER long, slow swallow of tea, holding on to the bottle while he took the cap off and on, needing something to do to with his hands. He wasn't accustomed to feeling off balance.

He had excelled in sports in high school, fearing nothing and no one on a field or a court. Seven colleges had approached him with athletic scholarships, three came through with academic offers. He'd wound up at the University of California, Davis, majoring in wildlife, fish, and conservation biology. During the summer he'd volunteered with Habitat for Humanity and fell in love with construction. Two tours of duty in Iraq followed graduation.

He had absolute confidence in his ability to handle whatever life brought his way. That belief lasted thirty-nine years, right up to the day he was laid low by a twelve-year-old with something Cheryl had described as wildly fluctuating hormones.

Until then, Shiloh rarely ever cried, for any reason. For the better part of her life she faced hospital stays and medical tests with stoic acceptance. Now all it took for her to turn into a sobbing bowl of mush was a video of an animal rescue on Facebook. Most days he was at a loss for what to do or what to say when Shiloh woke up sullen, then turned into someone whose laughter echoed throughout the house minutes before she burst into tears over the news that a blue whale had died and washed ashore at Pebble Beach. How was he supposed to make things better when the world they had occupied only months before had developed a fault line the size of the San Andreas? How did he respond when she sneaked out of the house in a tank top to watch a sunrise knowing she was taking her life in her hands?

The clock on the microwave nudged him to wrap up his conversation with Melinda and get on the road. He had a meeting with his lawyer that ranked even higher in importance than his meeting with Melinda.

Still, he couldn't resist one more attempt to convince Melinda that coming to Santa Cruz had been a mistake, one that would do Shiloh more harm than good. If their meeting had accomplished nothing else, it had let him see Shiloh was important to Melinda.

With studied patience he expanded his explanation of what Shiloh was going through, emphasizing her emotional vulnerability. "Cheryl thinks Shiloh's wild mood swings are connected to hormones," he said without elaborating. "She said she went through something similar with both of her daughters."

"Cheryl is the woman who lives in the cottage next door . . . ?"

"I got to know her and her husband when I was doing the first remodel of this place. They're great people. You'll like them." What a stupid thing to say, especially considering he'd come there to ask her to leave. Still, he finished what he'd started. "Shiloh and their son, Bobby, met on a Monday and were best friends by the end of the week."

"He must be one unflappable kid if he's managed to make it through her hormone stage and they're still friends."

Her smile didn't just come from her lips, but from her eyes. Another physical trait she shared with Shiloh. Jeremy stared too long for her not to notice, especially when he made a point of looking away. He was trying to reconcile the image he had of the mercenary sixteen-year-old who had sold her baby for twenty thousand dollars and the woman who would do anything to see her again. Did she come to apologize? If so, she was going to be disappointed at his reaction. He could handle everything Melinda had done leading up to the adoption, but he could never forgive the last-minute demand she'd made for more money.

"I remember what I was like," she said. "Mainly because my father spent the rest of his life trying to understand how I could have gone to bed one night his sweet, accommodating daughter and woke up the next morning convinced he and my mother were old and out of touch and didn't have a clue what it was like to be a teenager. The abrupt change nearly drove him crazy. My mother took the tears and tantrums in stride. She was the most easygoing person I've ever known. I wish I'd inherited just a little bit of that from her." The smile faded, replaced by a yearning. "Is Shiloh easygoing?" she asked.

He didn't want to answer her. He didn't want her to know intimate things about his daughter no matter how easy they were to tell. The stories and hopes and dreams were his. He hiked himself up to sit on the counter and stared at her. "She used to be."

"If she used to be, she'll be that way again," she said with complete confidence.

Jeremy shook his head. Just like that, as if Melinda had been there for the entire transformation, she took what he and Shiloh had been going through and reduced it to its simplest form—the painfully awkward stage of a girl transitioning into a woman. He wanted to be gracious and accept her insight for what it was, but he was too irritated.

She may have put in the labor to bring Shiloh into the world, but he'd put in the time. Shiloh was his daughter and had been from the moment he'd held her in his arms.

She made a face, letting him know she knew she'd made a mistake. "I'm sorry," she said. "I'm acting as if I know Shiloh already when I don't. It's just that from what you've told me—"

"I'll be more careful from now on."

"Jesus—I hope you're not always this prickly," she said. "I'll have to rethink my impression and it won't be good."

"Okay, I'll give you that one," he said. "You sound just like her." Trying to pretend they had nothing in common was as foolish as trying to pass a hurricane off as a summer storm. He could see Shiloh in Melinda in a hundred ways, from their slate blue eyes to their wavy light brown hair, but most of all in the way they made the same fluttering movements with their hands when they were anxious or upset. Who did that? In thirty-nine years he couldn't remember ever seeing anyone else make that particular expressive gesture.

"How long did the hormone thing last with you?"

"For me, not very long. There were too many other things going on with my parents for them to give me and my problems the attention I thought I deserved."

"Like?" It was more than curiosity. He had always wondered what life experiences had pushed her to the point she would one day sell her baby to strangers.

"My father lost his pension when the only company he'd ever worked for went bankrupt. His lungs were in such bad shape no one would hire him, and it fell to my mother to find a job that would keep them from losing their house. It was demeaning work at low pay, but between her income and my father's disability, we survived." Melinda shrugged. "You can see there wasn't a lot of time, and not much tolerance, for me to swim in the pool of self-indulgence."

"Sounds a little harsh." And compelling. Not something he wanted to feel where she was concerned.

She sighed. "Why are you doing this? If you want to know something, just come out with it."

He leaned forward, planted his hands on either side of his legs and stared at her. "Why did you give Shiloh away? How could you?"

Melinda leaned back in her chair and crossed her arms to keep them still. "What difference does it make when you got exactly what you wanted?"

When he didn't answer, even after she'd given him plenty of time, she added, "I've never understood that question any more than I understand people who think it's okay to ask why someone committed suicide."

Jeremy flinched. She was right, of course. Her reasons were her own, to share or not share as she saw fit. Melinda made another fluttering motion with her hand. It was a gesture that connected her to Shiloh as powerfully as a DNA test. Every hand motion, every tilt of her head, every lopsided smile provided irrefutable proof of a connection.

"Shiloh has gone through a lot of rejection," Jeremy said. "I'll be damned if I'm going to set her up to go through more. Whether it's the lupus or hormones, she's been an emotional mess for months now."

Melinda changed the direction they'd been heading. "Isn't it really rare to develop lupus so young?"

He nodded, grateful to be talking about something less personal. "She was in pretty bad shape by the time one of her doctors figured out what was going on."

"How could you possibly think you could tell me Shiloh was sick and I would just pack up and leave?"

"It wouldn't be the first time that—"

Instant, fierce anger hit her with the force of a broken bat. "How can you say something like that? I've never—"

"—it's happened to Shiloh," he added with studied patience.

Her anger disappeared as quickly as it had appeared. "I understand why this would be a bad time for you. I know what it's like to take care of someone so sick you're afraid to leave them alone to get a cup of coffee or go to the bathroom. If you think telling me that Shiloh has an incurable disease is going to help you win this argument and get rid of me, think again."

"This isn't working," he reluctantly admitted. "It's been a shitty day for both of us. I shouldn't have come, but I thought you deserved more than a phone call."

"I guess I should thank you for that much at least. You could have sent a text."

He ignored her sarcasm. "I owe Shiloh an explanation."

She stared at him. "No."

"No?"

"I'm not leaving Santa Cruz without seeing her."

Chapter Seven

*J*eremy left the soapstone counter and came around the island to sit on the stool next to Melinda's. "I realize you're disappointed."

"You can't begin to imagine what I'm feeling. All these years went by and I never tried to contact you. Not once. I thought about it. Sometimes it was all I could think about. But I couldn't do that to Shiloh."

She got up to put distance between them. Unable to come up with any other reasonable action, she took a glass out of the cupboard and filled it with ice water from the refrigerator door. "Then out of nowhere," she went on, "you call. Not only do you want to set up a meeting, you want it right now, without a word of explanation. I had a hundred questions but was terrified to ask even one. What if I said something that made you change your mind? Four days later, here I am."

"Shiloh can be incredibly persuasive at times."

"She's twelve years old and you're . . . what? Forty? You're telling me that she has that kind of control over you and Tess?"

Jeremy almost smiled at her rebuke. He'd been curious if Shiloh's stiff spine was inherited or something she'd developed through a lifetime of fighting her illness. Plainly it was something she'd gotten from her mother. Her biological mother.

Melinda started to say something, stopped, drew her lip in between her teeth, and for a minute seemed to fold into herself. "Does she look like me?"

He could see what the question had cost her and felt guilty about the answer. She was looking for a connection he didn't want her to make. "No, not really."

Melinda nodded. "Do you have pictures?"

He lied a second time. "Not with me."

"When can I see her?"

He hesitated. "I told you—"

"You told me what you want, not what Shiloh wants. Convince me that she's changed her mind and I'll reconsider leaving."

Jeremy hesitated, indecision battling expediency. "There's no way I'm going to drag her into the middle of this, not with her being as sick as she is. And sure as hell not while she's still in the hospital."

She changed the subject, as much to unbalance him as get

answers. "You said it took months to reach a diagnosis, but how did the doctor finally settle on lupus when it's so rare under five years old and mimics so many other diseases?"

Her knowledge of the disease took him off guard. Outside the people he'd met in the medical profession, it was the first time anyone had asked him that question. "She had an extraordinary doctor who looked past the obvious."

"My cousin had lupus. I helped take care of her when I was pregnant with Shiloh and her mother agreed to let me live with them." The "had" created an instant, ominous silence that Melinda rushed to fill. "She went through a rebellious stage when she reached her teen years and died from a drug overdose."

"I see signs of that in Shiloh already," he said.

"Drugs?" she said disbelievingly.

They'd slipped into a civil discussion that gave him hope she could be reasoned with after all. "Rebelliousness. She hates the restrictions the disease puts on her. She keeps saying all she wants is to be normal. Whatever the hell normal is."

"Normal is not having to tell your friends you can't go to the mall without a hat and long sleeves and sunblock because of the fluorescent lights. Worse is that you have to avoid sunlight, which means you put up with a hundred lame jokes about vampires." She gathered her braided ponytail and twisted it into a bun that immediately came undone. "And that's just the beginning," she added softly.

Jeremy had come there hoping to be able to dismiss Melinda as an uncaring, greedy opportunist, but she wasn't cooperating. "Your cousin must have been grateful to have someone to talk to about what she was going through." He put the glass on the counter. "I used to imagine Shiloh came from an extended family. But then it didn't make sense that no one pitched in to help you keep your baby."

Melinda stuffed her hands in her pockets, glancing down at her tired-looking running shoes. She made more money than she had time to spend, keeping most of it in conservative investments, imagining that one day she would help put her daughter through school. "It's complicated," she finally said.

For Jeremy, Melinda's inexpensive shoes and off-brand jeans revealed as much as reading her diary. Having been married to a woman who looked at labels before price tags, he had developed a prejudice toward high fashion—not a great role for the father of a daughter who looked as if she belonged on the cover of one of the teen magazines.

He avoided acknowledging that the older Shiloh became, the more he could see how important it was for her to be around other women. While the two of them had made it through the braid stage that hit hard when she was in fifth grade, it wasn't easy. Anything more complicated than a three strand was beyond him until he found a class at the YWCA in Watsonville and mastered styles from fishtail to Dutch to five strand.

It was the boyfriend talk he dreaded, and he could see it coming with the speed of a bullet train. The female friends he turned to for advice on how to approach the changes that were happening to Shiloh's body talked in terms he didn't understand. The physical part, things he didn't know even after being married to Tess, he got out of books. The emotional stuff was beyond him. More often than not he dropped her off at Cheryl's to figure things out.

Melinda gave him a puzzled frown. "There's no family on your side?"

"There was my mother, but she died six months ago. She thought Shiloh walked on water."

"There are psychiatrists who believe children see death as another form of abandonment. What about Tess's family? Are they out of the picture, too?"

"Tess doesn't have a lot of immediate family, and what she does have, I'd rather weren't around."

"We all have our share of those."

"What's the 'too' supposed to mean?" he asked.

"It doesn't take a genius to figure out that you're not together anymore." *Just a little time to put it all together.* "She didn't come with you to meet me, she never communicated with me by text or phone or email, you haven't talked about her, and you go to your friend, Cheryl, for advice. Are you and Tess divorced or just separated?"

His first reaction was to tell her that his relationship with Tess was none of her business. "We're not together at the moment. Leave it at that."

"That's fair. I don't like people sticking their noses in my business either. But Shiloh's another matter. Nothing is off the table as far as she's concerned."

"Don't push me on this," he warned. "Just because I asked

you here doesn't mean you're entitled to any part of me or Shiloh."

She wasn't thirsty, but went to the sink to refill her glass then returned to stand next to her stool. "Let's stop playing this idiotic game. If you're hoping this is just another phase Shiloh's going through you never should have contacted me. You started something with the wrong person if you thought I would throw up my hands in defeat and walk away."

He leaned back against the counter and crossed his legs at the ankles. "I love the way you think you have me figured out."

"Am I wrong?"

"I already admitted I made a mistake. Luckily, it's not too late to do something about it."

"Think again." Melinda got up and walked from one end of the kitchen to the other, pacing and thinking. She stopped directly across from him with only the island separating them. "I'm not leaving until I've seen my daughter." There. She'd said the actual words. For the first time ever she said out loud that she was a mother and that she had a daughter. She felt liberated. From now on if someone asked her if she had children, she wouldn't hesitate telling them, yes, she had a daughter.

"How do you intend to explain my absence?" Melinda settled on her stool and immediately got up again. She could see she'd finally gotten through to him. "Send me away and I automatically become the most important person in Shiloh's life."

"Don't be so sure. I've been at this a long time. I'll do whatever it takes to make sure she never feels abandoned again."

Abandoned? What in the hell was that supposed to mean? "I still don't understand why you called me."

They were going around and around, repeating the same questions and answers, the results no different at the end than they had been in the beginning.

"Shiloh caught me at a weak moment. Now that you're actually here I realize what a huge mistake I made. I came here today hoping to appeal to your better side. Plainly, that's not going to happen."

"Low blow, Richmond," she said.

"It's the truth, inconvenient as that may be."

"That's nothing more than a self-serving way to tell me you're going to lie to her about why I left."

She'd put him in a room with no exit. His only choice was to strike back. Hard. "Self-serving? Interesting choice of words for someone who decided it was easier to give her daughter away than find a way to keep her."

If it weren't so melodramatic, if there were anything she could gain by it, she would throw something at him. "Said with all the compassion of a fundamentalist zealot."

He wearily wiped his hands across his face. "I'm sorry. That wasn't deserved."

Almost choking on the words, she broke down and said, "Don't make me leave her again. Please—not without telling her she's the most important part of me and always will be.

I've never stopped thinking about her. I couldn't bear her not knowing that."

"I need some time to think about this. How long are you staying?"

Hope washed over her. He'd originally approached her saying she could stay two weeks. Did he mean to give the impression it was negotiable? "Forever?"

He almost smiled as he moved to leave. "Trust me—that's not the answer I was looking for. I'll get back to you in a couple of days."

"Or sooner?"

"Oh my God. How far back does this pushy streak go in your family?"

Melinda found her smile. "Generations—all on my mother's side. My father believed the goodness in people would come out on its own and didn't need nudging from him."

"Smart man." Jeremy took a faded and tattered cap from his back pocket and put it on. Melinda could just make out the lettering—#1 DAD.

Chapter Eight

Jeremy stunned Melinda into speechlessness when he called fifteen minutes after he left. Not bothering with a greeting, he told her the name of the hospital, how to get there, and that he would meet her in the lobby at four o'clock that afternoon.

She arrived twenty minutes early. An hour later she still hadn't seen or heard from him and was beginning to wonder if she'd imagined his call.

He hadn't hinted at what made him change his mind and she'd been afraid to ask. She had managed a shaky "Thank you" in lieu of good-bye.

For the fifth time, Melinda crossed the lobby and looked outside, scanning the walkway and parking lot, not seeing anyone who remotely resembled Jeremy, or his battered truck. She vacillated between anger and fear. *He could have called to let me know he was going to be late* turned into *what if he's changed his mind yet again about letting me see Shiloh?*

For twelve years Melinda had tried to imagine what her daughter looked like. She'd stared into the faces of babies and then toddlers, becoming lost in the awkward early school years that followed when missing teeth and freckles marked faces in transition. An awkwardness that bordered on a peculiar grace followed the toothless stage. This was when legs seemed too long for the bodies they carried. And then another transition at eleven and twelve. These were athletic young women exiting a soccer field with effortless grace, their hair and uniforms disheveled, filled with an energy they were too young to appreciate. Never once had she pictured the pain-etched face of a child dealing with an incurable disease.

She had looked to her own family for clues to a connection, but what she longed to see was her beloved Daniel. Just a flash of his blue eyes or the left-cheek dimple that appeared when he was particularly happy or streaks of sun-colored hair would do. If her daughter had none of her father's physical features, then the way he laughed over corny jokes or his avid curiosity about everything from a black-and-yellow millipede to the mythological source of dragons would be enough. The smallest familial gesture passed from father to daughter became poignantly important when memories were all she had left of the boy she'd loved beyond reason.

There were times she was overcome with missing him, the

loss hitting her like a blow to the back of the knees that left her a crumpled mess and unable to function. Daniel died never knowing that the first and only time they'd made love they had created a beautiful little girl. Melinda would give everything she owned, every dime she'd worked so hard to save, her retirement, her future—for five minutes to tell him about his baby girl.

If love could be imprinted like a tattoo, Shiloh would have left the hospital covered in images of a family she would never know.

If only . . .

Melinda didn't see much of Daniel that summer. He was either staying with his mother and her new husband in North Carolina or being dragged around the country with his father whose job it was to oversee mine closures. Daniel marked the miles traveled by how long it took his father to deliver one of his lectures about what it took to be a real man.

Evert Lee Clausen was a man's man. Ask anyone and they would tell you there was no finer example of someone Kentucky born and bred. He'd be damned if he was going to have people point at his kid and wonder if he was some kind of nancy boy. Things like that rubbed off. The acorn doesn't fall far from the tree. Like father like son. Those weren't just sayings in these parts, they carried weight. If Evert Lee didn't stop the gossip before it set roots then one day there would be people point-

ing fingers at his one remaining son and swearing they always did think he walked a little swishy or looked at one of them longer than was right or necessary.

Melinda didn't say anything about Daniel's relationship with his father for the better part of three years before she unloaded on her own father. It wasn't as if she was breaking a promise. Daniel never asked her not to tell anyone. He trusted her. And up to now she'd never given him any reason to think he couldn't. But no matter how long she thought about it and tried to come up with something to say to help him, she couldn't.

Her father listened, asking a question here and there, but mostly not saying anything. When she was finished, he thought about what she'd said for a long time, scratching his beard, adjusting the cannula tubes that snaked over his ears and lay against his bony chest, and shifting his position on the end of the sofa. He never found comfort in the maneuvering but it gave him time to construct his answer.

"Evert Lee is an asshole," he finally, simply said. It was one of the words he rarely used that always triggered an immediate apology. But not this time. She wished Daniel was home so she could tell him he had a powerful advocate. In her world her father's opinion was godlike. He was never wrong. If he said Evert Lee Clausen was an asshole, then the man was an asshole.

With the care and tenderness she would have shown a new baby, Melinda hugged her father, not letting go until she felt him struggle to fill his lungs. She leaned back and planted a kiss on his stubble-filled cheek.

"Thank you, Papa."

"You're welcome, sweet girl."

She stood and picked up her backpack. It was Tuesday and the library van had been in town since eight o'clock that morning. It had never happened, but whenever she was late, she worried they would leave before she got there to pick up her father's books.

"Your lunch is in the fridge. You want me to—"

"Whatever needs to be done, I can take care of it."

"I made you an Elvis Presley sandwich and cut up some of those carrots Miz Donaldson gave us from her garden." *To her father, peanut butter and banana on white bread was the equivalent of barbecue on a sesame seed bun to most men.*

She was halfway out the door when he called, "Melinda?"

"You need to go to the bathroom?" *She knew how much it embarrassed him to ask for help with his private goings-on, so she did what she could to make it sound as normal as combing his hair.*

"If you want to bring Daniel home now and then, I'd be all right with it. He seems like a fine young man."

She caught her breath in surprise. As the disease had taken more and more of the strapping man her father had once been, he'd drawn deeper into himself. At his request, friends stopped calling. Neighbors knew

*not to bring bounty from their gardens unless they saw
her mother was home. Mary Ann Campbell refused to
stumble over pride when it came to feeding her family.
Still, she accepted the gifts at the back door, and did so
quietly and without fanfare.*

"Thank you, Papa."

*He nodded. "You best let him know it wouldn't be a
good idea to tell Evert Lee. I never did like that son of
a bitch and never did nothing to hide it."*

*He didn't apologize for the "son of a bitch" either.
He was letting her know that as long as the words fit
the man, it was all right to use them. She wasn't sure
how her mother would feel about her using son of a
bitch or asshole no matter what the circumstance, but
she liked it just fine.*

"Did you get my book list for next week?"

She patted her pocket. "Got it right here."

*"Take a minute to stop by and tell your mother I
think she's the most beautiful woman God ever put on
this earth."*

*Melinda's mother worked six days a week at what
passed for the town's only remaining grocery store and
service station. She mopped the floors, cleaned the toi-
lets, ran errands, and stocked the shelves. And for the
privilege of working fifty hours a week, she was paid
a dollar less than minimum wage, half what the owner's son was paid for standing behind the cash register
charging customers twice what something was worth*

for the advantage of buying local, cleaning his finger-nails with his pocket knife.

Melinda stood with her hands on her hips and gave her father a half grin. "You know I'm not going to do that. If anyone heard, they'd think I was weird."

"There are worse things."

The grin faded. Worse things—like the way her mother had aged. What happened to the girl in the family album who looked as if she'd stepped out of a movie? In every picture she was smiling. Not the kind of smile that focused on lips and teeth, but the kind that came from her eyes. Even now, with the pictures fading beneath the plastic covers meant to protect them, it was impossible to resist wanting to know that girl.

"I could give her a note. That way you could write whatever you wanted." She was teasing him, but he wasn't responding the way he usually did. "All right. I'll tell her."

"And tell her that I love her."

Fingers of fear inched up her spine. "She's going to think it strange that I'm the one telling her when you could say so yourself tonight when she comes home."

He forced a smile, recognizing where her thoughts had led her. "Never pass up an opportunity to tell someone you love them, Melinda. Today might be the day that they're the most important words someone can hear."

"I love you, Papa."

"Thank you, sweet girl. I love you, too."

Melinda made it to the book van in record time, skipping the woods in favor of the gravel road that led into town. She stopped by the market to give her father's message to her mother, but she was over in the next county buying cigarette paper and loose tobacco for the store and wouldn't be back for two or more hours depending on the delays caused by the construction crews working on the bridge.

She glanced at the ancient Coca-Cola clock with the slogan THE IDEAL BRAIN TONIC *written along the bottom panel. Twelve thirty. She'd told Daniel she would meet him at the McElroy place at noon. She never doubted he'd wait, she just hated making him.*

Daniel's mother dropped him off at his father's house every third week. As likely as not, Evert Lee was on the road the first two or three days Daniel was home. This gave Melinda and Daniel afternoons at the McElroy place, a stone house they'd discovered deep in the holler behind Melinda's forest.

With her father's help, she'd researched the house and discovered it predated the Civil War. Thirty years earlier the last of the McElroy clan had petitioned for the house to be turned into a historical landmark. The coal company caught wind of what was going on and sent a team of lawyers to kill the idea, convincing the elected officials the house was of no real significance and stood in the way of continued prosperity in the county.

Future exploration depended on keeping the lands open.

Wanda McElroy had the last word when she died and left the house and the entire hundred and sixty acres surrounding it to The Nature Conservancy. Following her request, the Conservancy left the house the way it had been given to them and within a decade it was overgrown with wild grapes and mountain olives and a tangle of domesticated blackberries. Only kudzu could had done a more complete job of hiding the historic jewel from view in the lushness of summer.

Melinda and Daniel found the house in the winter, coming across it by accident during one of their Saturday explorations. They'd been following the creek that ran through the property, a route they'd taken a half dozen times in summer, but never during winter.

The air was eyelash-freezing cold with hoarfrost covering bushes and trees in magical patterns. Daniel followed what looked like a path to a log covered in frost flowers, looked up and spotted exposed walls of precisely cut and stacked stones. Without leaves to hide the house, doors and windows and the remnants of a pillared porch became obvious.

A miracle of sorts had protected the greater part of the roof with the exception of a couple of holes here and there. Half the windows and doors were gone, but it looked to be the work of vandals rather than time and neglect. The walls and chimney were as solid as the day they'd been mortared. Come summer, with the bushes in full leaf and sending out tendrils of new growth, she and Daniel spent an entire weekend cutting a path to the opening where the front door had been.

Their reward was the discovery of a fully furnished household in varying stages of decay—a kitchen table collapsed into a cast-iron cookstove, a patchwork quilt that disintegrated when Melinda ran her hand over the tumbling blocks pattern, and a copper pot that had captured rainwater and snow and provided a home for a thriving swamp sunflower.

They tested the floor and found several places that swayed and creaked but none that gave way. After checking the chimney for nests and finding it remarkably clear, they built a fire from the deadwood around the cabin and shared their lunch, sitting on a blanket Daniel had taken from the back of the linen closet at home. Between visits they kept the blanket stuffed in a heavy plastic bag deep in the cupboard beside the sink, hoping to discourage squirrels in search of nest-building material. Daniel insisted that leaving the blanket at the cabin was safer than sneaking it in and out of his house.

Daniel was there now, waiting for her.

Melinda stood in the doorway of the grocery store/ gas station, torn between waiting for her mother and keeping her promise to Daniel.

"Shut the fuckin' door," the man behind the counter

yelled. "Can't you see you're lettin' in flies? You born in a goddamned barn?"

Melinda glared at him, leaving and slamming the screen door so hard it bounced against the wall.

"You broke somethin' and it's coming outta your mama's paycheck," he yelled at her.

A dozen profanities danced on the end of her tongue, but none that she was willing to say out loud and let her mother hear about later. Instead she took off at a run, heading home to check on her father one more time to make sure the new oxygen tank delivered that morning was working okay before heading to the cabin to meet Daniel.

Her father was sleeping when she got home. As usual, she struggled to understand how someone who did nothing but sit on a sofa and read books could be so tired all the time. Granted, every breath required effort, but she remembered not that many years ago when he would leave for work before sunrise and not come home until neighbors who worked on cars or painted houses or drove trucks were headed for bed. He'd come through the door wearing the bathrobe he kept in the washhouse, stop to do a really bad imitation of Michael Jackson's moonwalk, grab her mother in an enthusiastic embrace that ended in a kiss, and say, "What's for dinner?" No matter how tired he was he'd make time to go over her homework and help her mother with leftover chores.

Melinda slipped out of her backpack and tore a sheet of paper from her tablet. She was in the process of writing her father a note about meeting Daniel when he gasped and went into one of his coughing spells.

It was a bad one. Worse than any she could remember.

She checked the dial on the oxygen tank. It showed empty. How could that be? She went into the kitchen to call the emergency number hanging by the phone. The woman who answered told Melinda that the driver had called in sick that morning and that the deliveries were postponed a day.

"He can't wait that long. The tank is empty now."

"I'm sorry. I'll put you first on the list for tomorrow. That's the best I can do."

"That's not good enough," she shouted. "I need that tank out here right now. My father can't breathe. He can't wait until tomorrow."

"I told you—there is no one here to make deliveries. It's not like I can snap my fingers and make someone appear."

"If something happens to him I'm going to sue your ass." She instantly knew it was the wrong thing to say.

"If you're really all that worried about him, call 911." She hung up before Melinda could answer.

She pressed her forehead against the wall beside the phone and bit her lip so hard it bled. For years, almost as if it were a nightly prayer, her father made her promise she would not call 911 if something happened to him.

He said it was because he didn't want to die in a hospital hooked to machines being charged five dollars for a box of tissues and thirty dollars for a Band-Aid.

Did he know what watching him die would do to his daughter? Did he stop to consider how her memories of him would turn into nightmares that would haunt her the rest of her life?

Melinda picked up the phone and dialed the number for the store. Her mother could never make it home in time, but she could, and would, call an ambulance. Saying a prayer that her mother was back from picking up the tobacco, she discovered the trip had been extended, all the way to the other side of the county for pickled pigs' feet and jerky. She wouldn't be back for hours.

Melinda heard her father's rasping breath as his lungs worked to expand and then collapsed. There was no way he could wait until the next day. He would suffocate without his oxygen. It wasn't fair when he still had so many books to read and so much to teach her. It wasn't fair that her mother would lose the love of her life.

There were two ways to die with black lung disease in Eastern Kentucky: at home or in the hospital. The hospital was for people who had insurance or who were willing to sell everything they owned, including their house and land to pay for the privilege of being hooked to machines that would only prolong the dying process.

Her father had made her mother promise to let him die at home. He would die in peace knowing the house he'd built for her one brick, one two-by-four, one shingle at a time, belonged to her and not some bank.

Melinda knelt in front of her father, begging him to let her call for help. Already he was turning blue and mentally drifting. She put her hand on his forehead. He was cold. Scary cold.

She grabbed a blanket and tucked it under his chin and across his shoulders before she bolted out the front door and ran into the forest looking for Daniel.

Chapter Nine

Melinda's heart went into fight-or-flight mode when her phone vibrated against her hip. She glanced at the number as she moved to a quiet corner of the lobby.

Jeremy. Finally. "Where are you?"

"My meeting went longer than I expected."

"And now?"

"And now I'm calling to let you know." He plainly didn't like or wasn't used to being questioned.

She moved into a corner between the stairs and elevator and pressed her forehead against the cool, marble-sheathed wall, seeking the little privacy that could be found in the lobby. "How much longer?"

"An hour, more or less, depending on traffic."

She held back a frustrated sigh, exhausted by the tightrope she walked just thinking about him. "Are you leaving now or is there something you have to take care of first?"

His voice developed an icy edge. "I told you I'll get there as soon as I can."

"There's something I have to take care of at the house that can't wait. I'll get back here as soon I can. Please wait for me."

"I should have started with this, but I just talked to Shiloh's doctor and she told me Shiloh probably won't wake up for several more hours, which would make it the middle of the night. None of us are going to be at our best by then, especially Shiloh. She never comes out of a sedative in a good mood. I can tell you from past experience it's not the way you want to meet her for the first time. It would be a lot better for everyone if we tried again in the morning."

Once more he held the hand with the aces. If she didn't cooperate, if she didn't make it appear she was doing so willingly, all he had to do was turn his back and walk away.

Jeremy waited for Melinda to say something. When she didn't, he added, "If you wait until morning, I'll ask Cheryl if she's available to take care of your cat while you're at the hospital."

Melinda felt a hand on her shoulder. She looked up to see a woman with a concerned frown staring at her. "Are you all right?" she mouthed.

She nodded, adding what she hoped was a reassuring smile. The woman gave her shoulder a quick squeeze and left to catch the elevator. The simple kindness made Melinda's heart twist with gratitude.

"How did you know I have a cat?" she asked Jeremy, delaying while she searched for a way to tell him she didn't care about Shiloh's mood, she cared only about being there when she woke up.

"I saw her on the sofa. She looked in pretty bad shape so I figured you brought her with you to try to save her."

"She's small," Melinda acknowledged, then defensively added, "But she's strong. And determined."

"Sounds like you two have a lot in common." His cell started cutting out. "What's her name?"

She panicked. What kind of person didn't name their pet, even if the relationship was only temporary? *The same kind of person who doesn't name her baby because she's terrified it will make leaving even harder?*

"Heidi," she said. Where had that come from? She didn't know anyone named Heidi, had never read the book, didn't even know the plotline. Worst of all, she was pretty sure the kitten wouldn't like such a frilly name. She was more a Skuld or Athena or Daenerys.

"I'm going to lose you in a couple of minutes." Underlining the warning, the static increased. "What did you decide?"

Because she felt she had no real option, Melinda said, "I'll wait until tomorrow."

"I'll call if anything changes." In response to her silence, he added, "Otherwise, I'll meet you in the lobby around nine."

"Around?"

The phone cut out preventing her from hearing his answer. Assuming he had bothered answering . . .

THE NEWLY NAMED Heidi stood in the middle of the living room carpet and looked at Melinda, her impossibly tiny body displaying an amazing amount of attitude.

Melinda scooped her up and nestled her under her chin. If the responding purr was any indication, Heidi was as quick to forgive as she was to chastise.

But she was hungry and let Melinda know the only way she could, by stiffening her front legs and letting out a plaintive meow.

"Okay, I'm on it."

Already Heidi recognized the snap and ripping sound of a can of food being opened. She perched on Melinda's shoulder and turned toward the sound, letting out an even louder meow when Melinda spooned the food into a bowl and mixed it with the gruel the vet had recommended. With a leap that almost landed her in the sink, Heidi jumped from her shoulder perch and made a dive for the food. Melinda scooped them both up and put them on the floor at her feet.

Heidi gulped and choked and gulped again, finishing with a gag that brought everything back up. Melinda grabbed the bowl and washed it. Heidi sat perfectly still, plainly puzzled by what had just happened.

"It's called gluttony," Melinda said, immediately feeling a

sharp stab of guilt. Starvation eclipsed table manners. Was it any wonder that Heidi consumed whatever she could, whenever she could? Making her wait, forcing her to go through all too familiar hunger spasms must have been beyond frightening.

Melinda mixed the remaining half of the food into the bowl and sat down on the floor next to Heidi, feeding her small bites on the tip of her finger, wincing when the occasional sharp tooth mistook flesh for food.

"It seems like I'm forever apologizing to you," Melinda said. "And you always forgive me."

Heidi cleaned the last of the gravy off Melinda's finger and went to work licking her paw and wiping her face. In a heart-stealing effort, Heidi worked to clean bits of food from her cheeks, stopping to catch her balance several times before she was finished. She shook when she stretched, but the leap to Melinda's shoulder that followed was marked with absolute confidence.

Everything about Heidi was unexpected. Until she'd come into Melinda's life her only experience with a kitten had been the orange tabby the housekeeper gave Daniel for his thirteenth birthday. When his father discovered the kitten he gave Daniel two choices—he either got rid of it himself or watched while the dogs did it for him. As far as Evert Lee Clausen was concerned, cats were vermin, only good for target practice and then only if they had sense enough to run. Sissies had cats. Men owned dogs. Hunting dogs. The bigger and meaner, the better.

Chapter Ten

Jeremy leaned over the hospital bed and kissed the tip of Shiloh's nose. She opened her eyes and made a face.

"Eeeuw, gross, Dad. People don't kiss other people's noses."

He laughed. "Yes they do. I used to kiss your nose all the time when you were a baby. Besides, I don't hear you complaining when Coconut does it."

Coconut was the dog Shiloh had found sitting on the beach two years ago. She had been there for three days, staring at the wooden steps that led to the beach, waiting for her person to come back and claim her. Late on the second day, with the sun racing to dip into the Pacific, Shiloh put on her hat and long-sleeve shirt and took the forlorn-looking dog a bowl of water and a ham sandwich. They'd been inseparable since.

"Where is Coconut staying?"

"With the Wellses."

Shiloh reached up to tuck her hair behind her ear, the IV tubes making the movement awkward. "When do I get out of here?"

"Tomorrow. Maybe."

"Depending on what?"

"The labs from your bladder infection coming back clear." From the outset he'd told her the truth about her disease even when lying would have been easier. There were times he'd questioned that decision, but he'd never regretted it.

"Did she come?"

Jeremy brought the chair he'd been sitting in closer to the bed. "Yes."

"And?"

"I asked her to wait in the lobby until I could get here. I was late and she had to leave." Seeing a questioning sadness come over her, he added, "She'll be back."

Shiloh tried to smile through trembling lips. "Did she say why she had to leave?"

"Remember Grandma telling you about the kittens she rescued when I was around your age and how hard we worked to save them?"

"What has that got to do with—"

"Melinda has a kitten just like that."

"She has a kitten?" This brought a successful smile. "What's it like?"

Jeremy hesitated. He'd taught Shiloh never to judge people by their appearance. Did that apply to cats? "Different."

She frowned. "What's that supposed to mean?"

"If she was a bat, she's be the best-looking bat that ever flew out of a cave."

"Oh."

"But I have a feeling once she grows into her ears and puts on some weight she's going to be an okay-looking cat."

"Even if she isn't, that would be okay, too. She could be the smartest cat in the world."

He leaned over to plant a kiss on her forehead. "I like the way you think."

"Taking care of a cat like that is a good thing, isn't it?"

"Your grandmother would have thought so."

Shiloh took his hand and wove her fingers through his. "I miss Grandma."

"Me too," Jeremy said. More than he'd believed possible.

"Do you think she would have liked my mother?"

Jeremy flinched at the "my mother." Exactly what he was afraid would happen already had. "I think it would be better if you called her Melinda for now."

"Why?" When he didn't answer, she added, "You don't trust her, do you?"

He considered the question. She had a point. "I don't know. I need some time to make up my mind."

Shiloh smiled slyly. "Don't worry, Dad. I'll still love you best."

Could she be right? He laughed because he didn't want Shiloh to see how close she'd come to the truth. They'd never fought, at least not until six months ago when she started digging in her heels about meeting her biological mother. Now it seemed they censored everything they said to each other. She questioned his motives for not letting her meet her mother and he questioned her motives for wanting to.

"Tell me about the cat," Shiloh said, plainly eager to hear about anything connected to Melinda. "You know I've always wanted a cat."

"No, I didn't know that." There'd been times in the past couple of years she'd been so ravaged by her lupus shifting and settling in different parts of her body that he would have bought her a car if she'd asked, anything to bring just a moment of joy. A cat would have been easy.

Jeremy leaned back in his chair and brought one leg up to cross the other. "It's about half the size of my hand and way too young to be away from its mother. Cats like that need a lot of care if they're going to survive. We were up all night every night taking care of the three that we found. And then what seemed like overnight, they were feisty little creatures with unbelievably sharp claws and teeth who were ready to take on the world."

"Grandma said you cried when they were old enough to go to their forever homes." Shiloh wiggled into a position in the bed trying to sit up. Jeremy took a pillow out of the cupboard and put it behind her back.

"She let me keep the runt of the litter," he said.

"What happened to her?"

There was no way Jeremy was going to tell Shiloh that his beloved cat had simply disappeared one day, a likely meal for the fox that roamed their urban neighborhood. "Are you really interested in hearing about something that happened when I was your age?" He grinned. "Isn't that what you refer to as ancient history?"

"I want you to tell me about my mother. What is she like? Does she look like me? Is she nice?"

They hadn't met yet and already Shiloh was calling her "mother." Jeremy had a sick feeling this wasn't going to end well. No one could live up to Shiloh's expectations. "Stubborn, the way you are. Yes, but not as much as I expected. And yes, as far as I know."

"Do you like her?"

How to answer? Of course he didn't like her. How could he? With a dismissive gesture she could rob Shiloh of everything he'd worked so hard to give her—confidence and belief in herself were just the beginning. "I don't know her. Give me time."

"You don't need time when you interview a new client. You said it only takes a minute to tell what someone is like if you're paying attention."

He leaned forward to rest his arms on the mattress and stare at her. "You would be a whole lot easier to deal with if you weren't so damned smart."

She grinned. "So tell me—do you like her?"

"I like what I've seen so far."

"What does that mean?"

"When I told her I didn't think this was the best time for her to meet you, she didn't argue, she just refused to leave."

Shiloh's eyes lit up. "Even after you told her I was sick?"

"She doesn't care." He ran his hand over the stubble on his chin. He really did need to find time to shave. "That's not right. She cares that you're sick but she doesn't care why."

"You told her everything? That I'm not like normal kids and that I never will be?"

"It turns out you have a distant cousin who had lupus. Melinda stayed with the family while she was pregnant with you. She knows what lupus is, Shiloh, and she doesn't care."

The excitement in her eyes turned to worry. "That's because she doesn't know me. It's easy to say something like that when you think it's something someone wants to hear." She considered what she'd said. "What if my mother gave me away because she was worried I would turn out like my cousin? And now . . ." She didn't finish.

Jeremy reached for his daughter's hand. It would be so much easier all the way around if he stopped defending Melinda and let Shiloh make up her own mind. But he couldn't do that. She needed to believe she was lovable. "You promised me you wouldn't do this. You have more friends and more people who love you than anyone I know. Are you really going to allow one person to take all that away from you? One person whose only connection is DNA?"

"It's more than that and you know it. There has to be a reason she didn't keep me. Maybe I was an ugly baby when I was born, before you saw me. I've read that babies change really fast."

They had had this conversation a hundred times in a hundred versions. "She gave you away before you were born." When she started to answer Jeremy held his hand up to stop her. "Don't you dare try to tell me you didn't look pretty on the ultrasound. You were the most beautiful baby I'd ever seen. Even your grandmother said so and you know how critical she could be."

She rolled to her side to face her father. "I have to know why she didn't want me. It's important."

It would always be a puzzle to him how Shiloh could grow to accept and forgive being abandoned by her adopted mother at seven years old and agonize over a woman who had given her away after knowing her less than three days.

"Is she pretty?" Shiloh asked.

Luckily he was prepared for the question. "Of course she's pretty. She looks like you."

It sounded as little like a compliment as asking a woman how she dealt with big hips when she had such a small waist.

"What color is her hair?"

"Kinda brown and gold, like yours."

"Short or long?"

"Long enough for a braided ponytail."

"Is she tall?"

"Medium, I'd guess."

"Medium? What kind of answer is that?"

Jeremy laughed. "She's shorter than me and taller than you. And before you ask, she's thin and has big feet."

"Big feet?" Finally, a smile. "Come on, Dad. You can do better than that."

"Remember that toy you had when you were around five or six that you could bend and stretch and put in all kinds of crazy positions? She reminds me of that." What he could have said was that she crossed a room with long strides that made her look as if she were floating. When she'd reached for a glass, she'd done so with effortless grace that reminded him of his first girlfriend, who'd broken up with him when she had an offer to try out for the New York City Ballet. Jeremy saw her perform several years later and told her that it was obvious she'd made the right choice.

Shiloh thought about his answer. "She probably does yoga."

"Doesn't Cheryl still teach yoga?" Cheryl was the first person Jeremy had gone to when he discovered Shiloh was trying to find her biological mother. As the mother of three adopted children she was a wealth of desperately needed insight. She listened to his fears and agreed with many of them, but let him know it could do more harm than good to fight Shiloh.

So he didn't. And now he wondered if he'd made the biggest mistake of his life.

"She's here," Shiloh whispered.

"What?"

"Over there. Look."

Jeremy stood and turned toward the doorway. "You were supposed to wait for me downstairs."

She shrugged. "And you were supposed to meet me there at nine o'clock. It's going on ten."

Chapter Eleven

$\mathcal{S}$hiloh tried unsuccessfully to sit up to meet Melinda before resorting to pressing the button to raise the bed. She cringed when her dad helped her, believing it made her look like an invalid. Even though he made moving the IVs and blood pressure cuff connection look as if it were the most natural thing in the world, it wasn't. She knew there were other kids her age who lived the way she did because she spent time in the hospital with them. But she didn't know even one kid her age out in the real world whose life revolved around medical stuff.

She glanced at the woman crossing the room to see if she'd noticed how the simple movements made Shiloh stop and catch her breath. What kind of kid her age couldn't even sit up in bed without sounding like she'd just finished a hundred-yard dash, especially to someone who looked like she'd gone through Navy SEAL training?

But not even the monitors softly pinging and flashing around the bed or the IV stuck in Shiloh's arm seemed to bother this woman. She'd give up her new iPhone to know for sure whether Melinda was putting on a show, acting as if it didn't matter that Shiloh wasn't like other kids, or if it was how she really felt.

Melinda glanced at Jeremy before moving to stand next to the bed. It seemed like forever until she could put aside her obvious fear and offer a hesitant "Hi."

Shiloh had rehearsed and rejected a dozen greetings, but faced with actually seeing Melinda in person, she couldn't remember a single one of them. What came out was a return smile. "Hi."

Melinda took a deep breath while her heart did a crazy tap dance. Was this the physical reaction when dreams came true? What she'd imagined wasn't close to this reality. Happiness wasn't a soaring feeling, it was rainbows turning into showers of confetti and falling like snowflakes. She reached for Shiloh's hand, making the gesture seem as familiar as two longtime friends running into each other at Starbucks. For what seemed like forever, she stared at her beautiful daughter, dizzy with a sickening dread for all the things that could go wrong. It wasn't that she saw her own mother in Shiloh's high cheekbones, or her father in the crooked smile, or Daniel in her penetrating eyes. It was more that they were all there. "It's been a long time."

Instead of answering, Shiloh sent her father a look that openly begged him to give Melinda a chance.

Aware how easy it would be to say something that would put Jeremy in a defensive posture, Melinda focused on finding a place to tuck the nylon carrier she'd brought. She finally settled on a three-cushion sofa under the window, opening the newspaper she'd picked up in the lobby and carefully tenting the mesh openings.

She wiped her hands on her jeans before turning her attention to Shiloh again. "I'm such an idiot. I really should have called before I came, but all I could think about was getting here as soon as possible. Please tell me you're not allergic to cats."

"Not that I know of. We've never owned one, but one of my girlfriends has two and they always sit on my lap when I'm at her house."

"She's fine," Jeremy said. "Although I'm surprised you'd do something that could get you in so much trouble if you got caught."

"I saw a half dozen companion animals come through the lobby yesterday, cats and dogs." She looked at Shiloh and smiled. "I figured if I did get caught I'd tell whoever caught me that Heidi was a kitten in training."

"And you really believed you could get away with that?" Jeremy said.

"That, and the fact that I can slip in and out of a Kentucky drawl as easily as Ray Allen can make a three-point shot." She looked at Shiloh as if they were sharing a secret. "I've learned from past experience that all I have to do is look confused and talk really fast and throw in a lot of tryin' and buyin' and cryin' and a couple of y'alls and anyone born and raised above the Mason-Dixon Line or west of the Mississippi River automatically assumes my IQ is twenty points shy of average. People are nicer when they feel sorry for you."

Shiloh laughed. "Would you teach me to do that?"

Before Jeremy could protest, Melinda said, "It doesn't work when you're young and pretty. You'll have to wait until you're my age or grow a wart or two on the end of your nose."

"Tell her the real reason you brought Heidi," Jeremy said impatiently.

Melinda barely heard him, caught up in the heady excitement of having a dream come true.

"Heidi?" Shiloh asked. "My dad told me you had a cat, but didn't tell me her name. I loved that book. My grandmother used to read it to me whenever I stayed at her house."

"My Heidi is a kitten, which right now is several months away from being a cat. I found her in the Dumpster behind my condo when I was working in Juneau."

"Someone threw a kitten in a Dumpster?" Shiloh was horrified.

Jeremy looked from Shiloh to Melinda and back again. Melinda had instantly, easily created a connection with a daughter she hadn't seen in over twelve years. He was relieved and unsettled at the same time. For Shiloh's sake he wanted the meeting to go well, just not this well. He moved the chair so Melinda wouldn't have to stand, then went to sit on the sofa next to Heidi.

"I've decided it was an accident," Melinda said, settling into the chair. "I don't like thinking there are people who would do something like that on purpose."

"Me either. Is she okay now?"

"We're working on it. I was late for her last feeding and when I got home she let me know late feedings were not acceptable."

"Can I see her?"

Melinda brought her chair closer to the bed. She glanced down at her hands and saw they were shaking so hard she could easily scare Shiloh into believing there was something wrong with her. She tucked them under her legs. "Did you ever hear the expression 'let sleeping dogs lie'?"

Shiloh shook her head.

"It's an old-fashioned way of saying if everything is going well, don't do anything that might change it. With Heidi, if I wake her up now, she's going to want to eat and explore and find ways to get into trouble. And she's going to do some of it so loudly she's sure to draw attention and get both of us tossed out of the hospital no matter how thick I lay on the accent."

"So why did you bring her when she could cause so many problems?"

Melinda smiled. "Because I wanted to be here to see you as long as I could and kittens as young as Heidi need to be fed every couple of hours. Your dad offered to ask Cheryl to take care of Heidi for me, but she was tied up today."

"I have a dog," Shiloh said.

"What kind of dog is it?"

She looked at Jeremy for help. He shrugged. "Brown?"

Melinda laughed. "That's a good color. Is it the one I saw sitting on the porch of the cottage next door? She stares at the beach house like she's expecting someone. Could that be you?"

"She misses me when I'm gone. Dad was working at the beach house last year, and she probably thought I was there."

Flashes of the people Melinda had loved and lost showed themselves when Shiloh grew animated. She saw her mother in the way Shiloh tilted her head when she asked a question, and her father in the expressive way she moved her hands. Most of all, she saw an innocence and tenderness in Shiloh's eyes that was so much like Daniel's it filled her chest with longing.

"That's the hard side of loving someone," Melinda said.

"Did you miss me?" Shiloh asked, leading with her heart.

And there it was, the reason Shiloh had worked so hard to find her mother. She needed to know it had been as hard for Melinda to give her away as it was for Shiloh to see the mothers who had kept their children. "I missed you every minute of every hour of every day."

"Then why did you give me away? I don't understand." Unmistakable anger threaded its way through the question. Anger laced with pain.

Jeremy got up and moved to the other side of the bed. "We talked about this, Shiloh. You told me you understood you might not like Melinda's answers, but that you would try to deal with them."

"It's all right." Melinda was both surprised and grateful for Jeremy's understanding. "If it were me, I would want to know, too. I'll answer your questions and I'll tell you anything you want to know, but I think we should save those discussions for when you come home from the hospital."

"That's fair, Shiloh," Jeremy said. "You don't want strangers coming and going while you're talking about this."

As if on cue, a cute boy in his late teens wearing blue scrubs brought a tray with Shiloh's dinner. He propped her up with a third pillow he took from the cupboard and rearranged the furniture to accommodate the overbed table.

Shiloh stared at Melinda. "I'm sorry," she said, sounding as sorry as a hacker who'd cracked what was advertised as an impenetrable code. "I promised my dad I wouldn't blast you with a hundred questions on the first day." She lifted the lid covering her dinner plate. "Want to see my punishment?"

Melinda smiled. "My dad . . ." She swallowed at the pain that came with the memory. "Your grandfather was put on a low-sodium diet that almost made him give up eating."

"I'm on a low-sodium diet, too. I won't know how much salt I can have until the final tests are done." She poked at a piece of meat that loosely resembled chicken. "There's no way I can go to a movie and skip the popcorn. My life will never be the same."

"Did your father have kidney disease?" Jeremy asked.

"What makes you think that?" He was right, but how could he know something so specific?

"Low sodium usually means heart or kidney problems. I had a fifty percent chance of being right no matter which one I picked."

"Initially, it was black lung disease. It wasn't until the last stage that other parts of his body began to fail."

"Isn't that something coal miners get?" Shiloh asked.

"Yes."

"My grandfather was a coal miner?" Shiloh opened a container of bright red gelatin.

"Not by choice. My father was fifteen years old when his father left. He went to work in the mines because it was the only job available and the only way to keep the family together. He was the smartest man I've ever known and could have been anything he wanted to be."

"I didn't know they mined coal in Mississippi," Jeremy said.

"I'm not from Mississippi." Melinda had not only set her own trap, she'd sprung it. And now she was caught.

Shiloh frowned. "Then why was I born there?"

Jeremy stared at Melinda. "At the time, you worked pretty hard to give the impression your family came from Mississippi. Why would you do that?"

"It's complicated."

Jeremy came around the bed and reached for Melinda's arm. "I think we better take this out in the hallway."

Chapter Twelve

Melinda twisted free of Jeremy's grip, furious over his aggressive treatment, and did not follow him until he was through the door and halfway down the hallway.

He turned abruptly and waited for her to catch up. "What else are you lying about?" He ran his hands through his hair, leaving it even more unruly. "Goddamn it—I trusted you." To himself he added, "How could I have been so stupid?"

He gritted his teeth and stood toe-to-toe with her. "It's *complicated*? What in the hell does that mean?" When she didn't answer, he jumped to what seemed a logical, painful conclusion. "What happened that made you run away?"

"Tell me why that's important and I might answer."

He lowered his voice to a whisper. "Do you even know who Shiloh's father is?"

She glared at him.

"Were you raped?"

"You're such a . . . such a *man*. You think you have me all figured out and you don't have a clue." Until his call, she'd played by the rules, counting off the days and weeks and months until Shiloh was twenty-one and could make up her own mind whether she wanted to see Melinda.

"I can't see where that's any of your business," she said. "But I wasn't raped. I loved Shiloh's father. I've never stopped loving him."

"Past tense? I suppose that means he left when he found out you were pregnant? Or did his wife find out and chase you away?"

She'd never wanted to hit someone as much as she did Jeremy at that moment. Instead she listened to the voice in her mind that insisted she let it go. "He died. He never knew about Shiloh. If he had, he would have moved heaven and earth to protect her."

"Unlike her mother?"

"You son of a bitch. How dare you say something like that to me? You have no idea what I went through to protect Shiloh."

"Any more than you can begin to understand what I've gone through." He nodded in reply to a greeting by one of the nurses, his posture making it clear he wouldn't welcome an interruption.

"I never said I was from Mississippi," Melinda said. "And I don't remember you or Tess caring enough to ask about me or my family. The only thing you wanted was to get your baby and get away from that hospital as fast as your fancy car could carry you."

He started to walk away, turned and came back. The look he gave her acknowledged the truth in her accusation. "You must have known I was afraid you would change your mind."

She had considered the possibility and rejected it. Her main memories of that day centered around a mortifying shame. Shame over giving her baby away. Shame over the way the doctors and nurses and the other mothers at the hospital treated her. Shame over the way Jeremy and Tess took her baby and left without so much as a backward glance.

Melinda's aunt came to get her an hour later. During the entire ride home she tried persuading Melinda to stay, even offering to pay her to take care of her cousin and clean the house. Of course, because she was being paid, there would be new duties, including cooking and laundry. When Melinda insisted she was needed in Kentucky to take care of her father, her aunt cried at the thought of once again becoming the sole caretaker of her own daughter. Her social life would be curtailed without Melinda, her home no longer preacher's-comin'-to-dinner clean.

"How could I have known something like that? It never entered my mind that you had reason to be afraid of me. I was a naive sixteen-year-old with no one to help me. Your lawyer sure as hell didn't bring it up when he approached me and offered to pay my hospital bill and give me a bus ticket back to Kentucky."

"You could have said no. You weren't coerced as far as I know. Until you signed the papers, you were free to walk out of that hospital with your baby in your arms. There wasn't a damn thing I could have done about it."

"I did say no, but then he told me what great people you were and all the advantages my baby would have with parents who could afford good schools and took vacations in foreign countries and lived in a great neighborhood."

Even more important, and the real reason her mother had worked to get Melinda out of Kentucky as soon as possible, was the frantic need to hide her pregnancy. No one could know. The only way to protect her and Daniel's baby was to come up with a logical reason for leaving.

Evert Lee's influence didn't reach into Mississippi. No one would call him or even answer his calls if he tried to find her. Then, when the adoption was a done deal, it would be long past the time he could do anything about it.

"I held out until your lawyer gave me the letter you'd written telling me how much you wanted my baby that I agreed."

Jeremy moved closer and lowered his voice to barely above a whisper. "And then there was the money. Can't forget that."

"*What money?*" she demanded.

"The twenty thousand dollars."

She let out a snort of derision. "Is that what your billboard lawyer got out of you? If you really wanted to know where your money went, you would have asked to see a check with my name on it."

"Are you saying you weren't paid?"

She put her hands behind her and leaned against the wall. "As far as I know, he settled up with that backwater hospital, paid for a one-way bus ticket to Kentucky, and pocketed what was left. If my aunt hadn't made me a couple of sandwiches I would have been picking through lunch-counter leftovers on the way home."

Jeremy had a hard time letting go of something he'd believed from the day he brought Shiloh home and became her impassioned defender. Melinda selling her baby was the weight that had tipped the unfit mother scale, making it impossible to think of her any other way. "Before you signed those papers, you could have taken Shiloh and walked away."

"And gone where?"

"To your father or mother or even a friend. There's a lot of government help for unwed mothers."

A sudden rage came over her. "Are you trying to tell me that I should have kept Shiloh so you wouldn't be dealing with a sick child now? I wish to hell I had found a way. Every hour of every day I wish that."

Melinda glanced up and saw they had drawn a small crowd at the nurses' station. She crossed the hall to stand closer to Jeremy. In an even, determined tone, she said, "Give her to me now. I'll take care of her. And I'll show her what it is to be loved."

Years of frustration surfaced in Jeremy. "I want you out of

our lives. Go back to the beach house, pack your belongings, and leave. There are a couple of hotels by the airport where you can stay until you can get a flight out. If you try to see or call or text Shiloh before she's twenty-one I'll get a restraining order. How do you think that's going to look on your business résumé?"

"I'm not leaving without telling her why."

"Try and I'll call security to have you tossed out. Is that really the way you want your daughter to remember you?"

Melinda's anger turned into a choking fear. She had nothing on her side, not even a belief he was an unfit parent. "What are you going to tell her?"

"I'll come up with something." He turned and walked back toward Shiloh's room. "I've had lots of practice where you're concerned."

She started after him.

He whipped around and confronted her. "Don't push me."

"I need to get my cat."

He let out a bitter laugh. "Of course the cat would be at the top of your priority list."

She moved to step around him. "I've known some mean men in my life who were just plain stupid in their meanness. You're not stupid, you're cruel."

He put his hand on her shoulder. "You're not going back in there. I'll get your cat and you'll leave." His eyes narrowed. "And you won't come back. Got it?"

A sob caught in her throat. In a choked whisper, she said, "At least let me say good-bye. Please."

"No."

Out of the corner of her eye Melinda saw the nurses busy themselves, shuffling papers and studying charts on computer monitors. A light flashed over the doorway in the room next to Shiloh's. No one got up to answer the summons.

Melinda had suffered shame and heartache and blind anger, but she'd never known humiliation. Until now. She avoided eye contact with the nurses fearing what she would see. She could handle curiosity and dismissal, but not sympathy. That would be her undoing. As long as no one tried to comfort her, or offered her so much as a compassionate look, she could hold her head high and leave with a modicum of dignity.

Jeremy came out into the hallway, closing the door to Shiloh's room behind him. Without a word, he handed Melinda the cat carrier, making no attempt to hide what he was doing.

She drew herself up to her full height, turned, and headed for the elevators, saying a quick prayer they weren't all stuck on the first floor.

SHILOH COULDN'T MAKE out every word, just enough to understand what was going on in the hallway was the end of her dream to have a mother. What her dad didn't understand was Melinda didn't have to be perfect, just someone who would make Shiloh feel like she belonged. There were kids at school with divorced or separated parents, but she didn't know anyone who had been outright rejected by their mother.

Twice. Most mothers fought for their children. Not Shiloh's. A tear slipped down her cheek. She reached for a tissue and wiped it away. The last thing she wanted was her father to start questioning her. He would just blame Melinda and insist he'd been right about not contacting her.

Why hadn't Melinda tried harder to stay? Was it the lupus? Was the fight with her father just an excuse, something she could tell her friends? *How sad it was that their meeting hadn't worked out. She'd tried everything she could think of to get to know her daughter, but it just wasn't meant to be.*

Tears fell from both eyes now. Shiloh grabbed another tissue. What was wrong with her? Why was she so hard to love?

Chapter Thirteen

As Melinda turned onto the eucalyptus-lined road that led to the beach house, a fog of despair followed her. How was she going to go back to the life she'd been living? How was she going to walk into her beautiful, sterile apartment and have any sense of coming home?

Her daughter wasn't a nameless, faceless person anymore. She was a fragile beauty with Daniel's expressive eyes, her only physical connection to her father. Finally, after years of imagining what her daughter looked like, wondering if she would reflect Daniel in the way she moved or smiled or shyly dipped her chin, whether she had dark hair or blue eyes, whether she was tall and lean or short and rounded—Melinda knew.

But it wasn't how someone looked that tilted the scale in

the direction of who they were. Melinda brought an album of family pictures on every assignment, her visual diary of a time and place lost to everything but memories. Personal history had to be shared with someone who cared. Until now, there had been no one since her mother died. Melinda was the connective tissue between her own mother and Shiloh and the only one who could make her father and grandfather real people, not just statistics gleaned from some online research company.

Shiloh's biological family members were pieces of the whole, brought together with stories only important to the people who had lived through them. They were critical in understanding a person and discovering what made them special.

The world wasn't changed in any universal way because Shiloh's grandfather had spent every weekend for an entire summer building a shed on the hill behind their house. Melinda was the only one left to care that the shed held a shower and a washing machine and that no matter how tired her father was after work, even if he'd put in a double shift, he refused to enter the house without taking a shower and washing the coal dust off his clothes. He was terrified he would infect his baby daughter and wife with the black poison he breathed every day.

What kind of man cared that much? Did knowing how he sacrificed for his family make it easier to understand the sacrifice Melinda made to come home to take care of him when he was dying?

In winter he might be half-frozen from walking through snow to get to the house after his shower, but he still greeted her mother with a kiss and words whispered in her ear that made her cheeks bloom in a blush and her eyes light with a smile. Shiloh's grandmother and grandfather had a bond that went beyond romantic love. It sustained them when the mine closed and her father's nagging cough turned into a day-by-day, hour-by-hour battle to draw in every breath.

The changes in their lives were subtle, or so they had seemed at the time. Looking back, Melinda could see with poignant clarity the toll her father's illness had taken on her mother. There were smiles, but the laughter died. Exhaustion etched lines in her face.

Someone had to tell her mother's story. Someone had to care enough to listen. It was the only way Melinda knew to celebrate Mother's Day that gave it any real meaning.

She missed her father every day, the loneliness a constant companion. Her mother was an ache that never went away. She'd understood Melinda's sacrifice in a way no one else would or could. If she'd known how, she would have made Melinda's pain her own, absolving her guilt and erasing her longing. Instead she opened doors for the daughter she loved more than life itself that led to an unexpected healing.

"Why are you crying?" Melinda asked, stunned at her mother's reaction to the early Christmas present. "It's just a fancy phone." She reached across the Formica table, one of ten booths at the last family restaurant still

open in Walker County, and curled her hand around her mother's.

"I know," Mary Ann said, taking a napkin from the chrome napkin holder to wipe her eyes before summoning a smile. "I was just thinking how much it would have meant to your father to see you talking to him when you called. He loved all these fancy new gadgets."

A waitress Melinda didn't recognize came by with a coffee carafe and filled their cups. She wore miniature Christmas tree earrings that brushed her shoulders and a large silk poinsettia pinned to her bosom pocket. "You ready to order?" she asked, her hand poised to snatch a pencil with candy cane stripes propped behind her ear.

"How is the fried chicken today?" Mary Ann asked.

The waitress glanced over her shoulder toward the kitchen before she looked at Mary Ann and shook her head, the Christmas trees slapping her neck.

"Meatloaf?" Mary Ann ventured. "I've been cravin' a nice thick slice of meatloaf with baby peas and gravy and mashed potatoes."

The waitress rolled her eyes. "As long as you don't mind it being your last meal—ever—it might do."

"What would you suggest?"

"The house salad."

"The house salad it is," Mary Ann said.

"Make that two," Melinda added.

"Crackers or fresh homemade garlic bread?"

Melinda gave her a questioning look.

"The bread is the best thing on the menu." She smiled. "Says so right on the frozen package, just below where it says homemade."

A woman stopped by their table when the waitress left, a baby in her arms, a toddler hanging on to the hem of her oversize sweatshirt. Like the majority of women in the holler she was a poster child for fast food, preferably batter dipped and deep fried. "Hey, Melinda. Long time no see." She shifted the baby to her other arm. "You here for Christmas, or did you finally graduate from that school up north?"

It was obvious this was someone Melinda should recognize but she couldn't see anything even remotely familiar. "I'm here for Christmas and then it's back to school for my final semester," she said, buying time.

"Chrissy May's moving back home," Mary Ann said, recognizing Melinda's confusion. "Tyler volunteered for another tour of duty in Afghanistan. What is this, Chrissy May—the third time he's been over there?"

Chrissy May nodded.

Finally Melinda recognized the girl she'd gone to school with since the third grade. She struggled to hide her surprise at the startling change. How, in three and a half years, could the first two-time homecoming queen winner at Henry's Pond High School, a girl who could flirt her way out of a traffic ticket with the ease

*of a runway model marrying a millionaire, turn into a
woman with vacant eyes and sloped shoulders?*

"*Tyler said he figured he wouldn't be coming home
this time, 'cause his number was up. He's been right
about things like that—he knew his cousin Leroy
wouldn't see his twenty-first birthday—so I decided I
better be looking for someplace I could afford to live.
If I'm going to be alone, I want to be around family.
I'm tired of spending Thanksgiving and Christmas by
myself. And I really miss all the summer barbecues.*"

*Melinda smiled. "Especially Fourth of July with the
parade and fireworks."*

*Chrissy May shifted her baby to her other hip. She
lowered her voice. "My grandma told me if Tyler knew
what he was talking about and I really am going to be
all by myself I better start lookin' around for someone
to support me and help raise my kids." She shrugged.
"Here I am. Back where I started."*

"*Your mama must love having you home again,
especially with those beautiful little boys to keep her
company,*" *Mary Ann said.*

*Chrissy May opened the blanket covering the baby
and held her up to give Mary Ann a better look. "No
reason you should know, what with me being gone all
that time, but this one's a girl."*

"*Look at all that blond hair,*" *Melinda said. She
and her mother exchanged furtive glances. Babies were
something they never talked about, even when they*

were alone. Despite all the years that had passed since leaving Mississippi, the loss was like an open wound.

Chrissy May brushed the baby's downy blond hair to one side. "Her daddy says she's going to be a real looker when she grows up." She blushed. "Just like her mama."

"I'll remember Tyler in my prayers," Mary Ann said. "God willing, he'll be home to see his babies grow up into the fine young people they look to be."

"Thank you, Miz Campbell. Having you single Tyler out that way in your prayers means a lot to me."

The toddler tugged on his mother's sweatshirt. "I'm tired, Mama."

Chrissy May gave Melinda a look that crossed from envy to wistfulness as she took her son's hand. "Nice seeing you again, Melinda. I hope you get yourself a good job when you graduate and that you're happy living up north."

"Thank you. I'm excited to think I'll finally be doing something outside a classroom. Seems like I've been in school my entire life." She knew the second the words were out that it had been the wrong thing to say.

"I don't know what it's like to be in college goin' on four years with all the parties and foolin' around that happens there, but I do know what it feels like to be stuck in an apartment in a strange town with two babies and no friends. You think one's worse than the other?" She left before Melinda could answer. The

sound of plastic Christmas bells clattering against glass marked her exit.

"What was that about?" Melinda asked her mother as they watched Chrissy May head for her car.

"You never have been one to listen, Melinda. You have to see things for yourself. Now that you're a semester away from graduating I thought you could use a gentle reminder how small this town is, in every way."

"You set this up?"

Mary Ann took a drink of water, made a face, and put the glass back on the table. "Didn't have to. I knew if we sat here long enough, someone you went to school with was bound to come by. This place is what passes for entertainment around here now that the theater closed."

"You think I would wind up like Chrissy May if I came back?" She was disappointed and a little angry.

"Tell me your options. Make a list for me and start with how you'd put all those years you spent in college to use around here when there's not one local company that would give a woman a job that didn't involve running personal errands for the boss. Is that what you want? To become a glorified secretary for some man who refuses to give serious consideration to anything you do or say simply because you're a woman?"

The waitress brought their salads and basket of garlic bread. "You listen to your mama, honey. She knows what she's talkin' about." She moved on to another table before Melinda could answer.

"I'm going to start my own company," Melinda said, hoping it would satisfy her mother. "There are a lot of businesses in the region that are vulnerable to computer hacking. All I have to do is show them what could happen to their bottom line if—"

"You're too smart to believe anyone around here would hire you. Evert Lee still tells everyone he meets that you're responsible for Daniel's car going off that bridge. He's never going to let it go, Melinda."

"No one believes him. They know what kind of man he is and what he did to Cole and Abby."

"You know the people who live here, Melinda. You know how they think and how they act. There's not a man with any influence in Walker County who can handle a woman who's smarter than he is."

Melinda stared at the red and green and silver garland swags draped throughout the restaurant, at the lopsided artificial tree in the corner by the front door decorated with cutouts from old menus, and the thick layer of dust covering the neon sign in the window. Truth be told, she didn't want to live in this town again. If she could, she would walk away and never look back.

If only she could get her mother to walk away with her. Until then, Melinda would endure a crush of memories as painful as a wreath of poison ivy.

Chapter Fourteen

$\mathcal{M}$elinda had friends, but none so close she'd called any of them more than a couple of times the entire six months she'd been in Juneau. They were the kind of friends who were perfect companions for a dinner at one of the trendy new restaurants that seemed to open on a weekly basis in Minneapolis, or a night at a comedy club when she was desperate for a break from work. But none were the kind of friends who cared enough to listen if she'd wanted to talk about her mother and how she'd refused to leave the town that had broken her heart because her husband's ashes were scattered there.

Mary Ann couldn't leave him, not even when it was her beloved daughter who asked. Not even when she had to wait five months for a mammogram and four more months for a diagnosis. By then the particularly aggressive cancer had left her breast and settled in her bones and liver. Even then Mary Ann wouldn't leave and vehemently refused to let Melinda come home to care for her.

For the first time in her life, Melinda didn't listen to her mother and took an extended leave from work. They had a week together at home and three days in the hospital and she was gone. With her heart breaking with every step, Melinda hiked to the tree where they had scattered her father's ashes. She knelt in the damp mulch that surrounded the tree and cradled the wooden jewelry box that held her mother's ashes.

"Daddy knew how much I needed you and how lonely I would be with both of you gone. But I don't think he had any idea how much you missed him or how lost you were after he was gone." She let out a hiccuped sob as tears spilled down her cheeks and dripped on her coat.

"I know Daddy has already found Daniel, but I need you to promise me you'll tell him again that everything I did was to protect our baby. He can't wonder about that. He has to know and I don't think Daddy would tell him the way you will."

As she scattered her mother's ashes a weight settled on Melinda, the heavy awareness of what it was to be alone, truly alone. There was no one she could turn to with family questions or a shared "remember when . . ."

Melinda understood the how and why of friends drifting away. Six months was a long time. Friendships needed care and nurturing to develop into something deeper. FaceTime wasn't the same as spending time looking into someone's face.

So far she'd found ways to cope with the loneliness, some more successful than others. As much as she loved her volunteer work at the hospital, she paid a price every time she left. The babies haunted her and not only in her dreams, but when she should have been concentrating on a security problem for a client.

She'd tried garnering some enthusiasm for redecorating her apartment—the one the company had leased for her seven years ago, but it still looked exactly as it had the day she moved in. Her only contribution was a shelf filled with books, the same ones her father had once checked out of the library over and over again. She owned copies now, some new, some not so new, all of them paid for with her first check from Wyndham and Parker Security Systems. Next to the books was a framed photograph of her mother and father's wedding. Most days she purposely avoided looking at the photograph. Instead of seeing the love, she saw how alone she was.

She dated, but rarely went out more than twice with the same man, as much because of her job as a lack of interest in the men she met. She'd had a three-month relationship with a political science major in college that broke up when he put a bumper sticker on her car promoting a candidate she considered a fascist. He said it was a joke. She told him she wasn't laughing.

Melinda made her way to the front door of the beach house,

sidestepping flowers that dipped their heavy heads onto the walkway, dropping seeds the birds ate and scattered in yards and gardens throughout the cove. She barely registered the show being put on over the ocean where the sun lit the sky in oranges and pinks and a bold stripe of purple as it neared the end of that day's journey. The warm light coming through the sliding glass door filled the living room.

Freed from her carrier, Heidi took off down the hall to her litter box. Melinda headed for the kitchen and the kitten food. A spasm hit before she made it to the doorway. She put one hand over her mouth and the other across her stomach as a second and then a third followed. *No*, she silently pleaded. *Not now. Please.*

She swallowed, once, twice . . . then, acknowledging there was nothing she could do but give in, took off running toward the master bathroom.

Five minutes later, her face washed and teeth brushed, but still in the middle of berating herself for the insane way her body released stress, she looked at herself in the mirror. Why couldn't she just cry like everyone else? Crying was accepted, even encouraged. No one ever said, "Why don't you just throw up?"

And yet there were times she cried. Like now. Not gentle or dignified tears. These were the kind accompanied by breath-stealing sobs, companions of a broken heart. She could count the number of times she'd cried so hard she was convinced she'd never recover. But she had. And she'd gone on just as she always had.

She backed against the wall opposite the mirror, her full weight pressing against the towel and towel rack. As she slid to the floor, both came with her, the bar releasing with a popping sound. Heidi appeared in the doorway. She studied Melinda for a long time, tilting her head to one side and then the other.

Melinda reached for the towel on the floor beside her and buried her face in the thick terry cloth. Heidi crossed the room and climbed on her lap. She stood on her back paws and reached for the towel, catching her claws in the loops and pulling until Melinda uncovered her face and acknowledged her.

Melinda looked into her eyes and, with one last hiccuped sob, put her hand on Heidi's head and scratched her ears. "How pathetic am I that you're my only real friend and the whole time we've been together I've been trying to find a way to get rid of you?" Melinda winced at the thought. She could just imagine what Jeremy would think if he heard her planning to give away yet another helpless infant. He already believed she had the nurturing instincts of a cowbird.

"What am I going to do, Heidi? I can't leave. Not now. Shiloh needs me." She reached for a length of toilet paper to blow her nose. "And I need her."

The sun was long gone, the sky a fleeting crimson remnant of its escape by the time Melinda roused herself from the bathroom floor and took Heidi into the kitchen to feed her. This time the meal was followed by an impossibly loud burp.

"Keep this up and I'm not going to be able to take you anyplace nice to eat." Fresh tears touched the corners of her eyes as she attempted a smile.

Desperately tired, fighting a stabbing headache and throbbing sinuses, Melinda cleaned the kitchen and went into the living room, not bothering to turn on a light. When she curled up on the sofa, Heidi nestled into her side, always ready for a nap.

Melinda closed her eyes but sleep eluded her. She had to come up with a way to approach Jeremy that would let them start over and put their ugly encounter behind them. She tried, but couldn't fault his stubbornness. He believed he was protecting Shiloh from someone who would upend their world. What he couldn't see yet was that no matter how much he wanted to erase all of yesterday, it wasn't going to happen.

If necessary, she would rent an apartment and stay in Santa Cruz until he changed his mind about letting her see Shiloh. For as long as she could, she would work from home and if her job suffered, she would get another. She had the savings she'd put away for Shiloh.

All she needed was a place to stay, nothing fancy, a room above a garage would do, where she could work and wait until Jeremy changed his mind or Shiloh turned twenty-one.

She'd lost her father, the window to her intellectual soul. And her mother, who'd loved her without question, the way no one ever would again. And she'd lost Daniel, her soul mate in a world too jaded to recognize the concept. She would not lose her daughter. Not again.

Her life had been impossibly hard and filled with crushing disappointments, but she would go back in a heartbeat. She was loved in that world and she loved in return. Chores were never a burden, secondhand clothes were good enough. Pleasure came from a sandwich made with tuna on day-old bread and a spirited conversation over which Founding Father had the most influential wife. A good-bye hug from her mother was enough to make Melinda believe the birds sang just a little louder on her way to school in the morning.

Melinda closed her eyes and drifted back to a place where she'd been loved, throwing her emotional arms wide in welcome even as her mind shouted a warning that she could not go there without paying a crushing emotional toll.

Chapter Fifteen

Melinda found Daniel at the McElroy place. By the time she reached him she was gasping for air and nearly incomprehensible.

He grabbed her arm to hold her upright. "What's wrong?"

"I—need—your—help," she said between gasps. "My father is dying. He has to get to the hospital and he won't let me call an ambulance. I can't get him there by myself." She explained about the oxygen tank and how she'd tried to reach her mother.

Unlike most privileged children in Eastern Kentucky, Daniel's father made sure he understood poverty. Evert

Lee used it to wound his most tender child, insisting it was the only way to toughen him up.

Evert Lee took Daniel with him on his weekly trips to deal with the indigents he claimed were drawing the lifeblood out of the mining company. He wanted him to see babies crying with hunger at empty breasts and blank-eyed toddlers facing futures without hope. A harsh look at the real world would turn his son into a man and make him appreciate his God-given position in life.

His father's greatest pleasure went hand in hand with forcing Daniel to tell miners who had already lost everything that the company was taking their home, too. Anyone foolish enough to tie their mortgage to the company that dictated hours and income deserved whatever came their way.

Worse than the shame of being told in front of their families that they would be homeless was hearing it from a kid still a year shy of starting high school.

Daniel stood and reached for Melinda's hand. "Go back and stay with your father. If it looks like he's not going to make it, no matter what he says call 911. We'll figure out how to pay for it later."

"He won't let me."

"How's he going to stop you?" He took her other hand and held them tight against his chest. "I promise you won't lose your home."

"How can you promise something like that?"

"I just can. And I will."

She didn't have the heart to tell Daniel that there was no way her father would accept money from him. "Whatever you're going to do, please hurry."

Daniel put his hands on either side of her face and kissed her. His lips were soft and pliant, and even though it was meant to reassure her, not show her how he felt, the kiss was everything she had dreamed kissing him would be, just not here and not now. "I'll meet you at the house."

She nodded and took off, running in the direction she'd come from to get there, stumbling over a root hidden by rotting leaves and looking back to see if Daniel had seen her. He was long gone.

Melinda repeated a silent prayer for her father over and over again as she zigzagged past rocks and ran through creeks.

Overcoming a choking fear at what she would find, Melinda went inside and stared at her father, willing him to breathe and letting out a cry of relief when she saw her prayers were answered.

She carefully eased onto the couch to sit beside him, snuggling as close as she dared to keep him warm but not restrict his breathing. She'd never been this scared, not even when her mother hemorrhaged after miscarrying a baby when Melinda was eight. There had been blood everywhere. Worst of all had been the tears. Her mother wasn't supposed to cry like that. She was the *one who dried Melinda's tears and told her everything would be all right. It never was again.*

Melinda jumped at the sound of footsteps and loud thumping on the front porch. She raced for the door and gasped in surprise when she saw Daniel standing there, an oxygen tank cradled in his arms. She opened the door wider and stepped to the side. "How did you—?"

"I'll tell you later," he said. "Do you know how to hook this up?"

"Yes—at least I think I do. I've watched the delivery guy every time he's here."

Daniel stood the new tank next to the old one. "Hi, Mr. Campbell," he said in a confident voice. "It's me . . . Daniel."

Melinda worked on the tanks, her hands shaking so badly she had trouble taking the regulator off the old tank and putting it on the new one.

"I have a friend who uses oxygen," he went on. "She keeps a spare in case the first one gets low. She said she'd be happy to loan you her extra one until yours is refilled."

Melinda believed everything except the "happy to loan" part. He hadn't been gone long enough to have that kind of discussion with anyone. She turned the flow dial, heard the familiar hissing sound and rocked back on her heels intently staring at her father's chest.

She focused on every move the way a bank teller surreptitiously watches a burglar. His response to the oxygen wasn't a miracle, but it was closer to one than she'd dared hope. He opened his eyes and attempted a smile.

"Good work, you two. I don't know how you pulled it off, but I'm more grateful than I know how to say." He had to pause several times, but managed to finish. "I think I'll take a nap now." He looked at Melinda, and winked. "If that's okay."

She readjusted his blanket. "Of course it's okay. I don't need you awake to keep an eye on you. I'll be right here, holler if you need me."

"Protect yourself, Daniel," he said, before he closed his eyes. "There will be hell to pay if you're caught."

Melinda took Daniel into the kitchen. "What did he mean, protect yourself? What did you do?"

"Nothing you wouldn't have done."

So much for the "happy to loan" he'd tried to sell her. "That's not an answer."

"It's the best you're going to get. I don't want you to know anything else because I don't want you involved. If anyone asks you about how your dad got the tank, you'll be able to say you don't know and mean it."

"I'm not going to let you take all the blame—" She drew on her best defense, she got angry. Hands on her hips, she confronted him. "Just tell me, Daniel. I should at least know what I'm going to be accused of doing."

"I stole the tank."

Her eyes widened in surprise. Daniel didn't steal. He'd even refused to eat the cherries she'd picked from a neighbor's tree without permission. "How? From where?"

"It was easy. My aunt, the one who comes for a month every summer, is off visiting her daughter in Pikesville while my dad is in Ashland. She'll be gone until Friday."

"What aunt?"

"Linda Sue. She's my father's sister. She's been coming every summer since the divorce. Supposedly to take care of me, but I think she's really looking to get away from my uncle."

"And she uses oxygen?"

"My dad swears she doesn't need it, that she only hooks it up when she wants attention. Half the time the oxygen isn't even turned on."

Melinda went to the refrigerator and took out the pitcher of sweet tea her mother had made the day before. The tea wasn't as sweet as it should have been what with sugar nearly as expensive as coffee, but it was still better than the cheap cola sold at the Buy-A-Lot over in Pikesville.

She added ice and handed a glass to Daniel. "Won't she notice it's gone?"

"Not if she's still staying with her daughter. If she comes home early, I'll show her where my dad hides his sippin' whiskey."

"You're going to get caught," she said. Her anger turned into fear.

"I don't care."

She could see that he did. "Tell me what I can do to help."

He went over his hastily conceived plan. As soon as they heard the driver approaching to deliver the new tank in the morning, they would disconnect his aunt's tank and reconnect the empty tank. When he was gone, Daniel would load his aunt's tank back on his bicycle and head home. With just a little luck his aunt would still be at her daughter's house and he could skip the whiskey.

Everything went according to plan right up to the moment Daniel pulled into the driveway and saw the garage door open with his father inside leaning against the back fender on his candy-apple red, 1995, Cadillac DeVille.

Melinda took off for Daniel's house as soon as the new tank was hooked up. She waited at their usual place nervously pacing as the sun moved from tree to tree through the forest. He'd made her promise she wouldn't go to the house no matter how long she had to wait. It wasn't a casual promise, the kind you could convince yourself it was okay to break. This was the serious kind where friendships hung in the balance.

Only knowing she could make things worse than

they already were kept her from crossing the yard and ringing the doorbell. Instead, after more hours than she wanted to acknowledge, she picked up her bike and cast one last look at the house before heading home to check on her father.

Sometimes fate alters lives by days or sometimes only hours. Sometimes it's no more than the seconds it takes to pedal a bike noisily through low-hanging branches or over piles of the previous winter's leaves.

Bleeding and bruised from the beating his father had given him, Daniel ran behind the house and up the steep embankment, knowing it was a direction his father wouldn't and couldn't follow. He ran until he stumbled and fell from exhaustion and then got up and ran some more.

It was long past dinnertime when Melinda heard a car pull into their driveway and got up to see who it was. She'd been watching for Daniel all afternoon, her heart racing at every sound. When she saw the familiar red Cadillac she let out a loud moan, calling to her mother as she ran into the kitchen. Mary Ann looked up from dropping rounds of biscuit mix into a pan filled with peaches.

Melinda grabbed her mother's arm. "Daniel's father is here. You can't let him come in. Tell him Daddy isn't feeling well, or that I'm sick—but don't say anything about Daddy having an oxygen tank. Please, please, please make him go away."

Responding to the panic in Melinda's actions and voice, Mary Ann wiped her hands on her apron and headed for the front door. Questions would come later. She stepped onto the porch, closing the door behind her.

Melinda couldn't hear what was being said, but she could make out the anger coming from Daniel's father and the opposite tone coming from her mother. She was so caught up with what was happening outside that she almost missed her father calling her.

He motioned for her to help him remove the cannula. "Take all this business into the bedroom."

She hesitated.

"Now," he said with surprising strength.

She rolled the tank across the hardwood floors as quietly as she could, reaching the bedroom just as the front door burst open.

"Cross that threshold and I'll have you arrested," Mary Ann said in an even, icy tone. Evert Lee moved to push her out of the way. She blocked his path. "You may have half the people in this county afraid of you," she said, "but I know for a fact the sheriff isn't one of them. After the way you screwed his brother out of his pension, he would love nothing more than to haul your ass to jail."

Evert Lee took a step backward before he put his

hands on either side of the doorframe and leaned for-ward to look inside. "Daniel? You in there? Your life is going to be a living hell if I have to come in and get you."

"He's not here," Melinda said. "I haven't seen him since day before yesterday." It was what Daniel had told her to say.

"Don't lie to me. I know you two are out in those woods every chance you get doin' God knows what."

Melinda's father braced himself on the arm of the sofa and stood. "You're forgetting where you are, Evert Lee. You damn well better apologize to my wife and daughter and then get the hell out of my house. Come back and I'll have to call on my crazy cousin Monroe to pay you a visit. You remember Monroe, don't you? I know he remembers you."

At the first sign of light in the morning, Melinda took off to look for Daniel. She found him at the McElroy place, curled into a ball in the corner by the fireplace, covered by the green blanket they used for their picnics. A fence lizard sat on the windowsill watching her. She put her backpack on the table and approached Daniel, her hands trembling in fear over what she would find. The lizard took off, disappearing so fast she wasn't sure which direction he'd gone.

Sensing her presence Daniel stirred, letting out a soft moan before opening his one good eye. The other was swollen shut, a cut running parallel to the brow, dried blood from the wound crusted in his ear and scalp. His lip was split and distended.

Melinda put her hand over her mouth and dropped to her knees. She reached out with her other hand, her fingertips settling on his cheek. He flinched and she jerked backward, believing for an instant that she was the source of his pain. "I will never forgive your father for this."

Filled with a need to hold him, she took his hand and cradled it between her own. "I'm so sorry, Daniel." With a hiccuped sob, she added, "This is my fault. I never should have—"

"Stop it, Melinda." His anger seeped through the pain. "There's only one person this can be laid on, my good-for-nothing father." He carefully moistened his lips with his tongue, avoiding the split. My dad likes nothing better than beating one of his kids. You should have seen him. He let out a whoop every time a blow landed. He called me a fucking baby when I begged him to stop. I think he would have killed me if my aunt hadn't come home and threatened to tell my mother what he'd done."

Daniel's voice lowered and turned monotone as if he were drifting away. He inched forward over the splintered wood flooring and put his head in her lap.

She saw that he was crying. It was harder to look into his sorrowful eyes than at his bloodied face. A *man crying was akin to cowardice in Walker County, something no man would want another man or woman to witness. It was a measure of the depth of her love for Daniel that she saw through the tears and into his wounded soul. He had sacrificed everything for her. She had never witnessed anything as brave.* "What can I do?"

"Nothing."

Time passed slowly as neither of them said anything. "I brought an apple." *Could she have offered him anything more stupid? Daniel could no more open his mouth far enough to eat an apple than he could a SuperSonic Double Cheeseburger.* "I could bite off a piece for you. I brought a biscuit with blackberry jam and a hard-boiled egg, too."

"I'm not hungry."

He looked up, turning to see her out of his good eye then doubling over and holding his sides in an effort to contain the pain. She'd never seen Daniel like this and it scared her. It wasn't the first time his father had beaten him and likely wouldn't be the last. How many more times could he go through that kind of abuse and survive?

"What happened?" *Gut instinct told her there was more to his grief than the beating he'd endured.*

He didn't answer.

"Please, Daniel."

Still, he didn't say anything. She waited, feeling his heart breaking, desperate to find a way to help. Finally, she stopped trying.

Gently weaving her fingers into his, she said, "I came home from school when I was in third grade and told my father there was no way I was ever going back, that no one could make me, not even him. My teacher was like your father, a man who hurt people because he could, and because he liked it more than a trained dog likes catching a squirrel and hearing it scream in fear.

"He waited until I'd spent all my anger before he asked me why I was willing to let my teacher have all that power over me. I didn't have an answer. And my teacher didn't have power anymore. He couldn't have what I didn't give him. I hate your father but I understand why you can't."

Daniel struggled to sit up. "If he hadn't reached the shotgun first I would have put a hole in the middle of his fat gut."

An icy hand pressed itself against her spine. "I don't believe you."

"You don't know me as well as you think you do." He shook his head. "My father was laughing when he told me it was time I knew I was never going to see Cole again. The son of a bitch has known what happened to my brother since the night he left, but he's been waiting

for the right time to tell me. He said he didn't want to waste the moment."

Before Daniel could say anything more, Melinda carefully wrapped her arms around him. She didn't want to hear what would come next almost as much as he needed to tell her.

"Cole's dead."

"Oh, Daniel. I'm so sorry." Melinda held on as tight as she dared, making a decision in favor of emotional pain over physical.

"He parked his car in the middle of the Rappano Bridge, stood on the railing and jumped. There was a witness. He said Cole never hesitated. He just got out of the car and walked over to the railing and . . ."

"I don't believe it," she said. "Your dad is just looking for a way to hurt you. If it were true, how come we never heard anything about it?" Gossip was like hard cider to the people who lived in Walker County, better tasting when passed."

"The coroner's my uncle." Daniel winced when he tried to shift position. "He's been afraid of my dad since they were kids. It makes sense he kept his mouth shut."

She was desperate to give him something to hold on to. "Still, there must have been someone who—"

Daniel raised his arm and put it across his eyes. "Cole's face was so messed up from hitting the rocks it took two weeks for my uncle to figure out it was him." The rest was said barely above a whisper. "Knowing

Cole, he was hoping he'd be taken downstream and end up feeding the fish in Lake Walker. He would have liked that."

Melinda put her hand to her stomach and then her mouth. She swallowed over and over again, but it was useless. Finally she made it to the back window and did what she always did when there were no words.

Chapter Sixteen

Melinda walked the length of the cove, accompanied by seagulls and a mix of long- and short-billed shorebirds. Midway, she stopped and stood on the packed sand at the edge of the incoming tide. A foamy rush of water washed over her feet and climbed her ankles before racing back to join the next wave.

Birds with thin inwardly curved bills ran forward, dipping deep into the sand, withdrawing crustaceans and worms and snails in rapid movements then racing out of the way of the next incoming wave. Occasionally their prey was large enough to identify, but for the most part, their beak movement made it obvious the hunt had been successful. Cumulatively and determinedly they consumed enough to sustain them.

The foam developed a pink hue as low-hanging clouds picked up color from the early-morning sun that topped the hills behind her. As if painted with an enormous brush dipped in containers of orange and pink and purple, the colors filled the sky and minutes later disappeared almost as quickly. A flock of pelicans skimmed the waves that broke offshore, emerging through a paint pot of color and disappearing minutes later into blues and grays of incoming fog.

Reason dictated that a sunrise lasted as long as a sunset, but it never seemed that way to Melinda. With a sunset, just when it seemed the show was over, a lingering spray of color would catch what had been ordinary clouds and turn them into shimmering silk.

During her few short years with Daniel, their favorite time together was spent sitting with their backs propped against the shagbark hickory tree on the rise above the cabin, talking about their future while the glow of a setting sun filled the sky around them. A sunrise didn't welcome lingering, but came with demands to start the day.

Melinda turned to look at the beach house perched on the cliff behind her. She'd been there less than twenty-four hours and yet felt a connection so powerful it confused her. She'd loved Juneau, attributing her unusual feelings to the exotic and unexpected journey of exploring mountains cloaked in rain forest clouds, or ocean water suddenly exploding with a pod of humpback whales bubble net feeding. But it was more. Being at the ocean, whether in the wilds of southeast Alaska or along the sprawling Monterey Bay, she felt a sense of belonging she hadn't felt since losing and leaving all that had bound her to Eastern Kentucky.

It didn't surprise her in the least that she would find her daughter near an ocean.

She'd been awake all night going over every abbreviated moment she'd spent with Shiloh at the hospital. How had she and Jeremy taken so many wrong turns when all either of them wanted was what was best for Shiloh? Was he to blame for allowing himself to be manipulated into contacting her before he was ready? Should she have recognized the hazards that went hand in hand with a hastily arranged reunion?

But how could she? Jeremy's phone call was the fulfillment of a dream she'd had from the day she'd put Shiloh in his arms. A dream she'd secretly believed would never come true.

Another row of brown pelicans appeared from behind the cliff that marked the southern end of the cove. They followed the pattern of those that had already passed, skimming the tops of waves for the updraft, in the process creating nearly effortless flight. She watched them until they were out of sight, then wandered over to sit on the log she'd spotted earlier. The weathered gray wood looked as if it had been sanded and polished by decades of use, begging stories, created or true, to be told about when and how and why it had washed ashore at this precise location. Another flock of pelicans appeared, this time headed in the opposite direction. The irony prompted a laugh. Like the pelicans, she didn't know whether she was coming or going.

The peaceful sounds of the morning were abruptly shattered with a cacophony of loud barks. Melinda turned to see a knee-high brown dog with floppy ears making a beeline for her. She braced for an impact, but it never came. Instead the dog circled her, making excited hopping movements as it rounded the ends of the log, reminding Melinda of YouTube videos of dogs greeting soldiers who had come home after a long military assignment.

She lowered herself to her haunches to put herself at the dog's level and wound up sitting in the sand when she lost her balance. Determining her body language as an invitation, the dog crawled into Melinda's lap, tilted her head up and covered her chin in sloppy dog kisses. "Good morning to you, too."

"Coconut, *no*," a woman shouted as she ran toward them. She wore shorts and a sweatshirt with GREENPEACE written across the front in rainbow colors. Free of cosmetic trappings, her gray-streaked dark blond hair tied up in a casual ponytail, she was quick to smile. Melinda put her at anywhere from thirty to fifty.

The woman worked on a scowl as she approached. "Bad dog."

Coconut appeared to take the reprimand as encouragement and pressed into Melinda's side with increased enthusiasm until she saw a purple-and-white polka-dot leash appear out of the woman's pocket. Instantly, she dropped her head. Dejected, she trotted back to sit at the woman's feet and patiently waited for her confinement. With the leash attached she became the epitome of the well-trained dog, walking at the woman's side, her tail whipping the air, her tongue lolling from side to side.

"I'm so sorry," she said, extending her hand to help Melinda stand. "I took her off the leash before I saw you and that's like leaving a dozen five-year-olds alone at a birthday party. We usually have the beach to ourselves this time of the morning."

"No problem." Melinda tried brushing the sand off her damp chinos but saw it was useless.

"I'm going to hazard a wild guess . . . by any chance, are you Melinda Campbell?"

Melinda hesitated answering. "Yes."

"I'm Cheryl, your next-door neighbor. And this is Coconut, Shiloh's dog." She reached down and scratched the dog's ears. "Jeremy told me to expect you. He said you'd be staying at the beach house for a couple of days."

A lump filled her throat. "When did he tell you that?"

"Last week."

She caught her lip between her teeth then let it go with a deep sigh. "There's been a change in plans."

"I was afraid of that." Cheryl reached over and gave Melinda a touch on her arm. "Shiloh didn't handle any of this the way it should have been handled. She took advantage of her latest hospital stay to maneuver her dad into making a decision he wasn't ready to make. But then she's had him wrapped around her finger from the beginning."

"Maybe she didn't have any other option." Melinda stopped to pick up a flat round shell with a palm leaf design on the surface. It looked like an ephemeral piece of art. She tucked it in her sweatshirt pocket knowing it was a mistake to gather physical memories but unable to stop herself.

"I picked up a blueberry coffee cake at Gayle's last night. If you help me eat it, I won't have to commit the unpardonable sin of putting what's left in the freezer. No one else in the family likes blueberries so the only time I indulge is when I can get a friend to indulge with me."

The "friend" part took Melinda by surprise. Her first inclination was to decline the offer. She didn't make friends easily or willingly, especially not when it involved revealing details of her private life the way any conversation with Cheryl was bound to. But if ever she needed someone to talk to, it was now. She looked down at her sand-encrusted slacks. "Give me ten minutes to get out of these wet clothes and take care of my kitten."

"Kitten?"

"It's a long story." She actually smiled. "If you're lucky, I won't bore you with it."

"Take as long as you need. The guys are at the nursery today and won't be home until dinner so we have all day."

"The guys?"

"My husband and our son, Bobby. Shiloh and Bobby became best friends almost from the moment they met. She was exactly what he needed at the time to keep him from a gang of boys at school that were getting in all kinds of trouble. He's turned into the sibling she wanted but never got."

Melinda moved toward the stairs, wisps of hair blowing

across her face as the calm air changed into a gentle breeze. One day she would ask Cheryl about Shiloh and Bobby's relationship and what made it special, but not now—not yet. "And the nursery?"

"We grow wholesale orchids. The kind you buy at your local grocery store."

Poignantly aware it might be one of the last times she had the opportunity, Melinda turned to look at the ocean before climbing the stairs. She glanced at Cheryl. "As much as I would love to spend the morning with you, I don't know that it's such a good idea. I was supposed to move out of the house last night."

"Does that mean you're packed and ready to go?"

"No."

"Or that you intend to spend the rest of the morning packing?" she added slyly.

"No."

Cheryl smiled. "Good for you. I wouldn't either. Now, it seems to me that leaves you plenty of time for cake and coffee and conversation. If nothing else, it will help pass the morning."

Melinda looked down at her pants and the tenaciously clinging sand. "I'll be over as soon as I clean up."

"Great." She caught Coconut before she could take off to check out a jogger with a golden Lab in tow. "Something you need to know is that right or wrong, Jeremy will do whatever he feels is necessary to protect Shiloh."

"I got that."

Disheartened that her beach time had been cut short, Coconut followed Cheryl to the back porch where she patiently put up with having her paws and haunches sprayed and then wiped down.

Melinda stood on the front porch at the beach house and tried for the second time to brush sand off her pants. She succeeded enough to step inside and strip behind the closed door. Heidi heard her and came running down the hallway, stopping several feet away and staring. As if approaching something alien, she made her way across the carpet, ready to pounce.

It took several seconds for Melinda to realize what was wrong. Heidi's path to Melinda's shoulder had been cut off at the ankles. There was nothing to hold on to, nothing to climb that wouldn't bring a shriek of pain from Melinda. Heidi knew this because she'd tried and the result had been exceedingly unpleasant for them both. With Melinda half-naked, how was Heidi supposed to get from point A to point B?

Melinda bent and scooped Heidi into her arms. "I don't want to hurt your feelings, but I met a dog today that just might be a little smarter than you are."

Heidi had already discovered the betrayal by thoroughly sniffing Melinda's sweater and giving her an accusing look when she tried to feign innocence. She climbed higher, perching on Melinda's shoulder and head butting her, staking her claim.

Melinda choked back a threatening sob as she tried to remember when she'd last experienced anyone or anything caring about her enough to feel possessive.

Chapter Seventeen

"Coffee or tea?" Cheryl called to Melinda as she came through the back door.

"Tea."

"A woman after my own heart."

Actually, it was the open shelves in the kitchen, lined with plain and fancy antique teapots, that had clued her in. Sitting in the middle of the room was a rustic kitchen table finished in a light walnut stain that looked as if it had been rescued from a flea market refuse pile. The kitchen, and what Melinda could see of the living and dining rooms, were decorated in shabby chic. Not the artfully put-together pieces purchased from a decorator's gallery, more an assortment of beloved hand-me-downs gathered from family basements and attics.

"Shiloh called me this morning," Cheryl said, as she added a healthy scoop of black tea to a rooster pot to steep. "She wanted to make sure you were still here."

"What did you tell her?"

"That as far as I knew you were." She took two mismatched plates from the cupboard, added a piece of blueberry coffee cake, forks, and cloth napkins, and put them on the table. "At least your car was still in the driveway. She asked me to find a way to convince you not to leave."

Cheryl sat across from Melinda, tucking one leg under the other. "I probably shouldn't tell you this, but she was crying." She poured their tea, passing the sugar and milk along with the steaming mug. "Shiloh never cries."

"Something we have in common," Melinda said. Along with her mother and, according to her father, her grandmother.

Cheryl smiled. "With me it doesn't matter if it's a book or movie or some dumb television show. There are times I've broken down watching the evening news. And don't even get me started on those Clydesdale horse beer commercials."

Melinda tried, but couldn't manage to get even one bite of the blueberry coffee cake past the lump in her throat. "Is that what this get-together is all about? Shiloh crying?"

"Partially," Cheryl admitted. "But there are some things I think you should know to help you understand what's going on with Jeremy. As he sees it, Shiloh has been abandoned twice already, and he'll do whatever it takes to make sure it doesn't happen a third time. He's protective when it comes to his daughter, sometimes overly so."

Melinda let out a frustrated sigh. "Abandoned? Why is it so hard to understand that a woman can give up her baby for adoption out of love? I didn't abandon Shiloh. I did the only thing I could to protect her from a brutal grandfather who would have emptied his considerable bank account to get custody if he'd even suspected I was pregnant with his son's child.

"Not a day has gone by that I haven't thought of her. Not a birthday or Christmas or Halloween passes that I don't fantasize what it would be like to have her with me. I've created theme parties in my head for every one of her birthdays, going so far that I made up imaginary friends she would invite and the games they would play."

She tested the tea and found it cool enough to drink. "Birthdays were important in our house when I was growing up. For years my mother said we would do something extra special to celebrate when I turned sixteen."

"And did you?"

Melinda stared at Cheryl over the steaming mug. "I had Shiloh. Our birthdays are a month apart."

Cheryl held her mug up for a toast. "Happy birthday."

Melinda smiled. "Thanks."

"Do I need to ask what you'd like for a present?"

"No . . . I think it's fairly obvious."

"I don't think anyone who's gone through what you have could begin to understand how hard it's made everything that followed," Cheryl said.

"I've put myself to sleep at night mentally shopping for

the material I would use to create a Hermione Granger Halloween costume, hand-stitching a Gryffindor emblem on her hooded robe and painting her wand—because, of course, any daughter of mine would love Harry Potter as much as she loved the time we spent reading the books together." Why was she babbling all these intimate thoughts and feelings to someone she'd just met?

Melinda made her usual, dismissive hand gesture. "I'm sorry. I shouldn't be unloading on you like this. I know it makes me sound as crazy as I feel sometimes."

Cheryl got up and opened the back door then pulled the screen closed. The air that stole into the room was cool and slightly damp, and filled with a salt-tinged fragrance that made anyone considering a nap inclined toward a walk on the beach instead.

"I'm not judging you. There are as many reasons a woman decides she can't keep the child she brought into the world as there are babies. I'm sure Jeremy didn't tell you because there's no real reason he should, but all of my children are adopted. Each one came to us in a different way and for a different reason and each of them has dealt with it in a different way."

Melinda tilted her head in curiosity. "How do they feel about their birth mothers?"

"It depends on which day you ask. The girls vacillate between hurt and anger, but they are never neutral. Not yet. It's going to take time because their pain is real, and as much a part of them as their extraordinary talents. You can't compare them to Shiloh. Their backgrounds are nothing like hers. They came to us as teenagers after years of mental and physical abuse."

Cheryl gathered the crumbs on her plate with her fork and took one last bite. "We learned early on that it doesn't matter how many times Andrew and I would tell them that they shouldn't judge someone until they'd walked a mile in their shoes, they couldn't understand. Not really.

"It doesn't matter how uncaring or abusive or neglectful a mother is," Cheryl went on, "she occupies a unique position in a child's world. I'm sure you've read about Steve Jobs. His entire life was altered because he couldn't deal with being given up for adoption even though he was raised by wonderful parents."

"And what about Bobby?"

She smiled. "From the minute he was born, Bobby has known both of his mothers. It's made a world of difference."

"You agreed to an open adoption?" Melinda knew what they were, but couldn't imagine they succeeded.

"We suggested it."

"And it's worked?"

"Better than we had hoped. Bobby accepts he has two mothers and isn't confused where either of them belong in his life."

"How did you—?"

She smiled. "I'll tell you about it one day over coffee cake you actually eat."

Melinda couldn't let go. "Other than letting me know Tess

is out of their lives, Jeremy hasn't said anything about her. I have no real idea what she's like, but from the bits and pieces of things I've picked up, I don't think she would have agreed to an open adoption."

Cheryl leaned back in her chair. She studied Melinda. "There's a story behind that relationship that's even uglier than the way Tess left six years ago. I can tell you some of it but you'll have to get the rest from Jeremy."

"Jeremy has been a single parent all this time? Shiloh hasn't had a mother since he and Tess were divorced?"

Cheryl shook her head. "No mother since she turned seven, and no divorce."

"I don't understand how everything could fall apart so fast. The adoption agency assured me that all the babies they handled went to stable, loving families. They even offered to let me meet other mothers who'd gone through the process." Looking back, she realized she'd been so young and so desperate she must have heard what she wanted to hear. Without her own mother or father to guide her while she hid in Mississippi, she'd made one bad decision after another.

"I don't know anything about private adoptions," Cheryl said. "All I know is that Andrew and I went through months of interviews and background checks when we adopted out of the foster system here in California."

"You said Tess didn't handle the separation well? What happened?" Melinda automatically assumed Tess had done something classless, like sending a text.

"Tess could become the next Mother Teresa and she would

never perform enough good deeds for me to forgive her for what she did to Jeremy and Shiloh."

Melinda wasn't sure she wanted to hear what came next.

"Tess took off the day before Shiloh's seventh birthday and Shiloh hasn't seen her since. For a long time I think Jeremy blamed himself, but he finally realized the only thing he'd done wrong was to fall in love with someone as egocentric as Tess and believe he could build a life with her. They didn't adopt Shiloh because they couldn't get pregnant, Tess didn't want to. She thought pregnant women were ugly."

"And Jeremy thought he could save their marriage by bringing an innocent baby into it? He used Shiloh?"

"I suppose there's some of that, but it's a small part. Jeremy was meant to be a father. He's one of those men who could have a half dozen children without any of them feeling neglected. It took him over a year to talk Tess into adopting. I think he'd convinced himself that once the baby was a part of their lives, Tess would come around." The shell wind chimes on the porch caught the breeze and played a brief melody.

"I barely knew them when this was going on," Cheryl went on. "Jeremy was in the middle of working on an addition to one of the other houses in the cove when Shiloh had a flare-up that marked the end of her remission. Within days she was back in the hospital. Jeremy told the owners of the house that he would help them find someone to finish the work, but they refused to let him go."

Coconut came into the room to check on them, pushed her nose against the screen, and took several deep sniffs. Satisfied all was as it should be, she sat next to Cheryl, put her muzzle on her thigh and commandeered a quick ear scratch, rewarding Cheryl with a contented sigh.

Cheryl absently ran her fingers through Coconut's fur as she picked up the story. "In the time Jeremy had been working on the house he'd made several friends with the other homeowners. If there was a party, he and Shiloh were invited; if there was a school holiday, neighbors vied to have Shiloh stay with them. She charmed couples whose own children had moved away and left others who still had children at home wondering how they could teach them to be as caring and intellectually curious."

"It sounds a little like a fairy tale," Melinda said.

Cheryl laughed. "I never looked at it that way, but I guess it does."

"So I assume they waited for Jeremy?"

"They went a step beyond. Shiloh became their project. She spent most of her time with one couple but everyone pitched in." Cheryl gently put her hand on the teapot, decided it didn't need to be rewarmed, and refilled their cups.

"You're probably wondering why I'm boring you with all of this, but there's an important subtext. Your time here is like a short sentence encapsulated in quotation marks. It's important you see and feel and experience the paragraphs and chapters that preceded your coming if you want this to work."

Melinda leaned back and let out a pent-up sigh. Embarrassed, she admitted, "I came here filled with family history

I wanted to share with Shiloh. I failed to take into consideration she had her own history she'd want to tell. Thanks for reminding me."

Cheryl brought her other leg up and tucked it under the first, yoga fashion. "I want this to work. For all of you."

"This Botswana thing is a done deal?" she asked.

"Bad timing, huh? But it's one of those now-or-never situations, and I really believe Bobby would benefit the most of all of us. Although, I have to admit, I'm pretty excited about seeing all those animals wandering around without cages."

"The first time I was outside Kentucky was when I went to Mississippi to have Shiloh. I've been to fifteen states since. I would love to see Botswana."

"We'll be there a minimum of three years and we'll have a guest room. You're welcome to stay whenever you want." Her eyes lit up. "It would be fabulous if you could find a way to talk Jeremy into bringing Shiloh for a visit. He desperately needs to be convinced Shiloh can lead a more normal life than she has now."

Melinda understood what Cheryl was doing and wasn't sure how she felt about it. Unwilling to have her hopes built any higher, she changed the subject yet again. "You said the people who live in this cove helped take care of Shiloh. What was wrong with her that time?"

"The lupus settled in her joints. It's not that a lot of damage was done, but the pain was debilitating. Luckily, she had every kind of care she needed, and more. One of the men is a retired Stanford English professor. He worked with the teachers at the private school Shiloh attended. One is a world-class artist. He taught her the basics of drawing. The list covered a part-time nurse and a writer who worked with her on a memoir.

"Shiloh has had a multitude of mother figures since Tess walked out," Cheryl added. "Some of them male. She's been well loved."

Chapter Eighteen

$\mathcal{U}$nable to sit still any longer, Melinda got up to clear her plate from the table. She maneuvered around Coconut who, satiated with petting, had moved on to take possession of the braided rug in front of the sink. She reached for the kettle and held it up. "Do you mind?"

"Not in the least. I've never felt possessive about my kitchen. If someone had the urge to prepare a five-course meal and wanted to do it here, they'd be welcome to whatever they could find." She chuckled. "Of course I would expect to be the beneficiary of their effort."

Melinda might not be able to get the coffee cake past the lump in her throat, but she felt as if she could drink a gallon of tea, the hotter and stronger the better.

Cheryl joined her, helping with the tea brewing by adding a large scoop of fragrant rooibos tea. As naturally as a hen tucking a wayward chick under her wing, she slipped her arm around Melinda's shoulders and gave her a hug. "I shouldn't say anything, and I won't go into details, but with everything else that Jeremy has going on in his life right now, I have a feeling you're exactly what he needs. It's important for him to see you fight for Shiloh even if he refuses to give an inch."

Melinda was nearly undone by the simple kindness. She wasn't sure about Jeremy, but she liked to think she could make a difference in Shiloh's life. Impulsively, she asked, "Did Tess leaving have anything to do with Shiloh's lupus?"

"According to the letter she left for Jeremy, it was the only reason. She said she hadn't signed on to be the mother of a sick child. She listed a dozen reasons it would be unfair to ask her to stay but never once mentioned how Shiloh was supposed to deal with losing another mother."

The kettle whistled. Startled, Melinda forgot the pot holder when she reached for the handle. Cheryl caught her hand. "Whoa," she said. "The last thing you want is to go into the hospital at the same time Shiloh is coming out."

They took their tea outside on the back deck and stood at the railing while they waited for the fog to finish its journey inland. "I love mornings like this," Cheryl said. "For me fog is like being wrapped in an ephemeral blanket."

"I've never thought of it that way. Mostly my mind goes to how dense the fog is and whether or not it's going to screw up my commute." She glanced at Cheryl. "Sad, huh?"

"To each her own. Being a stay-at-home mom allows me the luxury of contemplation. No matter how bad things are going at the nursery or how frustrated I am when Bobby tells me he's not going to Botswana with us and there's nothing we can do to make him, I can escape out here to recharge myself. You, on the other hand, have to earn a living."

Yes, there was that. Despite their unusually familiar closeness that made them more like siblings than boss and employee, if she didn't return her boss's calls, and do it soon, she wouldn't be making a living, she would be living off her savings. It didn't matter that she had taken vacation time to come here—the first vacation she'd taken in five years. In her boss's mind, a major part of her job was constant and instant availability. "You said Tess left Jeremy a letter . . ."

"Ah, yes, the infamous letter. Jeremy tried to keep it quiet, but there was a gossip network at the school Shiloh attended that rivaled the most lurid London tabloid. The way Tess left Jeremy and Shiloh was too good not to make the rounds."

"I wondered why it was so hard to find anything personal about him online. It was almost as if he'd hired someone to remove anything that didn't have a direct connection to his construction company."

"That doesn't surprise me. He skips most of the award banquets and I can't remember the last time he attended one of the charity fund-raising dinners in Silicon Valley where they put everyone's picture online. I know he's invited to them, but—" Cheryl's eyes narrowed as she peered through the fog, poised to give chase to something only she could see.

Melinda's gaze swept the gray, but she didn't see anything unusual.

"There's a gull that comes by every day around this time. He's after a nest of baby birds that hatched last week in the lilac bush."

"I didn't know gulls would do that."

"They will go after small, full-grown birds, but another bird's young are the most vulnerable and disposable."

"How are you going to survive three years in Africa?"

"Trust me, I've given that a lot of thought. There's no way I'm going out on safari unless the guide promises me he'll leave if a predator is going to make a kill." Satisfied the gull had moved on, Cheryl sat down on one of the cushioned Adirondack chairs. "Where were we?"

"The letter," Melinda prompted, taking the other chair.

"Shiloh was only seven when all this happened. It's hard to know people are talking about you at that age. Jeremy was miles beyond angry and as soon as possible switched schools, sending Shiloh to a private academy he couldn't afford."

Melinda loved knowing this about Jeremy. "Would it be better if you didn't tell me what else was in the letter?"

"Probably, but if you don't know, you will never understand why Jeremy feels the way he does." She did another visual sweep of the fog-shrouded beach and rooftops. "Somehow you and Tess have merged in his mind and he has a hard time separating his feelings where you're concerned. When he thinks about the way Tess abandoned Shiloh, you get thrown into the mix. He knows it isn't fair to you, but most of all he sees what it's done to the person he loves more than anyone in the world, making her doubt her worth because she was abandoned twice. In his mind, to defend you is to defend Tess."

"Jeremy made his feelings clear last night," Melinda said. "Of course I had no idea where he was coming from, but now that I do, I can see that he's not likely to change his mind."

Cheryl took a minute to run her fingers through her hair. "You need to hear the rest. It wasn't like Tess left her note for Jeremy on their bedroom pillow. That would have been too easy. Instead she made a big deal out of giving it to Shiloh when she dropped her off at school that last day. She made Shiloh repeat her instructions until she had them memorized. First, her father would be the one picking her up that night. He would look for her on the bench under the oak tree and he would be very angry if she wasn't where she was supposed to be when he arrived.

"Second, and this was the most important part, she was to give her father the letter as soon as he picked her up. Since it wasn't the first time Tess had been late, Shiloh's teacher waited a half hour before she got concerned and tried calling. Unfortunately, Shiloh remembered her mother's letter at the same time her teacher found the address book she kept for all the kids in her class. Thinking, hoping it was an explanation for the late pickup, the teacher opened and read Tess's farewell letter to her husband and daughter. You can imagine how fast that story traveled through the school."

Melinda worked to contain the wave of rage that consumed her. How could Tess do something so cruel to the trusting little girl she'd promised to love and protect? What kind of monster was she to do this to a seven-year-old dealing with a life-threatening illness? There were a hundred ways she could have left Jeremy, why choose this one?

Coconut came out to join them, immediately laying claim to the worn decking between the chairs, letting out a contented sigh, and falling asleep.

"When she's here, our dear sweet Coconut is the official greeter for the residents of the cove. Self-appointed, I should add." Cheryl reached for Coconut's leash, hooked one end to her collar and the other to the chair.

Melinda let her mind drift to an image of the chubby-cheeked baby she'd held in her arms for those three short days. As if she, too, somehow had known their time together was limited, her baby gifted her with fleeting poignant memories. She smiled and cooed and studied Melinda's face with surprising intensity.

At times, guilt almost overwhelmed Melinda. Why hadn't she worked harder to find a way to keep Shiloh and still protect her? There had to have been a way.

She'd traveled this road too many times to go back there now. There wasn't anything else she could have done. Every decision she'd made had been to protect her and Daniel's baby from the man who had killed his own son. That was as true and as real now as it had been then.

She would not beat herself up over something Tess had done.

"Are you all right?" Cheryl asked.

"What was she thinking? What kind of woman is she?"

"That's easy," Cheryl said. "She was thinking about herself. That's all she ever thought about. My take on this is that Tess wanted to end her marriage in a way that would destroy any hope Jeremy might have for a reconciliation."

"She must have stopped loving him a long time before this happened. Do you know why?"

"I can guess. Jeremy became her protector in college. Knowing someone's dark secrets turns you into a threat no matter how often you reassure them none of it matters. He knew she grew up in a trailer park with a father who was in prison for selling drugs and a mother who was an alcoholic. She couldn't disappear into the fantasy life she created for herself while she was living with someone who knew the truth. Until Shiloh came into their lives and opened Jeremy's world, he would have sacrificed anything and everything to make Tess happy."

"She strikes me as the kind of woman who doesn't just walk away when there's money to be had. Why not divorce Jeremy legally and get what she could when she could?"

"A couple of years into their marriage she started a small company that sold high-end shoes and bags to the kinds of stores where you have to make an appointment to shop. An entrepreneur who represented a chain of these stores in Asia approached her with an offer that all but guaranteed to make her one of the world's most successful fashion wholesalers. If she had tied up her company in divorce proceedings she would have lost the contract."

Melinda picked up her tea. It was cold, but she didn't care. Her mind worked better when she had something to do with her hands. "I wonder how long it took for her to come up with her exit line."

"I think things like that came naturally to her."

"What a friggin' bitch." She glanced at Cheryl. "Sorry, that's the kind of thing I usually keep to myself." Melinda swore, but rarely in front of anyone. As a woman traveling and working alone, it was foolish, and potentially dangerous, to try to pass herself off as one of the boys.

"Oh, don't stop there—shit, hell, damn, bastard are always good tension relievers for me." She grinned. "I try not to let Bobby hear me when I'm on a rampage, but I don't beat myself up about it if he does."

"She could have come up with a hundred ways to leave Jeremy without involving Shiloh. It's almost as if she purposely wanted to hurt her," Melinda said. She couldn't let go of a question with incomprehensible answers.

"I've always wondered why she agreed to the adoption. According to the people I've met who used to know her, she never wanted kids."

"Could it be she loved Jeremy?" Melinda could see the appeal, especially if she tried to imagine what he was like before the weight of the world settled on his shoulders.

"Maybe in the early days before he brought another person into the mix. Especially when he put the other person ahead of Tess. No one got away with something like that."

Coconut raised her head and cocked her ear toward the

beach house. Recognizing the sound of Jeremy's truck she took off, forgetting she was on a leash and choking herself when she came to the end. Cheryl checked to see that she was all right and then handed the leash to Melinda.

"What do you want me to do with her?"

Cheryl answered with a conspiratorial smile. "Use her as an icebreaker between you and Jeremy. She's really good at putting things into perspective."

Chapter Nineteen

Jeremy met Melinda on the front porch. "I see you're still here." He lowered himself to his haunches and tried to tamp down Coconut's out-of-control excitement.

"And you're not surprised."

"No, I guess I'm not."

Hope soared. "You could have called."

"My mother taught me that apologies should be made in person," he said through a symphony of whines, head butts, and slobbering kisses. Melinda foolishly released the leash, assuming Jeremy was in control. Realizing she was free, Coconut took off for the truck, dragging the leash behind her, snagging flowers and leaving a trail of broken blossoms.

Coconut circled the truck, stopping to bark when she reached a door, then moving on again when it didn't open.

Jeremy shook his head. "She'll go on like this until she sees for herself that Shiloh isn't hiding inside. It's a game they play."

Melinda waited on the porch when Jeremy went to indulge Coconut. He opened both front doors and let her climb around the truck until she was satisfied Shiloh wasn't there.

Melinda didn't understand the change in Jeremy's attitude, which made her afraid to accept it at face value. She almost laughed out loud at her thought process. What possible difference did it make whether she liked or trusted his attitude? She had to work with what he gave her.

She took the key out of her pocket and unlocked the door. "I found the coffee, if you're interested."

"I am, thanks." He motioned with his hand, indicating she should go first.

Heidi heard the door open, and as always, came bounding down the hallway. She spotted Coconut immediately after she saw Melinda and came sliding to a stop on the hardwood floor. As if genetically programed for that precise moment, she turned sideways, arched her back and came up on her toes. She glared, growled, and then hissed in an admirable attempt to intimidate an adversary thirty times her size. The more Heidi hissed, the faster Coconut wagged her tail.

With her heart in her throat, Melinda didn't know whether to grab Heidi or Coconut. Jeremy settled it when he crouched down, gathered Coconut to him and tucked her head under his arm. She freed herself, looked at him, and then at Heidi. The expression was unmistakable, *look what I found—a new toy.*

Jeremy sat down, his legs stretched out to form a V, with Coconut sitting between them. He put his hands on the sides of her head and gently massaged her ears while making her look at him. "This is a good thing," he said softly. "Her name is Heidi and she's going to teach you how to behave when you meet a four-legged bundle of pure attitude for the first time."

Coconut looked up at him and whined, no more interested in a lesson in manners than a visit to the vet. *Don't you see this great new toy? Why aren't we playing with it?*

Heidi took a couple of hesitant sideway steps toward them, her eyes never leaving Coconut. Melinda held her breath trying to decide whether Heidi was brave or foolish and whether she could safely wait to find out when instinct demanded she rush in to rescue the kitten that had emotionally rescued her.

Seeing how frightened Melinda was, Jeremy said, "I've got her. She just needs to realize this is Heidi's territory for now and that she doesn't have free rein anymore."

"How can you be so sure she's willing to let that happen?"

He chuckled. "Coconut understands she's out of her league. I've never seen a cat with more spunk."

While they speculated on the outcome of the lopsided confrontation, Heidi continued to sidle up to Coconut, stopping inches away to make several guttural hisses and actually spitting, something Melinda thought was limited to snakes in the animal world.

Melinda rocked back on her heels. Her fragile six-week-old kitten, still no bigger than a three-week-old, had turned into a panther.

Coconut pushed against Jeremy, trying to bury her face under his arm. "It's okay," he told her. "She's too little to hurt a big dog like you."

Heidi took a final step forward and sniffed, moving from one end of Coconut to the other. The yowls and hisses faded, replaced with cautious curiosity. Coconut tolerated the examination, even reciprocated when Heidi gave off an invisible clue that she would allow it. A final hiss elicited a tail thump.

Coconut tilted her head and licked Jeremy's chin. "Good girl," he told her.

Heidi turned to leave, each step calculated and measured. She looked away, but gave the distinct impression she had eyes in the back of her head. When she neared Melinda her retreat turned into an unmistakable swagger. "I'm impressed," Melinda said to her self-assured cat, slipping her hand under Heidi's softly rounding belly. "But I wouldn't push my luck if I were you."

Feeling more confident, Coconut crawled off Jeremy's lap and, with her head lowered the requisite degree of subservience and her tail making appeasement overtures, made her way across the room an inch at a time. She avoided direct eye contact with Heidi but her intent was obvious. She'd found a substitute friend as a placeholder for Shiloh and she was ecstatic.

Melinda glanced at Jeremy. "You said you were here to apologize?"

"Something like that."

"Me too."

"Oh yeah?" He focused on Coconut. "I have to admit I wasn't expecting that. I was the one way out of line."

Melinda unfolded her legs and moved to stand when a sickeningly familiar dizziness enveloped her. Her heart sunk. *No, no, no—please no,* she mentally begged.

She recognized what was happening and knew there wasn't a thing she could do about it. In less than a second she would pass out.

"Damn" was all she could manage before she doubled over and hit the hardwood floor with a thud that sounded like a walnut cracking.

She woke up less than a minute later. Jeremy had laid her flat and was hovering over her with an enormous construction flashlight that he moved from one eye to the other. She made a face and blocked the light with an outstretched hand.

Heidi jumped on her stomach and hiked to her chin, pointedly sniffing Melinda's exhaled breath when she arrived. Melinda moved to sit up. Heidi meowed in protest and Jeremy gently put a hand on her shoulder to keep her from moving. Coconut sat next to the sofa, openly curious but unconcerned.

"Cut it out you two," Melinda said. "I'm fine. This happens all the time."

"Really?" He gave her a skeptical look, but didn't push.

"Maybe not all the time, but it's not the first time. I haven't eaten a lot lately and it makes me a little light-headed."

"So I can call off the ambulance?"

Melinda lifted his hand off her shoulder. "Please tell me you didn't do that."

Coconut made a hesitant approach to check on Melinda, her tail tucked tight between her legs. Heidi swatted the tip of her nose with sheathed claws. Coconut reciprocated with a broad tongue swipe that left Heidi rolling on the floor. "Looks like they were working on a peace treaty while I was out," Melinda said.

Jeremy stood and held out his hand. "I guess you could call it that."

She came up too fast, wanting to impress him with how quickly she'd recovered. Instead she fought a dizziness that almost had her on the floor again. "Sorry," she said. "I normally have sense enough to go a little slower when I first wake up."

"When was the last time you ate?"

She tried to remember, going over the food she'd been offered, the salad she'd bought at the airport and then ignored, the cookie the flight attendant had given her with a cup of black coffee. Of all the times in her life she'd ignored food, this had to be one of the most foolish.

"I don't know," she told him. "I get sick to my stomach when I'm upset and food gets stuck in my throat. You'd think I would learn."

He shook his head. "How often do you pass out like this?"

"What?"

"Please don't play dumb. I'm not going to think you're a hazard unless you stop eating again."

"This is the third time it's happened. Once when I was working really long hours chasing a hacker in Nova Scotia and I simply forgot to eat."

"And the other two times?"

"One time," she corrected him. "After my mother died and I had to get her house ready to sell." She turned to look out the sliding glass door and locked gazes with a house finch. She'd done what she could to clear closets and drawers, but there wasn't anything she could do about the memories.

"Damn. I came here to make sure you were gone and—"

"And to apologize?" she suggested.

"Yeah, that too. The last thing I thought I'd be doing is playing short-order cook."

"I'm perfectly capable of taking care of myself."

"I can see that." He cupped her elbow and maneuvered her into the kitchen and onto a stool. "Sit here while I make you something to eat."

Other than holidays or celebrations at friends' homes once or twice a year, no one had prepared a meal for her since her mother died. "I can help."

"You'd just be in my way." He went to the refrigerator and took out cheese, chives, milk, and a carton of eggs. With deft, practiced movements he chopped a tomato and diced an avocado and set them aside.

"This happens to be Shiloh's favorite breakfast."

She smiled. "You're not going to believe this, but it's mine too. Minus the avocado. They weren't all that plentiful where I grew up and I never developed a taste for them." Still feeling light-headed, she leaned forward and rested her chin on her hands. "Let's talk about this apology thing. I don't want one, I just want to see Shiloh."

He let out a frustrated sigh. "There are going to be ground rules. Lots of them."

"I can handle that."

Intuitively, he knew where to find things in the kitchen, opening drawers and cupboards as if he'd arranged them. The omelet came together seemingly effortlessly. Melinda was impressed.

He put a pair of plates on the counter. "What if I told you that you couldn't see Shiloh unless I was there?"

So much for the quiet, intimate moments that were the foundation of friendships. But she certainly couldn't argue that he was being unreasonable. "I wouldn't be happy about it, but like I said, I'll follow whatever fair rules you come up with."

"You know it might have been smarter not to add a qualifier to that sentence." He put her plate next to his on the counter. "Eat."

She was stunned at the sudden, overwhelming feeling of hunger that came over her. She became aware of every meal she'd missed in the past week and it was almost impossible not to consume the omelet with the same gluttony Heidi had shown when she had been forced to wait for a feeding.

"Promise me you won't do this to yourself again—at least not while you're here—and I'll rethink letting you be alone with Shiloh." He got up and went to the refrigerator for a carton of orange juice.

When he started to pour them both a glass, Melinda said, "None for me."

"Are you allergic?"

"No."

He put the carton back. "This is what I was talking about. Do you make a habit out of not eating? I don't want to have to worry that Shiloh is going to witness you starving yourself and passing out. She has enough to worry about without adding a mother with an eating disorder."

Melinda ate her last bite of omelet, put her plate in the sink, and went to the refrigerator. Purposely she took out the orange juice carton and filled her glass. Staring at him over the rim she didn't put the glass down again until it was empty. "Good?"

Jeremy couldn't conceive how two people who'd spent a total of four days together over almost thirteen years could possibly be so much alike. He hated admitting it, even to himself, but Shiloh was the image of her mother. "Good enough for now."

"What do I have to do to convince you to let me see her alone?"

"Why is that so important? What difference does it make if Cheryl is there? Or me, for that matter?"

"I want to answer questions I don't think she would ask with other people around."

He leaned into the counter. "Like?"

"Why I didn't keep her."

"Why didn't you?"

"My father was dying, and from the time I was nine years old, it was my job to take care of him. My mother worked, but she hardly made enough money to pay the utilities and taxes and buy food. Even though we had a car, she walked five miles back and forth to her job six days a week. It didn't matter if it was summer or winter, she refused to waste money on gasoline."

Melinda found a tiny piece of the yellow sponge and rolled it on the counter the way Heidi rolled the foam golf ball she'd found under the bed in the back bedroom. Without looking up, she went on, "When the weather turned bad, she left the house earlier. Her boss would throw a fit if she came in late and she was terrified to give him any reason to fire her."

"I assume jobs were hard to come by," Jeremy said.

"They were so scarce people simply stopped looking. I was home for spring break my sophomore year in college when I overhead two men talking about how lazy mountain people were and what a mistake it would be to build a plant where you couldn't count on the labor."

Jeremy's normal hostile posture softened. "So you gave Shiloh away because you couldn't take care of her and your father at the same time."

"If that was all it was, we would have worked something out."

"Then what?" he pressed. "Help me understand."

She resented having to defend herself. Why couldn't he accept her answer when she told him leaving her baby was the hardest thing she'd ever done? "My reasons are complicated and would take more time to tell than either of us want to spend right now."

"Then give me the abbreviated version."

"Daniel's father drove two of his three children to suicide. If he had known about Shiloh, he would have moved heaven and earth to get his hands on her just for spite. There was no way in hell that I was going to let that happen."

Jeremy ran his hand across the stubble on his chin and said more to himself than to her, "Finally, something that makes sense."

He folded the towel he'd taken from under the sink and put it away. "All right. You can spend some time alone with her. But only while she's in the hospital. And not today. She's still upset about last night and I want to give her time to work it through. I'm counting on you backing off if you get the impression she's not handling the meeting well. I'll be in the lobby. All you have to do is call."

"Don't you have a job?"

"You know I do."

When it became obvious he wasn't going to say anything about the stress he had to be under juggling a construction company, a daughter in the hospital, and a woman he would just as soon got on the next plane to Minneapolis, she said, "Fair enough." She stood and moved toward the door. "For now."

Melinda slowed, stopped, and turned to look at him. She had made a transition from poised for battle to recognizing she owed Jeremy an acknowledgment for all he was going through. "I know how hard this is for you and I understand why you wish you'd never found me. I also know there's no reason for you to believe I will do whatever necessary to protect Shiloh." She blinked back threatening tears. "Even if it means leaving and staying away until she's older and better prepared to have me in her life."

"I hope you mean that," he said.

She reached up and pulled strands of hair in her ponytail in opposite directions to straighten it, because it gave her something to do. "I know what I want," she said, pulling the band from her hair and running her fingers through the mass in a useless effort at orderliness. "What do you want?"

He hesitated a long time before sitting on the stool she'd just left. She took the one beside him.

"I thought about this a lot last night," he said. "What I really want is for you to spend a couple of days with Shiloh, long enough that you're both satisfied and ready to get on with your lives. And then I want you to leave. Most of all, I want my life and Shiloh's life to go back to the way it was."

Coconut followed Heidi into the kitchen and pressed against Jeremy's stool as she watched the kitten reach for Melinda's leg and crawl up to her lap. Melinda lifted Heidi to her shoulder and reassured the kitten when she seemed confused by all the hair. She motioned for Jeremy to finish telling her what he wanted.

"You can send the occasional text and give her a gift card on her birthday and Christmas and I'll make sure she does the same for you. But summer vacations are out. And when she has another flare you will not come rushing to the hospital to play the mother role then disappear after you feel you've put enough points on the scoreboard."

"Ouch."

"Sorry—I know that sounds harsh, but that's the way it is."

"Okay, I've listened to what you want. Now it's my turn. I can either go through your list point by point or cover it all with a simple no. I'm willing to compromise. I understand why you don't want me drifting in and out of your lives, but now that I've seen Shiloh and talked to her I can't pretend she doesn't exist. What you don't understand is that I've been holding long conversations with Shiloh for years. Just last month I told her about the whales that come to Alaska for the summer. Every day I tell her how special her father was. I have a bookshelf filled with books my father shared with me when I was her age. I want to share them with Shiloh. I know how to make the world's best spiced peaches. It's a recipe that's been passed down in my family so many generations no one knows where it came from originally."

"Why am I not surprised you won't just fade away?"

She knew it wasn't the time or place, but she laughed anyway. "Because you knew what I would say before you started your list. What was that anyway, an exercise in frustration?"

"More like hope rides a golden horse."

She thought about his answer. "I don't understand."

"It's from a story I made up for Shiloh when she was first diagnosed with lupus."

She swung around on the stool and stood, fighting both a powerful stomach spasm and tears gathering on her lower eyelids. "I like that you made up stories for Shiloh," she said softly. "It's something my father used to do for me."

"We're forgetting what Shiloh wants, whether she wants you to stay, or once she's satisfied her curiosity, she would just as soon you left."

Melinda couldn't tell if he was being cruel or simply stating a fact. Either possibility was too painful to bear.

Chapter Twenty

Melinda sat tucked into the corner of a three-cushioned hospital sofa, her arms wrapped around her legs, her chin on her knees. Intently staring at Shiloh, she studied every detail of her face, assigning her nose to her grandfather, her cheeks to her grandmother, her lips to Daniel. In reality her daughter was a masterpiece of combined attributes that had come together to create a unique young woman.

A nurse came into the room, frowning when she saw Melinda. "I was expecting Jeremy."

"He's on his way."

The nurse checked the monitors and IVs and made notes on her iPad. She glanced at Melinda. "Family member?"

There wasn't an easy answer. She let it go with a simple "Yes."

The smile of relief said it all. The nurse was interested in Jeremy. For women hitting the nest-building stage in their lives there was nothing sexier than a nurturer, a man who would father her children and care for them through runny noses, temper tantrums, and soccer practice. Add the physical attributes of an athlete who had the ability to appear comfortable in his own body and the combination became damn near lethal.

"I don't remember seeing you here before," the nurse said.

"Night before last was the first time."

"I heard," she said cryptically, letting her know the confrontation between her and Jeremy had made the rounds. With her notes and physical check of Shiloh completed, the nurse picked up her iPad and started for the door.

"Is she doing okay?" Melinda asked.

"I can't talk to you about the patient unless you're on the medical release list." She propped the chart on her hip. "Are you?"

"No . . ."

"That's something you'll want to take care of as soon as possible." With that she glanced one last time at the monitors. Satisfied, she left.

Melinda waited, watching the open door and listening intently for footsteps before she unfolded her legs and got up to check on Shiloh. She reached through the bars and slipped her hand into her daughter's.

Was this real? Was it truly possible that she was standing next to her daughter, that she could touch her and talk to her and breathe the same air?

Shiloh's hand was cold and unresponsive and if it wasn't for the IV and blood pressure cuff, Melinda would have tucked it under her arm the way her own mother had done for her when she arrived home from school after a snowstorm. She remembered the loving kindness as if it had happened yesterday.

Cold hands and frozen cheeks were as much a part of winter in Eastern Kentucky as cardinals and woodpeckers. Storms laid deep carpets of snow, but it wasn't the snow angel kind, it was wet and mean and bitter. The carrot and donkey goad that led Melinda home from school was knowing her father would have hot cider and a blanket he'd hung next to the fireplace waiting for her. He would take Melinda's thrift-store wool coat and almost useless gloves and hang them by the fire, repeating a silly prayer he'd made up entreating the powers that be to dry the coat and gloves before Melinda left for school again in the morning.

She thought of this time as existing in an iridescent bubble, before the mine closed and her father became too sick to work anywhere else and her mother took over as breadwinner. It was the beginning of the end of her childhood.

Melinda bent lower and brought Shiloh's needle-bruised hand to her cheek. "I'm sorry this happened to you, Shiloh."

The name set uneasy in her mind and on her tongue, but she was getting used to it. She knew the lupus wasn't her fault any more than it was Jeremy's, but she couldn't get past a persistent, nagging guilt.

Gently, she returned Shiloh's hand to the sterile white blanket. The monitor pinged a warning that something had changed. Melinda glanced at the numbers and saw Shiloh's heart rate had spiked. Someone would be in to check on her. Reluctantly, Melinda went back to the sofa and took up her position in the corner.

It was the same nurse who'd been there earlier. After checking Shiloh's leads and seeing the heart rate had returned to normal, she left. But not without a warning backward glance.

Melinda turned to stare out the window. Life went on. A seagull landed on the statue that flanked the entrance. Her cell vibrated with an incoming call. She pulled it out of her pocket and glanced at the screen. Her boss. Knowing he was going to press her about a recently acquired client in New Mexico, a job she could handle from California, she tried to ignore the call. After leaving a voice mail, he immediately called again. This time she answered knowing he wasn't going to give up.

"Come on, Randy," she greeted him. "This is the first vacation I've taken in years. I deserve some time off."

Randy Wyndham, co-owner of Wyndham and Parker Security Systems, was sensible, for the most part, but always capable and determined. "All I want you to do is talk to this guy. He needs convincing that waiting a couple of weeks isn't going to allow every hacker in the Eastern Bloc to break in and steal their secrets. It's going to take ten minutes out of your day. Tops."

Melinda got up and paced, going from the window to the bed where she put her hand over Shiloh's, to the open door where she glanced down the hall to the elevators. "What is it that you don't understand about being on vacation, Randy?"

"Yeah, okay, I get it. You're tired of all work and no play and you're looking to put a little excitement back in your life. I'm not saying you have to drop everything and fly down to Albuquerque—unless you want to, of course. All I'm asking for is ten minutes." He waited, then chuckled. "This is where you're supposed to jump in and say of course you'll go, you've always wanted to see Albuquerque."

"Wrong. Remember I was the one who said I would quit if you ever tried to send me back to Las Vegas. I am not a desert kind of person. Besides, why me? With all those golf courses down there it seems to me Howard should be packed already." Melinda knew why. She was the only one at the company they could count on to take this kind of last-minute assignment. There were others who traveled, but they demanded time to get their lives in order and not one of them would go anywhere for more than three months without accommodating their families.

"Think about it for a day or two. There's a nice bonus involved and maybe even a raise."

"This must be some special client."

"I'll fill you in when you call me back."

She was tired of fighting him. "Don't expect to hear from me before Friday."

"Thursday would be better."

"Friday," she said and hung up before he could say anything more.

For long seconds she focused on the blank screen. Her mother had been captivated with the FaceTime feature on the cell phone Melinda had received as part of her signing package. Wyndham and Parker Security Systems had approached her months before she'd graduated college, offering a Prada computer case filled with electronic goodies worth several thousand dollars. They'd sweetened the deal by including a signing bonus that would take care of her move to Minneapolis. When she'd hesitated, they'd upped the offer to include the first year's rent on a high-rise condo with a spectacular view of the Mississippi River.

She still didn't answer directly, asking for more time. They automatically assumed she was either considering another offer or holding out for more money and benefits. She didn't tell them that her decision rested on scheduling her mother's breast biopsy through her doctor at the free clinic in Pikesville.

The hiring manager waited a week before he came to her with what he said was the company's absolute final offer. It involved a generous raise in the initial salary with regular bonuses tied to everything from Christmas to her hiring anniversary. In addition she would receive a percentage of the profits after two years, an additional week of vacation after three years, and two more weeks of paid family leave beginning six months after her first paycheck. The enticement was the family leave, something that would have been invaluable were her father still alive and something she had no way of knowing at the time that she would use so soon. No one, nothing, not even the years she'd spent taking care of her father, could make her believe she would need family leave for a long, long time.

She should have known better.

She should have remembered the story her father had created for her when she was too young to share his books any other way. He'd told her about the three Fates. As always, he wove the story around her, making her an intimate necessity in the telling. She loved hearing how the Fates had waited the requisite three days after she was born before visiting her room and weaving her destiny into their tapestry.

But they'd been distracted and hadn't paid attention to the number of threads they'd used that represented tragedy and joy. The pattern should have been balanced with yellow and blue and red. Instead Melinda was given brown and black and gray.

When they realized what they'd done, Lachesis, who measured the thread of longevity, gave her twice the length of the baby they had visited that morning.

But would this child want to live longer with sadness marking the road she will travel over her lifetime, Atropos, the goddess who held the abhorred shears that cut the final thread of life, had asked.

Clotho spoke up. *See these threads?* Clotho showed them a gray that shimmered as if the sun had been spun into its core. The black sparkled as if it had been laced with stars. The brown draped across her hand as if it carried no weight. *I will use these to weave love into her tapestry,* she said. *Not a mortal love, one that only the gods know. It will sustain her and guide her and when she comes to the end of her life, she will look back through all the sorrow and find happiness.*

As soon as Melinda was old enough to realize the story was not one most fathers would tell their impressionable daughters, she tucked it away, waiting for a time the message, at least the message her father had wanted her to hear, became clear. When that happened she would share her hard-earned knowledge over hot chocolate and oatmeal cookies and bask in the pleasure of seeing her father's eyes light with pure pleasure.

Her father was only days from dying when she thought to ask him about the story of the Fates and what he'd hoped to teach her. He smiled behind the breathing mask, took her hand, and whispered, "It's too soon, sweet girl. You have miles to go before you truly understand the tapestry those gray and black and brown threads have created for you."

He'd been gone nine years. Melinda still couldn't think of him without pain wrapping long, sinewy fingers around her heart. She had been the light in his eyes, his window to the outside world, and the conduit for his voracious, curious intellect. He'd given her dreams of a life far away from the coal fields and made her promise she would seek them out. She was in college before she realized every book he'd requested from the mobile library was meant to broaden her world, not his.

She was his caretaker for over six years starting when the black lung disease set in with a vengeance and tethered him to an oxygen tank. At the suggestion of their lawyers and accountants and financial advisors, the coal company her father had worked for his entire life intentionally went bankrupt, leaving the miners without jobs or compensation or medical coverage while the executives paid themselves obscene salaries and bonuses before the final papers were filed.

Some unemployed workers were able to pack up and move out in the middle of the night, a step to avoid the bill collectors that circled the town like vultures. They called all hours of the night to make sure no one would sleep through to sunrise. Even that tactic collapsed when the phone company cut off service.

Others, like her father, hunkered down, surviving on unemployment or disability insurance and food stamps while struggling to keep their chins off their chests and maintain the little pride they had left.

The house her father built for her mother sat beside what had once been a perfect valley, a spot originally cut by centuries of storms and droughts, that time had turned pristine and lush and peaceful. At the base of the valley ran a river where her father could drop a fishing line and five minutes later have enough trout to feed the family for two days.

Unfortunately the river ran along the base of a mountain-top coal-removal operation and turned out to be the ideal receptacle for a hollow fill where rock and soil and toxic by-products that had been stripped from the mountains could be dumped.

The river and fish disappeared along with any possibility the house could be sold. By then half the homes in the area had been abandoned, the FOR SALE signs attached to garages and trees so weatherworn they were unreadable. The men and women who'd stayed behind watched helplessly as their homes and property and families fell apart.

Chapter Twenty-One

Melinda pulled in a deep lungful of air and let it out as a sigh. She glanced at her watch. Jeremy was a half hour late, surprising considering how protective he was with Shiloh. A second nurse came in, this time to check on a beeping monitor. The tag on her pocket identified her as Marisse Brouhns, NP. She was older and looked more approachable than her predecessor, more mother than prom queen. She checked Shiloh and the monitor before turning to Melinda and giving her a reassuring smile. "These machines have a mind of their own sometimes," she said. "They'll start beeping just for the hell of it. Drives me nuts. I can only imagine what it does to the families."

Melinda knew all about cranky medical equipment. Her

father had one particularly malicious monitor that waited for him to fall asleep before sounding an alarm. "The noise doesn't seem to bother her," Melinda said. "She's been sleeping since I got here."

"It's the sedative." Marisse put her hand on Shiloh's arm in a tenderly familiar way. "She's especially sensitive to the one they used on her today. She could be out for hours."

As much as Melinda wanted to hear what Marisse had to say, she felt guilty letting her think it was okay to give her protected health information. "I should tell you—"

As if Marisse could read her mind, she said, "When Jeremy was here this morning, he signed papers making you an authorized recipient of Shiloh's medical information. In case anyone should ask, the permission has been added to her file."

Melinda was as surprised as she was confused. How . . . *why* had he done the extreme about-face, going from telling her he'd changed his mind about letting her see Shiloh to clearing a path to make their journey easier?

Before Marisse figured out she'd made a mistake, Melinda rushed to take advantage of the opportunity. "Can you tell me about the tests themselves—how many there were and what they were for? And in particular, why all the new tests when I was told yesterday that she was ready to go home?"

Marisse was about to answer when she was distracted and turned to focus on a sound coming from the hallway. "Sorry. That's mine. I'll be back as soon as I check it out."

"Thanks," Melinda said, but Marisse was gone before she could acknowledge her. She got up and crossed the room,

standing in the doorway, her gaze sweeping left and right
and then back again. A woman with premature gray hair sat
hunched forward at the nurses' station studying a computer
screen. Seemingly oblivious to the alarm sounds of heart
and blood pressure monitors and respirators pumping air in
rhythmic precision but coming instantly alert when one of
the patterns changed.

As did Melinda.

It didn't matter whether a hospital's sounds and smells
came from a cancer or respiratory or children's ward, there
was a dark familiarity about them. It was a place like this,
only without privacy or comfortable seating or meticulously
clean rooms where her father, and then her mother, had come
to die. They'd entered the small rural hospital during the final stages of their diseases, denied even a whisper of hope
that they would ever leave.

Melinda went back into Shiloh's room, compulsively looking at the machines before studying her for signs she was
about to wake up. There wasn't a twitch or groan or the
slightest change in breathing pattern. Again, she looked at
her watch. Where the hell was Jeremy?

She put her hand on Shiloh's foot and caught her breath in
surprise when there was a reaction. She looked up and saw
Shiloh staring at her, eyes wide and curious.

"You're awake," Melinda said, frozen in place.

"How long have you been here?" Shiloh asked.

"A couple of hours."

Shiloh sat up and looked around. "Where's Heidi?"

"Cheryl has her for the day."

"Where's my dad?" She brought her hand up to finger-comb her hair. "He told me you couldn't be here without him."

Melinda moved around the bed, her hand reaching for the metal bar. She ached to feel the earned intimacy of Shiloh's hand reaching out to hold hers but fear kept her from even trying. Melinda knew she wasn't the kind of person others felt comfortable touching. She received handshakes when hugs were the accepted greeting at parties or receptions, or sometimes neither when she'd been invited to dinner at a friend's house. Rarely, she tried to blend in and open her arms in greeting. The awkwardness was excruciating.

"I don't know," Melinda answered. "He was supposed to meet me here a couple of hours ago, but I haven't heard from him."

Shiloh made a face. "He's probably still at the lawyer's."

A simple sentence loaded with a world of possibilities. "Sorry. I don't know anything about a lawyer," she said carefully.

Shiloh studied Melinda. "He didn't tell you?"

"About?"

"Tess? My other mother?"

"He told me she's been gone a long time and—"

"She's back. Her lawyer is trying to set up visitation rights—at least one weekend a month and half of the holidays."

Melinda's jaw dropped. "How did you find out about this?"

She blushed. "My dad hasn't figured out yet that I have really good hearing. He stands out in the hall when he's on the phone with Cheryl, but he might as well be sitting on the end of the bed."

"After all this time she wants back in your lives?"

"There's no way my dad is going to let it happen. He said she's after something—and he's damn sure it isn't me."

Melinda almost smiled at the "damn," knowing there was no way Shiloh would have used the word in front of her father. She was reaching for ways to show she was mature beyond her years and wanted to be considered an equal. Shiloh's emotional equilibrium could be upset with something as seemingly inconsequential as a casual gesture. "I don't know," Melinda said. "I'm pretty caught up in how special you are already. I can understand how anyone would like to spend time with you."

"Not my mom. She thinks I was a mistake."

Putting aside her fear of rejection, Melinda touched the side of Shiloh's face. "Not this mom. To me you were a gift. The most precious I've ever received."

Shiloh didn't turn away or try to escape Melinda's touch in any way. Instead she stared long and hard into her eyes before saying, "And you just figured you'd regift me to my dad and Tess because you didn't have time to take care of a sick kid?"

The words hit like a board filled with exposed nails. She wrapped both hands around the railing. "That's your solution? Hurt me and it will take away the hurt you're feeling? Believe me, it doesn't work."

Tears pooled in Shiloh's eyes. "Why did you give me away?"

"Because there was a man who would have taken you from me if he'd found us. I had to do whatever I could to protect you."

"What man?"

"Your biological grandfather. He had money and influence and half the people in the county terrified of him. All I had was my determination to keep him from getting his hands on you."

"I don't understand," Shiloh said. "Why didn't my father—?"

"His name was Daniel," Melinda said. To her he was frozen in time, forever the sixteen-year-old reaching to become a man. The older she became, the younger he seemed until one day she looked back and saw the child he had been. Her love had transitioned from passion to protection.

"Daniel's story is complicated, and not an easy one to tell," Melinda said. "He was only sixteen when he died. And never knew about you."

"Why didn't you tell him?"

"I didn't know myself, not for several months."

"That's why you didn't want me? Was it because you didn't want to take care of a baby by yourself?"

Melinda grew serious, almost angry. "We need to get something straight between us right now. There was never a minute—*not one*—that I didn't want you."

Shiloh blinked. She dipped her chin and studied a fold in the blanket. When she looked up again, her eyes were moist, but she was smiling. "How did my father die?"

Melinda's stomach spasmed the way it always did when she thought about that night. She swallowed, started to answer, and had to stop to swallow again. "His car went through the railing on the Rappano Bridge. It was one of the rickety old bridges that go all the way back to horse and buggy days and was desperately in need of repair. The railing wasn't strong enough to stop a bicycle let alone a car."

The rest she left unsaid. Shiloh didn't need to know the bridge was where Daniel's brother had committed suicide or that Daniel's father had put up a brass plaque proclaiming the crossing COWARD'S BRIDGE, after they found Cole a hundred yards downstream, his arms and legs broken in so many places he couldn't have made it to shore even if he had lived through the fall. The day before Daniel was due to come home from his mother's, Melinda and her mother went to the bridge in the middle of the night and stole the plaque, throwing it in the lake three miles downstream.

Shiloh didn't say anything for a long time. Finally, she asked, "Where is this bridge?"

"Harvard County, Kentucky."

Shiloh stared at her long and hard. "Was it an accident?"

The question startled Melinda. No one, except her father, had thought to question how Daniel had died. The town accepted the easy answer the coroner supplied, one that made for a county-wide funeral with only a smattering of gossip passed with the spare ribs and sweet potato pie.

Melinda watched the comings and goings from a fork in the sycamore tree on the hill above the Chapel of the Redeemer. Two hours was a long time no matter how important it was for her to be there until the very end. Even when her legs grew as numb as the branch she straddled, and her back as stiff as the trunk, she still hung on.

She tried shifting position and realized she could no more lower herself to the ground in an upright position than she could sit on her bike once she got there. She moved her legs and arms and shoulders in an effort to get them working again.

Melinda made her move as soon as the last of the congregation squeezed into the firehouse where the engine and hose tender had been removed and a feast laid out as if they'd come to celebrate a wedding. In her mind's eye she could see what she'd seen a dozen times before—food slipped into oversize purses outfitted with snap-lid plastic containers and tucked into bib overalls.

As far as the guests were concerned, anyone relinquishing an entire afternoon to listen to a lecture on the wages of sin and the roadway to hell was more than deserving of a thick slab of meat or two—or maybe even three, if it could be managed. Meat and a healthy swipe of mustard stuck between thick slices of home-made bread washed down with a beer or two. Was there anything better when watching a basketball game between the Wildcats and Tar Heels?

Melinda reached down and pulled her right leg up and over until it rested beside the left. She stopped to look skyward. "Well, Daniel, what did you think? Was it as bad as you'd imagined?"

"It was worse."

Stunned by something she knew was impossible, Melinda had to grab hold of a branch to keep from falling. Her heart made a deafening sound as she twisted to look behind her.

Her mother had found her.

"I thought you weren't going to go to the service," Melinda said.

"When you didn't come home for lunch I figured you were either here or at the cabin. I didn't want you to be alone so I came looking for you."

"I thought I could sneak in to say good-bye before the service started, but it was full up with all his mother's people from Pennsylvania," Melinda said. "Best I could tell, they were the first ones in and the first ones out."

"Free food will do that. Even when it's provided by the likes of Evert Lee Clausen." She looked up at Melinda, her hands on her hips. "Time you came down and got away from here. There's nothing more to see."

"I need to sit here a spell. My legs have gone to sleep."

Mary Ann pressed her back into the trunk and braced her hands on her knees. "Ease down until you can put your foot on my shoulder. I'll help you the rest of the way."

Melinda recoiled at the idea of adding her weight to her mother's small frame. "Give me a little bit. I can get down by myself soon as my legs wake up."

"I'm not leaving 'til you're walking by my side. You might as well do as I say."

Melinda knew it was useless to argue. As gently as she could manage, she lowered herself until she could take a quick step from her mother to the ground. Her knees buckled and she wound up sitting on a pile of windswept leaves. Instead of helping her to her feet, Mary Ann sat beside her and drew her into her arms.

What started as a trickle of tears coursing her cheeks turned into deep, breath-stealing sobs. Mary Ann held her daughter and rocked her and softly assured her Daniel had moved on to a kinder and gentler place.

Chapter Twenty-Two

M elinda?" Shiloh prodded. "You didn't answer me whether it was an accident."

Melinda mentally shook herself free of the memories. "Because I can't. No one can. Not for sure. He was alone. There were no skid marks. The coroner found no drugs or alcohol in his body. That's all any of us knew then or now."

The stigma that came with suicide would do nothing to make the road Shiloh traveled any easier, especially if she discovered her uncle had taken his own life very nearly the same way at the same place her father had. But the truth would protect her against the handful of people still alive who believed they knew what had really happened that night.

"He didn't leave you a note?"

Melinda shook her head.

"Did you love him?"

"He was everything to me." She struggled to come up with a smile when her heart felt as if it were breaking. "He would have been a wonderful father." There weren't a lot of gifts she could give Shiloh that would be lasting or memorable. She couldn't let this one go even if it felt a little like a betrayal. "Very much like the father you have now."

As if the vessel Shiloh had been filling with Melinda's answers had reached overflowing, she moved it aside and waited. "Do you want to know about me?" she prompted.

Melinda smiled. "I want to know everything about you."

She answered Melinda's smile with a grin. "Okay. But you know the most important thing already. I have the best dad in the world."

"I can see that."

"And the worst mom."

Melinda flinched.

Shiloh reached through the bars on the bed and put her hand on Melinda's arm. "Not you—Tess. She is selfish and mean and only thinks of herself."

"How do you know I'm not like that?"

"Because my dad told me you're not."

The obvious reply danced on the tip of Melinda's tongue, but she managed to keep from asking what else Jeremy had said about her. "Do you like to read?" she asked instead.

"Yes."

"Do you have a favorite book?"

"Lots of them," Shiloh said.

"Like . . . ?"

She smiled sheepishly. "Before I started school, my dad read me *Winnie-the-Pooh*, mostly at night before I went to bed, but always when I was in the hospital. I can still quote whole passages about life and love and friendship as seen through the eyes of a stuffed bear. Then Tess left and Cheryl convinced my dad we should move on to Judy Blume's books. She said there were things in there that we both needed to know."

"And were there?"

"Yeah—lots of them."

"What about *Harry Potter*?" Melinda was a huge fan.

"Of course," Shiloh said. "He's just about the most perfect hero ever written. Although, he never, never, *never* should have wound up with Ginny. How could he not have seen that Hermione was his soul mate?"

Melinda laughed. "I feel the same way."

"You read the books?"

"Not the way most kids did. I had to wait until they became available in the mobile lending library that came to our town every week. We were the last town on their route, which meant I was last in line to check them out after they were released. I had to wait four months before I got my hands on *Goblet of Fire*. Which was both good and bad. I loved them all but hated waiting for the next one."

"That's the way I felt, too." Shiloh made a face that was followed by an ear-to-ear smile. "The sedative is wearing off."

"How do you know?"

"I'm hungry."

Melinda pushed her chair back and stood. "What can I get you?"

"A pizza with everything on it."

"I'm pretty sure the cafeteria doesn't serve what you have in mind, but I'd be happy to check."

"You might want to find out if they took me off this stupid diet first."

Melinda sank back into the chair. How could she have forgotten? "Of course," she said. "Your dad said it was okay for me to ask medical questions, but it never occurred to me to ask that one."

"You'll learn."

The simple statement was like a pair of emerald earrings stuck in the toe of a Christmas stocking, a beautiful, unexpected gift. "Has anyone said when you get to go home?"

"They don't tell me things like that. I have to wait for the doctor to talk to my dad and then wait for my dad to tell me what the doctor said. I'm thirteen years old. It seems to me that's old enough to be making some of these decisions myself."

"Almost thirteen," Melinda absently corrected.

"How do you know . . . ?"

"I was there, remember?"

"Oh, yeah," she said as if she'd been caught with her mouth stuffed full of a forbidden salt-encrusted pretzel.

Melinda laughed. Shiloh did, too—loud enough to be heard by Jeremy as he waited for the elevator door to finish sliding open.

Jeremy stepped into the hallway and moved toward Shiloh's room. As soon as he realized where the laughter had come from, he stopped to listen, confused as much as he was curious. He recognized Shiloh's high-pitched giggling, but not the source of the lower echoing sound. The nurses on the day shift were too busy with a full load of patients and not inclined to linger with one who had been judged well enough to check out of the hospital in the morning.

He stood halfway into the doorway and waited to be noticed but soon realized Shiloh and Melinda were too wrapped up in each other to be aware of anything as mundane as another person coming into the room. He took advantage of the temporary invisibility to observe them together. A flash of something uncomfortably close to jealousy went through him when he saw how animated Shiloh was with Melinda, and how quick to smile. *Cheerful* wasn't a word he would have used to describe his daughter in a long, long time.

Melinda leaned back in her chair. "I could use your advice. I was going to ask Cheryl where I could shop for some summer clothes—shorts and T-shirts and sundresses—things like that. I have a feeling as soon as the fog lifts, the wool and flannel I brought with me are going to be suffocating."

"She's the perfect person to ask. She even knows where to take me when I want something that doesn't make me look like I cover up because I have to. My dad tries, but he just doesn't get it when it comes to clothes."

If there were a way, for purely selfish reasons, Melinda would try to talk Cheryl out of moving to Botswana. How many times could Shiloh lose the women in her life and not suffer lingering consequences?

"Cheryl likes you," Shiloh said. "A lot."

Out of habit, whenever she heard a compliment she didn't feel she'd earned, Melinda countered with an offhand denial. "How do you know that?"

"She told me. We talk every day. Or almost every day. Cheryl doesn't like texting. She said it's the easiest way she knows for someone to misinterpret what the other person really means to say."

"Smart woman."

"My dad said she wouldn't call so much when they moved. It's expensive, and there's a big time difference."

"You'll find a way," Melinda said. "Maybe you'll even get to go there for a visit."

Damn it. Jeremy didn't expect Melinda to be in tune with the list of Shiloh's limitations, but she should have had sense enough to do a little research before suggesting traveling to a country ill prepared to deal with someone with lupus.

"My dad wouldn't let me go."

"Even if your doctors said it was okay?" Melinda said.

Shiloh shrugged. "They wouldn't. It's not that my dad is overprotective, because he's not. At least not most of the time." She moved her hands in a familiar gesture. "He wants me to have the best life I can. I know that. And I know some-times I blame him for things he can't control or change."

"I'm sorry." Melinda came forward in her chair and propped her elbows on the mattress. "I've spent half of my life trying to change things that can't be changed. You'd think I would have learned my lesson a long time ago."

Chapter Twenty-Three

$\mathcal{J}$eremy eased backward, escaping without being seen. He'd been tempted to jump in with a lecture based on eight years of hard-earned knowledge about dealing with lupus, but saw no reason to embarrass Melinda in front of Shiloh.

He glanced at his watch as he headed for the cafeteria, nodding and absently smiling at the nurses and interns who greeted him on the way. He could use a cup of coffee, no matter that it tasted like water that had been run through the same grounds two or three times.

To keep his stomach from becoming an acid bath, Jeremy picked up an oatmeal cookie to go with the coffee and headed for his favorite table, the one tucked in a corner with a view of the courtyard. As soon as he sat down his phone vibrated with a call from his lawyer, Brian Morely.

Considering he'd just left his office, Jeremy was surprised to hear from Brian again so soon. Their meeting had lasted close to two hours and several hundred dollars longer than either had anticipated, leaving Jeremy determined to see the money charged to whatever settlement Tess managed to finagle from their divorce.

"Hey, Brian," Jeremy said in greeting. "What's up?"

"I just heard from Tess's lawyer and he said she's decided she doesn't want a divorce after all. Just a legal separation. My guess is that someone got hold of her and convinced her she'd come away with more money if she tried a new tactic. Or maybe this has been their plan all along."

"Why am I not surprised?" Jeremy ran his hand across his chin, surprised at the lack of stubble. He'd finally found time to shave and it felt strange. "I'm sick to death of dealing with her. Give me a ballpark figure of what you think it would take to get her to go through with the divorce."

"For a start, everything your mother left you and Shiloh."

"For a *start*? What the hell does that mean?"

"According to the papers I just received, if she does decide to go through with the divorce, she's going to lay claim to half of everything you own, including Artisan Homes."

"I started Artisan Homes five years before we met, which makes it property owned before the marriage, not community property. Same thing with the money from my mother.

What kind of lawyer does she have who doesn't know something it took me ten minutes to look up on the Internet?"

"One who figures he can inundate you with filings and demands until you throw up your hands in defeat."

Jeremy took a long swallow of coffee and grimaced. Other than being hot and brown, the liquid bore absolutely no resemblance to the brew he turned to for sustenance during days like this. "If she thinks she has me cornered because of Shiloh, she has a short memory."

"She knows you will do anything to protect your daughter."

Jeremy picked up an odd inflection in Brian's voice. "Everyone knows that," he said warily.

"There's no easy way to put this," Brian said.

"Then just spit it out."

"We've known for days now that Tess was going to file for joint custody . . ."

"And we knew we were going to fight her."

"We will, but her lawyer has brought something into the mix that could make it harder than we were anticipating."

Jeremy got up and dumped his coffee cup in the trash, along with the cookie. He leaned his shoulder against the wall and stared at a young man sitting in the courtyard, his elbows on his knees, hands covering his face. He didn't know the young man, but he understood the sense of defeat he projected. "What makes her think she can find a judge who will trust her not to abandon Shiloh a second time?"

Brian cleared his throat, stalling for time. Finally, he said in a rush, "The abandonment will be a moot point when she brings out evidence that she left the first time to save herself from severe mental and physical abuse."

"*What?*" Convinced he couldn't have heard Brian correctly, he asked him to say it again.

"For the mental part, she's saying you refused to let her find someone to take care of Shiloh, no matter how well qualified they were. You insisted Tess assume the role of constant companion for Shiloh even when Tess was offered a once-in-a-lifetime opportunity to expand her own company. She wants you to compensate her for the money she lost during that period and prorate what she's lost since."

Like all lies, this one survived on a sliver of truth inextricably woven into Tess's fantasy fabric. When Tess had come to him with the proposal she'd been offered, he'd wondered aloud how they would provide Shiloh the care she needed. He'd proposed cutting his hours and hiring another craftsman to handle the finish work. That way he could split his days off with hers. She'd asked how it would work when she had to travel. He didn't have an immediate answer.

The solution was obvious if impossibly expensive. They would hire a nurse when their schedules conflicted. She shouted at him that it was a luxury they couldn't afford. She needed every dime they could squeeze out of his income to invest in her company. It was her turn to shine and she wasn't going to let a sick child, one she'd never wanted in the first place, get in her way.

Pushed beyond reason, Jeremy said she was selfish and didn't deserve to be Shiloh's mother. The argument went downhill from there with each of them hurling unresolved disputes at each other like blind snipers. When it became obvious she wasn't gaining ground, Tess lost all restraint. She looked around for something to throw at Jeremy, settling on the Lalique vase his mother had given them for their first anniversary.

The vase shattered when it hit the corner of the bookshelf, sending a lethal piece of glass ricocheting back toward Tess, slicing into her arm like a dagger. Blood soaked the sleeve of her silk blouse, then coursed from her bicep to her elbow to her wrist. Her fingers created crimson streaks on her tan slacks where she pressed her hand to her thigh. Shock kept her from immediately reacting. Seconds later she let out a string of profanity long and strong enough to make a truck driver proud.

Their neighbor, who was president of his garden club and eager to win the upcoming award for best urban backyard, overheard what happened and came running. He rang the doorbell, knocked, rang the bell again, and headed for the back door.

Jeremy was too busy wrapping Tess's arm in a towel and keeping Shiloh out of the glass-strewn room to pay attention to the neighbor. His main concern was whether to call 911 or drive Tess to the hospital himself. He settled on taking her. By the time he pulled out of the driveway, he had an audience of neighbors, staring at Tess as she held a blood-soaked towel across her chest, elevating her arm. Shiloh sat in the backseat of their Mercedes wide eyed, confused, and terrified.

When they arrived at the hospital, a nurse immediately separated them, taking Tess into a private room and Shiloh into a play area. Jeremy they left to fend for himself. He found a bench across the hall from the room Tess was in and sat down, not realizing he would be able to hear everything that was said.

Tess had been too angry to cry after she threw the vase at him. Now, under the gentle urging of a matronly-looking nurse, the tears flowed like water breaching the top of a dam. Through hiccuped sobs, Tess told them about the fight, too overcome to provide details, but hinting what happened hadn't been an accident.

Miraculously, the police who arrived to question Tess and Jeremy caught the truth on the recording. It wasn't until they replayed the section where she described the weight of the vase and how she'd never expected it to shatter the way it had, that she admitted what really happened.

The vase wasn't the only thing that irretrievably fractured that night. His trust was like the shards he swept and discarded when they arrived home, each piece a reminder of what had been and would be no more. He vacuumed and wiped the floors and furniture with a damp rag, aware how tenaciously each daggerlike sliver could cling to its hiding place from the number of broken windows he'd dealt with in his business.

Tess put Shiloh to bed, reading her part of a chapter of *Winnie-the-Pooh*, and patiently waiting for Jeremy to complete the bedtime ritual with a good-night kiss. Instead of giggling when he told her "Don't let the bedbugs bite," she clung to him and refused to let go.

He kissed the top of her head, struggling for a normalcy he recognized she needed as much as he needed to provide it for her. "See you in the morning, Tinker Bell."

"I love you, Daddy."

"I love you, too."

"Can I sleep with you tonight?"

"You know how Mommy feels about that," he said.

"Why did she throw Grandma's flower thing at you?"

With all of his heart he'd hoped she hadn't seen what happened. Opting for the truth, he said, "I don't know."

"Will she do it again?"

He tilted his head and shrugged. "I really don't think so."

"How do you know?"

Now he smiled reassuringly. "Because the vase is broken into too many pieces to put back together."

She thought about his answer before she returned his smile. "That's a good reason."

He leaned her back against the pillow, pulled her blanket up, and tucked it under her chin. "I thought so, too."

"Will Grandma be mad?"

"Not if we don't tell her."

Shiloh turned to her side to better see him as he left. "She'll know."

Jeremy stared at her. "What makes you say that?"

"Grandma knows everything."

Jeremy laughed. "I'm going to tell her you said that."

She propped herself up on her elbow. "You don't have to. Know why?"

As if they'd practiced it a hundred times, they both said, "Because Grandma knows everything."

Shiloh's giggle was the best sound he'd heard in days. He smiled and blew her a kiss. "Go to sleep."

"What if I can't?"

He recognized what she was doing and almost promised to come back after he'd made one more pass through the living room with the vacuum and damp rag, but could see that despite her protests, she was on the verge of sleep. "We'll talk about it in the morning."

"Okie dokie" was followed by a yawn.

JEREMY SIGHED HEAVILY. "I can't deal with this right now. I told Melinda I would meet her two hours ago. Do you have anything open tomorrow?"

"Meet me here after five," Brian said. "I'll order a pizza. Unless you'd prefer Chinese?"

"Can she get away with this?" Jeremy asked, not caring what or when he ate.

"We'll talk about what she can and can't get away with tomorrow," Brian said. "In the meantime, forget about Tess and figure out what you're going to do with Melinda when the two weeks you've given her are over."

"Yeah . . . thanks. Just what I needed."

Chapter Twenty-Four

Melinda noted the way Shiloh moved her fingers as if she were engaged in counting something only she could see. She had been planning this day for a long time. If she really was as much like Melinda as she appeared, she even put herself to sleep organizing the order she would ask her questions. None of them surprised Melinda, not the simple things like her favorite food to the hard ones, like what Daniel said and did on the day he died.

"Do I have other relatives in Kentucky?" Shiloh asked.

"Some. My grandfather's people are scattered throughout Eastern Kentucky. Your grandmother's people are mostly in the Carolinas, Mississippi, and Louisiana. We were included on a couple of dozen Christmas card lists, but for the most part we were considered uppity by half of the clan and poor white trash by the other half." After she had Shiloh and her aunt put her on the bus headed home to Kentucky, Melinda never heard from her again. She found out about her cousin's drug overdose through a Christmas letter from her uncle's third wife who had assumed the role of family gossip. Melinda sent a card, but even that was returned.

"What about Daniel's family?"

"All dead." She was ashamed how easily she told the lie.

"Sounds like I do come from a defective gene pool after all."

It seemed an odd statement. "Who told you that?"

"Tess."

Of course something like that would come from her. Melinda shifted in her chair, drawing one leg up to tuck under the other. "I'm sure you've already talked to your dad and your doctor about this, but the experts on lupus haven't discovered a genetic link, just a predisposition. You had a third cousin who had lupus, but it seems a real stretch to think you're connected to her in any way that counts."

"You said 'had.' Does that mean she's dead?"

"Yes, but it had nothing to do with her lupus. She died of a drug overdose."

"What about your mom and dad? They were kinda young when they died, weren't they?"

"That wasn't genetic either. Where we lived and the air we breathed in Eastern Kentucky dictated how healthy we were. If my father had lived in Santa Cruz or in Juneau, or in

Minneapolis I don't doubt for a minute that he would still be alive."

"And your mother?"

"Her too," Melinda insisted.

"Are you okay?"

"I'm better than okay. I can't remember the last time I was this happy. I'm with my little girl again."

"Not so little," Shiloh protested. "And not exactly okay."

"Oh, Shiloh, I learned a long time ago that any day you can tell someone you love them or see something that makes you smile or even something that makes you cry, you've had a good day. Being stuck in a hospital sucks, but it's just about over. The nurse said you get to go home in the morning. And you get to heal a broken heart."

"I don't know anyone with a broken heart."

"Think about it. She's spent the past week with her head on her paws, staring at the beach house with her big sad eyes, cocking her ear every time she hears a car turn onto the road that leads to the cove . . ."

"Coconut," Shiloh said.

"She's been so desperate for you to come home, she's made a new friend."

"Who?"

"Heidi," Melinda said knowing how improbable it sounded.

"Your cat?" Her reaction made it sound as if Coconut had befriended a dragon.

Jeremy came into the room before Melinda could answer. "Sorry I'm late," he said. "My meeting went longer than I expected. And then there was a fender bender that took forever to clear."

"It's okay," Shiloh said. "I had the best company ever."

He worked his way over to the other side of the bed and kissed Shiloh's cheek. "What did you talk about?"

"First tell me what's in the box."

Jeremy handed a small pink pastry box to Shiloh. "Custom-made, just for you."

Shiloh grinned as she untied the bow and looked inside. "Oh, how cute," she squealed. "It's the best one yet." She handed the box to Melinda.

Melinda laughed when she saw the square cookie designed to look like Superwoman bending bars to break out of jail. What kind of man went to this much trouble for a daughter who was in and out of the hospital with frustrating regularity?

"It's a tradition of sorts," Jeremy said. "A way we celebrate coming home." He made it sound as if it were nothing un-usual or extraordinary.

"You remind me of my father," Melinda said.

Jeremy chuckled. "The gray hair or the creaking joints?"

"The thoughtfulness. He was the kindest man I've ever known."

Shiloh studied them, looking from her father to Melinda and back to her father. "My dad always does nice things for people, even when they're not nice to him."

"Who isn't nice?" Jeremy asked.

She hesitated, clearly uncomfortable with her answer. "Tess."

He cast a sidelong glance at Melinda, trying to gauge her reaction. "I'm sure that doesn't surprise you."

"No," she said cryptically. It fascinated her how readily children defended parents who abandoned them. An unanticipated flush burned her cheeks. Did Shiloh defend her the same way she did Tess?

"On to happier things," Jeremy said. "Time to divide the cookie."

Shiloh broke off a corner and handed it to Melinda. The next piece she gave to her father. The third piece was left twice as large as the other two. "I have to have the biggest one," she said. "I'm going to make a wish with mine."

"What are you going to wish for?" Jeremy asked.

"Can't tell."

Melinda put her cookie next to Jeremy's. It was slightly larger than his. "Seems to me that second place should mean I get a wish, too."

"Ha—obviously the two of you don't know that it's the smallest cookie piece that holds the most power to grant wishes."

Shiloh gave Melinda a long-suffering look. "He made that up."

"I figured as much." Melinda basked in the glow of normalcy and decided no matter who had the better chance of having their wish granted, she'd been given this moment. She would cherish and care for it the way she did all of her special memories.

Jeremy wiped a crumb off the corner of Shiloh's mouth

with his thumb. "I'm going to borrow Melinda for a few minutes. I want her to meet Dr. Sheu before she leaves."

"He just wants to make sure she approves of you taking care of me," Shiloh said to Melinda. "Dr. Sheu is almost as protective of me as he is."

"I like that," Melinda said, untangling herself from the chair.

"Behave yourself," Jeremy said to Shiloh as he leaned forward to kiss her forehead. "Don't make me sorry I agreed to spring you out of here a day early."

"Yeah, yeah, yeah . . . you're not fooling anyone." Shiloh grinned. "You want me out of here as much as I want to get out." She reached up and put her arms around his neck.

Melinda waited for Jeremy in the doorway, trying to give them as much privacy as she could in an environment that had none. Her gaze swept the nurses' station and the hallway. Was there something about hospital architecture that dictated they all look alike? What was the point of having the lower half of the walls painted a darker color than the top? The marks left by gurneys and equipment carts showed up as clearly on the darker green as they would have on white.

Even the coroner's office in Pikesville where her mother had sneaked her in to say good-bye to Daniel was painted dark green and off-white. Nine months later, with heart-breaking irony, she gave birth to Shiloh in a room painted the same colors. The rural hospital where her mother and father had gone to die was a duplicate of the others.

Only the artwork was different. Here there were photographs of baby animals with a powerful *awwww* factor, with several hung for no other reason than to elicit a smile. Hardly great examples of truth in advertising when children were dying behind closed doors.

Melinda hated everything about hospitals.

"Ready?" Jeremy said, coming up behind her.

"I'm glad you arranged another meeting. I have several questions I didn't get to ask the last time she—"

He guided her down the hall toward the elevators. "I lied. There is no meeting."

"I don't understand."

He reached around her to hit the up button, his arm brushing hers in a familiar way. "I wanted to talk to you about Shiloh coming home tomorrow."

The elevator door slid open and they stepped inside, joining three people dressed in scrubs. Jeremy pushed the button to the fifth floor. Melinda looked at him and frowned, saying a quick, silent prayer that he hadn't changed his mind about letting her stay the full two weeks. To break the awkward silence, she asked, "Are we going to the cafeteria?"

"I thought you could use a cup of coffee while we talk."

"You really don't like me, do you?"

He turned to look at her. "What do you mean?"

"I've tasted the coffee at the cafeteria."

The woman behind Melinda laughed so hard she almost choked.

"You too?" Melinda said.

The woman opened the cloth purse hanging from her

shoulder, dug out two tea bags, and handed them to Melinda. "Self-preservation. They have an off-brand tea that's almost as bad as the coffee."

The elevator stopped and the door slid open. Melinda called out a thank-you as the woman left with her two companions. She glanced at the digital panel over the panel numbers. Theirs was the next floor.

Chapter Twenty-Five

The cafeteria had less than a dozen people this time of day, almost all of them in scrubs, and yet Jeremy chose a table on the patio tucked between a dwarf orange tree and a wall, a place where they couldn't easily be seen or heard. He left her there while he went for hot water.

Melinda took advantage of the time he was gone to check for messages. She turned on her phone, and as she'd expected, there were half a dozen voice mails from Randy Wyndham, a man she always considered the employer from hell and who had reinforced her opinion in the past week. Unexpectedly, there were two missed calls from a New Mexico number, but no voice mail to go with them. She looked at the time and decided whatever it was could wait another hour or two.

Randy was moving closer to the point of considering her refusal a personal affront. No matter how many times she reminded him that in all the years she'd been with Wyndham and Parker Security Systems she had never taken a real vacation, he insisted she was exaggerating. His peaks of frustration slipped into cajoling followed by coercion. She stood her ground, having gone through similar temper tantrums with him in the past and discovering any sign of weakness was tantamount to a snowshoe hare lazily crossing a meadow while a hungry eagle circled overhead.

If she truly believed she was the only one at Wyndham and Parker who could handle the job she would figure out a way to pull it off. But there were three people currently at the home office that she knew for a fact were waiting to be assigned new clients, all of them capable of handling whatever was going on in New Mexico.

If she had the outsize ego that usually came with the people who did her job, she would have been flattered. Instead she felt trapped. And she didn't like it. She needed to reconsider how important it was to have a rent-free apartment she never used, no friends who missed her when she was gone, and a work environment where she was valued for her skill but rarely her opinion.

She stared at the oversize black screen for several seconds knowing she had time for a couple of messages saying she would be in touch as soon as possible. Instead, she pressed the button to turn the phone off and slipped it back into her purse just as Jeremy returned with two tall cups of hot water, wooden stir sticks, and several packets of sugar.

"Work?" he asked as he sat in the chair opposite her.

She nodded.

"Is there something you need to do there?"

"There are lots of things I need to do, but nothing more important than being here." She lowered her tea bag into the hot water, hanging on to the string as if there was a puppet on the end.

"You're nothing like I thought you would be," Jeremy said, mirroring her movements.

"Which was?"

He struggled with his answer, his hesitancy making it obvious what he'd thought wasn't good. "It's hard to imagine anyone who could give a baby away would be anyone I'd want to know."

"I get the picture."

"No, I don't think you do." He added two sugars to his tea. "My feelings toward you were kinder before Shiloh got sick. Even when it was happening I knew what I was feeling didn't make sense, but I couldn't get it out of my head that somehow you'd known Shiloh was going to have lupus and that's the reason you gave her away."

"At least you understand how crazy that is."

"It doesn't help. I like to think I'm better than that."

She wrapped her tea bag around the stir stick and waited

for it to stop dripping. "I came here desperately wanting to believe you were a perfect father and that you would walk through the fires of hell to protect your daughter."

She looked up to see him staring at her. "Never once did I imagine I would be the one you focused on when it came to protecting Shiloh."

He wrapped his hands around the paper cup, the tea bag still inside steeping. "I thought I had a few more years before you turned into the most important person in her life. Cheryl told me to expect an angry stage, but Shiloh seems to have skipped over that, at least for the most part. Instead she can't stop asking questions, none of which I can answer to her satisfaction."

She sipped her tea slowly, stalling for time. "You said you wanted to talk about Shiloh coming home."

He came forward, resting his arms on the metal table. "This is going to sound strange considering everything that's happened up to now."

Melinda waited for him to finish.

Instead he engaged in a series of delaying tactics from gathering the empty sugar packets and spent tea bags and wrapping them in a napkin to running his fingers through his unruly hair.

"Just spit it out," she said.

"Shiloh isn't coming home with me tomorrow. She's going to stay with Cheryl until I have a handle on this thing with Tess."

Her stomach spasmed in fear for what would come next. She ignored the part about Tess. "So I'll have to go over there to see her?"

"For the first few days. At least until the weekend. Then if you're still here, I'll move in when Cheryl and Andrew take Bobby to Disneyland." Before she could say anything, he added, "This is a trip they've been planning for a long time. It has nothing to do with you."

What he'd said made as much sense as the directions that came with the home entertainment center she bought herself for Christmas the year before. "So let me get this straight. You'll be staying at their house monitoring everything we say when I come over there to see her?"

He shrugged. "You didn't really think I would leave Shiloh alone with you for the entire day."

Acutely conscious that he could change his mind as readily as he'd made the offer, she said, "What are you afraid of— that I'll kidnap her?"

She waited for him to say something. When he didn't, she added, "Oh my God, you are. Do you realize how insane that sounds? Have you given the logistics of kidnapping Shiloh even half a thought, or is it something that occurred to you in the middle of a really stupid dream?"

He let out a heavy, weary sigh. "This thing with Tess obviously has me more rattled than I thought."

"What thing with Tess?" she asked carefully, caught between telling him what she already knew and revealing how she'd found out. She should have asked Shiloh if it was okay for her to know these kinds of personal details about Jeremy and Tess.

"She's back. It's long and complicated, and all you really need to know is that she's using Shiloh to manipulate me."

Chapter Twenty-Six

fter five years she just appeared?" She focused on her tea, taking several long drinks even though she wasn't a fan of chamomile tea.

"Longer than that," he said.

"What does she want?"

"She says she wants to repair our marriage and to be a mother to Shiloh again."

"Can you keep Tess from seeing Shiloh?" Melinda asked. "Legally, I mean."

"Brian, my lawyer, is working on that now. He's convinced the abandonment issue can be used in our favor, at least temporarily. I don't think she'll fight it. Tess no more wants to have anything to do with Shiloh than she wants to stay married to me."

What an idiot. How could Tess not see what she had in Jeremy and Shiloh? "Then what is she after?"

"Money. It took less than a day for the detective who works for Brian to discover Tess's company was in financial trouble. She either comes up with what she owes her creditors by the end of July or the company goes into receivership."

"Poor management or theft?"

"Textbook theft. Her business partner got into drugs and used operating funds to bail himself out. Tess was the artistic side of the company and her partner handled the finances. He could have been stealing from the company for years and she wouldn't have known. Tess couldn't balance a checkbook when we were together and I doubt she ever learned."

Melinda was like a bloodhound picking up a scent. "Do you have the kind of money she's after?"

"Not personally. I pay myself a salary that covers whatever Shiloh and I need, and then put the rest into a fund to cover emergencies. There's a separate account for Shiloh's college and the beginning of a retirement account for me. Whatever's left over, if there is anything left over, gets put back into Artisan Homes." Jeremy shook his head. "I have no idea why I'm telling you this."

It was the kind of revelation best left alone. Instead of commenting, she said, "It seems she would have known this."

"She does. But she also knows my mother died recently and it's reasonable to assume I was her only heir."

"I'm sorry. I didn't know."

He shrugged. "There was no way you could have known."

He plainly didn't want to talk about it, but after what seemed like an eternity, cleared his throat and began. "Have you ever heard of a rogue wave?"

She shook her head.

"It's a wave that appears with no warning and is several times larger than any of the waves that came before or after. My mother and her friend Howard used to spend every Sunday picking up garbage on the beaches between San Francisco and Big Sur. That last Sunday she found a half-starved juvenile elephant seal with fishing line cutting off the circulation to one of its flippers. She stayed with the seal while Howard headed back to the truck for a knife. He said he wasn't gone five minutes but when he returned, both my mother and the seal were gone. The remnants of the rogue wave were still evident in the rocks that had pools of water thirty feet above the high-water mark. A couple of surfers witnessed the whole thing. They tried to help, but she disappeared before they could get to her."

"I'm sorry," she said simply. "It must have been an especially difficult way to lose her."

"The seal showed up the next day on a beach two miles south of where the wave hit. One of the local marine rescue centers managed to catch the seal and save it, but there was never any sign of my mother." He looked down at his locked hands. "She used to joke that she wanted to be buried at sea but didn't have time to fill out the paperwork."

"Has it been six months?"

"Yes."

"Tess must know most estates are settled around six months."

"It took a lot of air out of her balloon when her attorney found out it could be years before the estate was settled."

"Why years?" She was asking questions that were none of her business, but he answered as if they were.

"You need a body for a death certificate. Without one you wait five years."

"It must have been terrible for you and Shiloh when they stopped searching."

"Once we accepted she was gone, we agreed that she was where she would want to be."

Melinda smiled. "She sounds like my kind of woman. I wish I could have met her."

"She and Shiloh had a special relationship. If they weren't talking on the phone they were texting. As soon as Tess was out of the picture, my mother would come down from San Francisco every other week. She'd stay for a couple of days insisting Shiloh and I needed a break from each other and in the same breath telling me I was a terrific father." Jeremy shook his head, looked up, and smiled. "She loved to shop almost as much as she loved being with her granddaughter. I looked in Shiloh's closet the other day and it's filled with clothes she's never worn but already outgrown."

Melinda finished her tea. "As far as shopping goes, there's need and then there's want. For a lot of women it's more than buying new clothes, it's a pastime. For some it's a bonding experience—the female equivalent of a tailgate party." Unexpectedly, she smiled, surprising them both.

"Where I come from there's a ritual involved for women who love to shop but don't have any money. My mother used to call it 'fingering.' She could spend an entire day going through the stores in Pikesville teaching me the difference between a quality sweater and one that wouldn't hold up through a single washing. The next time she might show me how to tell if something on sale was a bargain."

"I don't think my mother was the fingering type," Jeremy said. "If she saw something she liked, she bought it, no questions asked."

"You may never go fingering with Shiloh, but with your mother gone and Cheryl leaving for Africa, like it or not, you're going to have to learn to shop. Either that or turn Shiloh and a couple of girlfriends loose at the mall with your credit card."

This time it was his turn to laugh.

Melinda was filled with a wonderful sense of hope that she and Jeremy could find a way to become friends.

"Were you close to your grandparents?" he asked.

"I never met any of them. There were family dynamics combined with reluctance to travel and a whole lot of stubbornness tossed in the mix. My mother used to say her and my father's families were the Hatfield and McCoy clans reincarnated. My father used to tell me it was a blessing we were the outcasts."

She looked up and caught him studying her the way scientists studied a new species. "My mother would have been a wonderful grandmother to Shiloh, but she was so lost when my father died she couldn't fight anymore. Not even for me."

"As long as you've done the best you can when you can, never look back."

She liked that he wasn't afraid to show a softer side. "You're a philosopher, too?"

"Not even close. That was straight out of my mother's book of favorite homilies. She had one for every occasion. I just thought this one happened to fit."

She laughed. "I think I like you, Jeremy Richmond. You're as near to the man I wanted Shiloh to call father as I'd dare hoped."

He acknowledged the recognition with raised eyebrows and a surprised smile. "Thank you, Melinda Campbell. Considering the circumstances, that's a hell of a compliment."

Nervous and at a loss for words with the direction their conversation had headed, Melinda changed course. "So you think Tess is here because she found out about your mother and figured you'd come into money."

"It's the kind of thing she would have done before she left. There's no reason to believe she's changed."

"I'm sure Brian told her she has no right to any of that money, even if you were to reestablish your marriage," she said.

Thanks to her father and his curiosity and thirst for knowledge, Melinda knew scraps and pieces about some things that had little to do with her everyday life, and a whole lot about some things that had absolutely no practical use whatsoever, like the broad spectrum of divorce laws throughout the country. She'd never pinned him down about his motive, but suspected it was his way to introduce her to the law, opening another door of possibilities.

"How do you know that?"

"My father believed curiosity was a religion. He attended the services faithfully, and like all apostles, he spread the word to his flock." She chuckled. "The problem was he only had one parishioner—me. Consequentially, I wound up the beneficiary of a wealth of seemingly useless information, like who was entitled to what in a divorce in California."

"Tess operates on the belief the world will accommodate her needs. Why shouldn't she? In her mind, she's beautiful and talented and that puts her head and shoulders above ordinary women. Reasonable isn't in her vocabulary. Empathy is for losers."

Melinda used the side of her hand to scoop the napkin with the empty packets of sugar into her cup and took it to the garbage. "What about Artisan Homes?" she asked.

"Same thing. I started the company before I met Tess."

Melinda returned to the table and put her hand on the back of the chair but didn't sit down. "And her company?" she asked.

Jeremy folded his arms across his chest. It was almost possible to see his mind working. It didn't take long before a slow smile formed, transforming his face. "Four years after we were married."

"Of course it's not as if you want half interest in a failing business . . ."

He stood and pushed his chair under the table "Right now I'll do whatever it takes to get her attention."

When he looked as if he was ready to leave, she put her hand on his arm to stop him. The touch was far more intimate than she'd intended. Heat extended from her fingertips to her elbow.

No, no, no, a voice inside her warned. *Do not let this happen. Keep your relationship with this man clean and simple.* "We didn't finish our discussion about Shiloh."

Melinda waited, giving Jeremy time and fighting the urge to list the reasons she could be trusted to have Shiloh stay with her for an hour or two a day. When he didn't say anything, she added, "If you're afraid I'm going to tell her something she isn't ready to hear, I wouldn't do that. Why would I? I don't just know she's more important than the two of us. I believe it."

He took a winding road to deliver his answer. "Cheryl volunteered to take her to Sacramento to her cousin's house," Jeremy said, "but Shiloh's doctor doesn't want her traveling until she's sure there won't be a relapse with the bladder infection."

She went along with the odd new direction he'd taken. "I like Shiloh's doctor. We had a chance to talk earlier." She was trying for casual, but it came out wooden.

"She told me she thought you could be trusted to follow the medical directions they'll send home with her."

Understanding dawned. "I should have known running into each other outside her office wasn't an accident."

He locked gazes with her. "I figured all those questions she wanted answered would be better coming from her than from me." Jeremy stared at her long and hard. "Look, I know all of my restrictions and rules are a lot to ask."

"You're kidding, right? You have to know that time with Shiloh ranks up there with making a wish on a star and having it granted."

"That's what I'm afraid of," he said. "Two weeks from now the dream will be over, you'll be wide-awake, and you'll be headed back to Minneapolis. Can you handle that?"

"I'll deal with leaving when it's time to go."

He nodded, letting her evasiveness go for now. "Do you have any questions for me?"

"Of course I do, but I assume you'll be available on your cell."

"Along with Cheryl, who will be next door before and after Disneyland. When I told her I'd been considering letting Shiloh stay with you at the beach house for an hour a day, she said she thought it was a good idea."

"Anyone else involved in this that I should know about?" She closed her eyes and groaned when it hit her how snarky her answer sounded. "Never mind. I'll have you and Cheryl to help me if necessary."

"Just so you know, it's the 'if necessary' that scares the hell out of me. I'd rather you were a little less confident. How many thirteen-year-olds do you know?"

She didn't want to, but she understood his hesitancy. "Not many," she admitted, following him out of the cafeteria. "But there was one I knew really well, and it wasn't all that long ago."

When they stepped into the elevator, Melinda put her hand on Jeremy's arm again and felt the same emotional jolt. How many years had it been since she'd had even this casual kind of physical contact with a man? Could she really be so lonely that her heart grew heavy with longing with a simple touch?

"What comes next?" she asked. "Do I ask her if she's okay about staying with me or do you?"

"I figured when you left you could tell her you'd see her tomorrow and I'll take care of the rest." The elevator door slid open.

Melinda glanced at her watch. "I told Cheryl I'd be back before Heidi's five o'clock feeding so I'll tell Shiloh good-bye now."

She followed him several more steps before reaching out to stop him one last time. "Thank you."

"This isn't a thank-you kind of deal. I wouldn't even consider letting Shiloh stay with you under any other circumstances."

"I understand."

"Do you? I'm turning the most precious thing in my life over to a virtual stranger. Before today I couldn't conceive a possibility where I would do anything like this. Please don't make me regret it."

She wasn't a demonstrative person. She'd tried, but her hugs and comforting gestures turned out stilted at best and just plain awkward the rest of the time. Which meant that instead of putting her arms around him reassuringly, she shoved her hands in the front pockets of her jeans and rocked back on her heels. "Would it make you feel better if I gave Cheryl my car keys when Shiloh was with me?"

When she saw he was actually considering her offer, her jaw dropped. "Never mind," she said. "It was supposed to be a joke. But as you can see, I'm not good at telling jokes."

Physically, he answered by shoving his hands in his back pockets. The gesture spoke volumes. Here they were, two people facing each other in the middle of an ugly green hallway, their hands as restrained as their emotions.

"I'll think about it," he said.

Dear God, how could she have been so stupid? "I wasn't serious."

He smiled. "I wondered how long it would take you to change your mind."

He had a sense of humor. Her knees went weak with relief. "Honestly? I didn't even make it all the way through the offer."

Chapter Twenty-Seven

Shiloh was out of bed when Melinda and Jeremy came into the room. Sitting on the couch under the window watching the seagulls, she looked like the vivacious preteen she was. "I'm sprung," she said to Jeremy, holding her arms wide as she got up and crossed the room.

He wrapped her in a bear hug, propping his chin on the top of her head. "Nice try."

She tilted her head back to look at him. "What do you mean?"

"You're not leaving until morning, which is a whole day early as it is."

She shrugged and looked over to Melinda. "I tried," she said.

"And it was an admirable effort," Melinda said.

Jeremy stood with his arm around Shiloh and looked at Melinda. "Don't you have to get going? I thought you said something about needing to take care of Heidi."

Shiloh gave him a frustrated look. "Heidi is with Cheryl and Bobby."

With a quick glance at Jeremy in acknowledgment, she said, "I don't want to take advantage of Cheryl and Bobby. And Heidi is probably wondering what happened to me."

"Are you going to be here in the morning? It takes forever to get all the papers signed and we could talk while I'm waiting."

Before Jeremy could come up with a reason for her to stay home, Melinda said, "Yes. I'll be here."

Melinda stopped at the doorway, put two fingers against her lips and blew Shiloh a kiss. She turned to leave and even when tempted, never looked back. It was a lesson she learned in the most painful way possible. For more years than she wanted to remember she'd carried a mental picture of her father sending her and her mother out of his room with a smile that barely moved his lips. He'd talked them into getting a cup of coffee, insisted, actually, as if he knew what was coming. Minutes after they left, he died alone, the way he wanted. It was his last gift to the women he loved, that they would go through life without the burden of remembering the moment he drew his last breath.

Melinda was alone on her elevator ride down to the main floor. In the silence her thoughts drifted to feelings as powerful as if they were days old and not years.

Harold Clyde Campbell died on Valentine's Day. Somehow during the week before, he'd gathered the strength to draw a heart on the backside of the menu that came with every meal. The writing was indecipherable to Melinda, but not Mary Ann. When she saw what he had written, she leaned forward, kissed him, and whispered in his ear. Melinda was too far away to hear what her mother said, but she would never forget the intimate smile they exchanged.

Her mother understood the gift her father had given them but never accepted not being by his side. Through the weary tears that followed, she pressed his skeletal hand to her wet cheek and made a promise that she would never leave him again. Years passed before Melinda fully understood the depth of that promise.

Melinda was at the funeral home making arrangements for her father's cremation when the Reverend Jefferson Davis Riggins arrived at the hospital. It took him less than ten minutes to convince her mother he'd been visited by an angel delivering a revelation. The one and only way to keep her husband from forever looking up at her through the fires of hell was to guide him to Jesus with a church full of the faithful singing the Lord's praises.

How could her mother say no?

Unlike the normal Sunday church service, where Reverend Riggins worked himself into a hellfire-and-damnation frenzy with his diminishing flock of follow-

ers, he looked at funerals as a God-given opportunity to grow the fold. He had a rhythm, start slow and build until he was shouting and beating his chest, warning that the hard times in the valley were nothing more than fodder for the devil, a devil who laid in wait at the bottom of every liquor bottle, gleefully encouraging fornication—and worse.

The road to salvation could be attained only by faithfully attending Sunday service, as if their very souls depended on it. Which they did, he assured them. And it must not be forgotten that Sunday service went hand in hand with tithing, even if it meant going without a meal or two from week to week. Sacrifice showed God you were serious. As would walking to work, the greater the distance the better. With less money put into their gas-guzzling cars, there would be more for the collection plate come Sunday service. When it came to the church spreading the word of God, every dime, every dollar, dropped in the collection plate provided the preacher with the means to pave the road to heaven God had reserved for the great people of Walker County.

Melinda kept track of the time the Reverend Riggins harangued the people who'd come to honor her father. He was five minutes shy of an hour before he mentioned Harold Clyde Campbell by name. Melinda glanced at her mother. She gave her daughter an almost imperceptible nod before slipping into her coat and walking down the center aisle, her head held high, her tears unheeded.

A flash of panic crossed the preacher's face when he saw the look in Melinda's eyes. In a practiced, impressive segue he switched from fire and brimstone to, "What brings us together on this Saturday morning—our need to say a collective good-bye to a man who was a friend, a father, and a husband, Harold Campbell."

Melinda followed her mother, striving to demonstrate a grace equal to the one displayed by her exit. When they were outside, Mary Ann took her daughter's hand and gave it a gentle, grateful squeeze. Melinda leaned into her mother's shoulder, closed her eyes and tried to picture her father as the young man who had swept her mother off her feet and into a life of enduring, albeit bittersweet love.

She wasn't sure she believed her father's spirit had lingered to comfort her mother, but she liked thinking it was possible. What she did know, what she never doubted, was that they were not alone as they silently walked through the unnaturally quiet forest on their way home.

"How do you think you will remember him?" Mary Ann asked as they reached the peak of the hill behind their house.

Memories tumbled over each other in her mind.

There were so many . . . "How he cried when I came home from Mississippi without my baby."

"He knew there wasn't a miracle to be had that would let you keep her, but he never stopped praying for one."

"I don't think God listens when you pray for someone to die," Melinda said. "Even someone like Evert Lee."

"You're saying you think I'm wasting my time?" Mary Ann said.

"I guess what I'm really saying is we should think twice about what we ask for. If God has anything to do with Evert Lee dying, it will be done and over with. I'd prefer it be a long, slow process with plenty of time to suffer and think about what he did to his children."

"And the children of all the men he drove from their homes." Mary Ann stopped so fast Melinda ran into her, almost knocking them both into the creek. She was staring at her house and the number of cars parked out front. "I can't do this," she said. "I can't abide one more person telling me your father's dying was a blessing because he's not suffering anymore. I never heard such nonsense. It's like saying all those years we had with him in the end were a waste."

"Then just keep walking," Melinda told her. "I'll see to what needs to be done at the house."

Mary Ann pulled herself up to her full five feet four

inches. "If I don't go down there your father will be the talk of the county from now 'til next summer. I'd rather give them what they came to see and hear and be done with it."

Later that night as Melinda lay in bed, curled on her side and staring at the moon drifting by her window, image after image of her parents skipped across her mind like a flat rock on a broad lake. She saw them sitting next to each other on the chintz-covered couch, her mother knitting a vest out of yarn she'd rescued from a sweater worn through at the elbows. Her father watched her work, never expressing his embarrassment that the ambition-filled promises he'd made to take care of her had become as empty as the freezer he'd bought to hold the fish that no longer swam in the streams.

She heard them discussing the funeral service as if they were actually in the next room. Her father grumbled over Reverend Riggins's intimidating pitch for money from men laid so low since the mine closed that they bent arthritic knees to retrieve a penny stuck in asphalt. It mortified him that some poor soul might be coerced into a contribution when his only reason for being there was to partake in the food provided by church members after the service.

He'd chosen cremation over burial in the century-and-a-half-old family plot, believing the cost of dying was an obscenity they should forgo. He left the where and when of scattering his ashes up to Mary Ann, telling her to choose a place where they would both rest easy. She chose early summer when the mountain laurel was in full bloom and left the rest to Melinda.

On a morning she couldn't sleep, she took off an hour before sunrise, guided by a faint dawn. She wandered without conscious thought or direction but wasn't surprised when she wound up at the cabin. It was the first time she'd been there since the week Daniel died. That was the day she realized there were multilevels and intricate facets to grief, something she'd never fully understood. Her losses would be with her the rest of her life, surfacing on different levels, always there.

She didn't have to look for Daniel. He was everywhere, from a song to a shadow seen out of the corner of her eye. She heard leaves rustle when there was nothing to disturb them. Once she felt him calling her, his voice carried on a breeze, insisting she hurry or they would miss the sunset.

When falling leaves gave way to snow, Melinda put her head back, closed her eyes, and told herself the flakes that landed on her lips were directed there by Daniel. He was always with her and yet she was always alone.

She finally chose a northern red oak on the highest peak in the McElroy Nature Conservancy Preserve, believing her father's ashes would be a gift to the soil that would nurture the tree for a hundred years.

The last of her father's ashes caught in a sudden wind and circled the tree. Her mother said a final good-bye that ended with an ominous foreshadowing. "Don't wander too far, my love. I need to know you're waiting for me."

The elevator door slid open and Melinda was back in a world filled with plans and decisions.

She felt weighed down as she crossed the lobby. Would the pain over her father's loss ever lessen? Would there be a day when her first memories were his quick wit and intelligence and not his long, slow death?

Her mother knew she was dying and prepared Melinda for the inevitable. Chemotherapy and radiation didn't frighten her—she just wanted to die on her own terms.

Melinda read medical reports, did research on the latest treatments, and built a case to present to her mother to convince her there were solid reasons to hope. Women survived breast cancer all the time, more and more every year.

Her mother was asleep when Melinda arrived at the hospital, armed with arguments befitting a brilliant John Grisham attorney. She looked frighteningly shrunken and pale. Melinda pulled the folding chair provided for visitors closer, snaked her hand through the bars, and clasped her mother's needle-bruised hand. There was bone and skin, but no cushioning fat. She stared at the monitors and listened to the steady labored breathing escaping her mother's parched throat.

Slowly, a drop at a time, Melinda released the tears she'd been fighting for months. She buried her face against her arm as her tears turned to sobs.

Her mother ran her fingers through Melinda's glossy hair. "Please don't be sad," she said. "I'm ready to leave this place. Every dream I have I'm with your father. He's strong and happy and young again." Tears formed that she made no effort to wipe away. "There hasn't been a day since he died that I haven't longed to see him, Melinda. The pain never goes away and it never gets better."

"I'm going to wish you were here every day for the rest of my life," Melinda whispered.

"I'm sorry, Melinda. For so many things. Most of all, that we couldn't find a way for you to keep your baby. I have lived with that regret every hour of every day."

Melinda stayed with her mother until she took her last breath. For days after the cremation friends stopped by the house to bring baked goods and to visit over a cup of coffee. They used different approaches, but to a woman they told her how wrong it was to let her mother go without a church service. No one listened when Melinda told them her mother had made her own arrangements and that she'd distinctly forbidden Melinda to let Reverend Riggins so much as offer a prayer *at Sunday service. They insisted they were fighting for their friend's soul.*

She put a stop to the food and visits three days after her mother's cremation when she sneaked off one morning before the good women of Walker County were up and about. Word that Mary Ann no longer resided in her grandmother's jewelry box spread like moonshine at a Fourth of July picnic, and by suppertime, Melinda was alone again.

Chapter Twenty-Eight

Cheryl was on the porch hosing off Coconut's feet when Melinda pulled into the driveway an hour after she left the hospital. The minute Coconut saw her she did a happy dance that sent a spray of water in Melinda's direction. She waited while Cheryl dried the dog's paws and put her in the house.

"I'm getting good at this dog and cat thing," Cheryl said, returning the hose to a ceramic flowerpot. "If we weren't moving, I would look into getting a dog for Bobby."

"Did Heidi behave herself?"

Cheryl laughed. "I was worried there might be a territorial thing between the two of them, considering she was the new-comer, but she had Coconut whipped into shape within four minutes after she stepped through the door."

"You brought her over here?"

"I wasn't going to, but then she looked at me with those big eyes and wrapped herself around my ankles . . ." She shrugged. "What choice did I have?"

"Welcome to my world."

"Jeremy called and said you were on your way so I took her back about half an hour ago. She's been fed and should be down for a nap after all the running around she and Coconut did."

"Thank you." Melinda realized she wanted to give Cheryl more. "It was a good day."

She responded with a broad smile. "I'm glad."

"Now, I have one more favor."

"You need me to watch Heidi tomorrow morning?"

"Well, there's that, but what I need right now is a couple of suggestions where I can pick up some summer clothes."

"I'll have to run this by Jeremy, but it seems to me Shiloh would be the perfect person to guide you through the boutiques in this area. Some grandmothers teach their granddaughters how to make cookies, Jeremy's mother taught her granddaughter how to shop."

"I can't remember the last time I had a homemade cookie," Melinda said.

"I used to make them on a weekly basis for Bobby's lunch. Now I'm lucky if I find time at Christmas."

A memory of coming home from school to the smell of freshly baked oatmeal cookies almost overwhelmed Melinda. She couldn't have been much over eight years old when her ordinary life of cookies and Sunday drives transitioned to her mother leaving for work earlier than Melinda left for school and not coming home again until it was near bedtime. Her dresser held clothes from the thrift store in Pikesville and what cans there were in the kitchen cupboard were all stamped *out of date*.

"Back to the shopping," Cheryl said. "Can you wait until tomorrow afternoon?"

"Yes," Melinda said, instinctively knowing where Cheryl was headed before she could finish.

"You should be aware Jeremy will probably insist Shiloh take a nap when she gets home."

Melinda would wear wool and flannel-lined jeans however long it took to accommodate Jeremy's requirements. "Is that necessary?" Realizing she was asking Cheryl to judge his behavior, she quickly added, "Never mind. If that's what Jeremy wants, it's what we'll do."

"I want this to work out. Not as much as you do, I'm sure. But I can understand how much having Shiloh in your life again means to you. I'm in your corner."

Melinda decided it was time to leave before she did something embarrassing, like throwing up or crying. "I'll see you tomorrow," she said as she skipped down the stairs. "And thanks again for taking care of Heidi."

Melinda was halfway across the path between their houses when Cheryl called to her. "Why don't you come to dinner tonight? You can meet Andrew and Bobby."

"I'd love to."

"Seven o'clock okay?"

She grinned. "Midnight would be okay. What can I bring?"

"Just yourself."

Melinda nodded and waved and reached for the handle on the garden gate. Out of the corner of her eye she saw Heidi at the window. She was stretched full-length against the glass, her mouth moving in what looked like a plaintive cry.

"I'm coming," she called, even knowing Heidi couldn't possibly hear her.

As soon as she opened the door, Heidi was wrapped around her legs meowing and then almost choking as she switched to purring and then back to meowing. Melinda tossed her purse on the sofa and lowered herself to the floor, her back pressed against the cushions. Heidi crawled on her lap, marking Melinda's arms and chest and chin with her cheek as she head butted whatever she could reach, maintaining a steady dialog of meows.

"Are you bragging or complaining with all that meowing?" Melinda asked, running her hand down Heidi's back and cupping her head to give her a kiss. "I understand you were throwing your weight around with Coconut today."

Heidi put her paws on Melinda's chest and her head on her chin. When she pulled back to look at Melinda, she was drooling. Melinda laughed as she dug in her pocket for a tissue to wipe Heidi's face.

She couldn't pick the precise moment Heidi went from a problem to a gift, but she innately understood their relationship was special. They were connected the way lost souls who'd managed to find each other were.

"I had a pretty good day, too," she said as Heidi finished her journey to Melinda's shoulder and settled into her favorite spot against Melinda's neck. "Shiloh's father is willing to let me see her. Not as much as I would like, but I'll take whatever I can get. So, what do you think about that?"

Heidi tucked her chin in Melinda's flannel collar and let out a contented sigh.

"Me too," Melinda said.

FOR THE FIRST time, Heidi was more interested in sleep than she was food and willingly returned to her nest on the sofa as soon as Melinda was satisfied she'd eaten enough to last until the next feeding.

Incapable of arriving empty-handed, Melinda looked through the cupboards until she found a vase then went into the garden to gather a bouquet. When she was content the arrangement looked as happy as she felt, she checked on Heidi one last time and headed next door.

"Oh, they're beautiful," Cheryl said, putting the bouquet on the sideboard. "Julia would love knowing someone is using the garden." She guided Melinda into the living room. "As promised, the rest of the family."

Andrew stood and came forward to shake Melinda's hand. "Cheryl has been talking about you nonstop since you arrived."

Melinda smiled. "Knowing Cheryl even as little as I do, I'm going to assume it was all good."

"It was," he said, gifting her with a second welcoming smile.

The quick introduction was all it took for Melinda to see Andrew was the kind of man whose character overshadowed his appearance. If she never saw him again, she wouldn't try to describe how tall he was, or what color hair he had, or even whether he was handsome or ordinary, she would talk about how he'd made her feel comfortable and welcome. Most appealing was the way he looked at Cheryl and the love they exchanged in a glance.

"I'm Bobby," Shiloh's best friend announced as he came into the room, a game box tucked under his arm. "Shiloh said I have to be extra nice because she wants you to like me."

She could see that he was testing her. "Does that mean you're not usually nice?"

"Depends."

"Bobby—behave yourself," Andrew said.

"Forewarned is forearmed," Melinda said.

Bobby frowned. "I don't understand what that means."

"I'll tell you later." She motioned to the box under his arm. "What's in there?"

"Clue."

"I love Clue. My dad and I used to play it all the time."

"My dad hates games." Bobby shot a look at Andrew. "Want to take his place?"

As if to prove his point, Andrew got up and moved to the

oversize chair next to the fireplace. Coconut joined him, letting out a deep-throated, rumbling groan of exhaustion before dropping her head between his legs and immediately falling asleep. "I have to warn you," Melinda said. "I'm pretty good and I play to win."

Bobby laughed. "Tell her how good I am, Mom."

"Obnoxiously so," Cheryl said.

Melinda took a seat on the sofa opposite Bobby while Cheryl settled into the chair closest to the kitchen. "Let the game begin," she said.

Bobby gleefully rubbed his hands together. "I think I like you already."

"Oh, yeah? Tell me that when I've got your Miss Scarlet in the library with a knife."

Cheryl leaned back in her chair. "I can see I'm out of my league with you two."

"It's okay, Mom. We'll take it easy on you."

Melinda inwardly smiled at the "we."

Chapter Twenty-Nine

Jeremy slowly made his way down the eucalyptus-lined road that led to the cove and the beach house—and Melinda. She had set him back on his heels so far he found himself fighting for balance when he thought about her. She was nothing like he'd imagined. He'd been prepared to find fault to use as ammunition through Shiloh's teen years, even knowing it would have to be done very, very carefully. Criticizing Melinda, even hinting she was unfit, could shake Shiloh's belief in herself.

Jeremy had walked a tightrope in a hurricane for twelve and a half years. He'd created excuse after excuse to explain Melinda giving Shiloh up for adoption, knowing as soon as she was old enough to reason them out, they would be rejected out of hand.

He had no one but himself to blame for the mess he was in. He should have told Shiloh the truth from the beginning, that he had no idea why or how someone could carry a baby for nine months, give birth to that baby—the most beautiful baby in the world—hand her over to strangers, and walk away.

And what excuse would he have used to explain Tess? He had memories of loving Tess, but none of the feelings that should have accompanied the memories. Anger consumed him when she walked out—he didn't care that she was gone, their marriage had become a ritual by then, but he would never forgive her for the way she left. Before he realized that it was happening, his anger had spilled over and tainted Shiloh. It wasn't until Jeremy saw how scared she was to even mention Tess that he came to his senses. He took time off, left a message on his work and private phones saying he would check in periodically but was only available for emergency repairs should there be a 7.0, or higher, earthquake.

Before the sun was up the next morning he and Shiloh were headed east, picking up the Gold Rush Trail and Hwy 49 in Jamestown and spending the next five days meandering north through a major portion of the historic gold rush trail. Jeremy saved the best for last, a half-day white-water trip down the south fork of the American River. Despite reassurances from her doctor, Jeremy worried the entire time they were on the water. By the time they reached the end and he saw how happy she was, how normal she felt, his smile was as big as hers.

He marked the trip as the real beginning of his and Shiloh's life together without Tess. On the way home their conversation drifted, covering a little bit of everything and nothing. He discovered Shiloh was confused why her mother had left, but not traumatized. She asked who would bring snacks when it was her turn to provide them for her class, and did he know her new school only allowed healthy snacks? No cookies or cupcakes unless they were made out of things like carrots or dried fruit. But no nuts. Some people reacted to nuts the way she did sunlight and fluorescent lights.

She wanted to know what she was supposed to tell people when they asked if they could talk to her mother. Was it okay if she didn't tell anyone at her new school about the letter? Did she have to tell them she was sick? What if she didn't?

There were times when Jeremy felt overwhelmed by the weight of trying to protect Shiloh. He was a doer. Give him a problem and he found a way to solve it. Tell him something couldn't be accomplished and he figured out what needed to be done and did it. How was it that he failed over and over again with the person who meant more to him than his own life?

Did he really want to try to convince Shiloh that Melinda didn't know how to be a mother? On what basis? What had she done to deserve that kind of treatment?

Jeremy parked the truck across the street from Cheryl and

Andrew's house and watched shadow figures move past the curtained front-room window. For the length of a heartbeat he let himself acknowledge how lonely he was.

He longed for the summers Shiloh had been in remission and they had waited together for the sun to sink into the sea. This was their time, special and private. A time when they set out to discover a world most people didn't know existed, one where he and Shiloh would spread a blanket on a hillside overlooking all of Monterey Bay. Silently they waited for the creatures of the night to wake and take over their world.

Everything he did back then was focused on turning her lupus into something they could handle, even resorting to the old cliché about making lemonade out of lemons. He knew he was succeeding when Shiloh broke through her self-imposed silence and started asking questions again, almost all of them beginning with "why."

They were on one of their nighttime picnics when she asked how many ants lived in a colony and why so many more skunks than raccoons were hit by cars. He loved her voracious curiosity even when it meant he would stay up half the night looking for answers.

He knew one day she would want to explore beyond the world he'd created. Being stuck with your father was boring when there were cute boys and girlfriends and music that made you feel as if you belonged to something bigger. How could sitting on a hillside waiting for raccoons and skunks

and the occasional opossum to wander by compete with texting a friend about . . . anything?

He could handle the pajama parties and insanely loud,
headache-inducing, incomprehensible music. He even managed to stay calm in a room full of girls giggling and tossing
pillows at each other in a custom-designed bedroom, a Christmas gift from her grandmother. Jeremy didn't fold until Shiloh
came to him and told him she wanted to find her mother. Her
real mother.

From that moment his life changed. He was forced to acknowledge that no matter how hard he tried, his love and
caring and nurturing weren't enough. He was a damn good
father, at times even a great father. But it wasn't enough.

Feeling himself sinking in a downward spiral, Jeremy
headed for the beach. He studied the water. If he timed it
right, he could make it to the jetty and back again before the
tide turned and blocked his way.

Normally he jogged at an easy pace. Tonight he ran as if
he could escape.

He needed time to do things, not just think about doing
them. The custom tile for a kitchen remodel he'd been working on for over two months finally arrived and he hadn't been
at the house to look through the shipping crates. His client
had found "this wonderful little shop in Deruta, Italy," and
ordered the pieces months before she hired Jeremy. He could
have told her that he knew the shop and that they did ex-
quisite work but that they used the worst shippers in Italy
because they were cheap. It wasn't uncommon to have up to a

third of the tile chipped or cracked or broken in transit. If he couldn't work with what was left by using the damaged tiles for cuts and edging, the homeowner either chose a new tile from a local vendor or they all waited another six months to finish the project. The longer he put off looking at the tiles, the longer the subcontractors were on standby.

He ran faster.

And then there was Tess. What in the hell was he going to do with her? The fastest way to get her out of their lives was to pay her off, but the thought of selling his and Shiloh's home to come up with that much money stuck in his throat like an enormous bitter pill.

He went back and forth about whether or not to tell Shiloh that Tess was back in their lives. Did he have the right to keep it from her? Tess had been her mother. Legally, she still was. According to Brian she had no chance for custody, but that wouldn't keep her from dragging Shiloh into the mess out of spite.

He was gasping for air yet pushed himself harder. Tripping on a piece of kelp, he righted himself and went on, using the pain as an escape. Finally, when his legs gave out, he stopped. Doubled over and gasping for air, for the first time he focused on the show in front of him.

The entire water surface appeared covered in a sparkling silver blanket. Despite the stitch in his side that made standing difficult, he put his hands on his hips and came upright. He was rewarded with a moment of magic as five shadows broke the surface and spouted with such force Jeremy could feel the vibration. Whales were consistent visitors to Monterey Bay, stopping for a meal to sustain them as they migrated from Alaska to Mexico and back again. But Jeremy had never seen them come into the cove.

He looked around to see if anyone else had witnessed the incredible show. Even in this, he was alone.

Chapter Thirty

Jeremy sat on the bottom step where he'd left his shoes and socks and brushed the sand from his feet.

"Dinner's ready," Andrew announced from the top of the stairs.

"How long have you been waiting for me?"

"Nine and a half minutes."

Jeremy laughed. Most women would go crazy married to a man as punctual as Andrew. Cheryl not only put up with him, she indulged his fixation, buying him a watch for his birthday that focused on each passing second almost as precisely as the atomic clock in Boulder, Colorado.

"Did you see the whales?" Jeremy asked as he shook out

his socks and put them on, accepting there was no amount of shaking or brushing that would keep him from cleaning sand from between his toes later that night.

"I did. Put on quite a show."

Jeremy knocked his shoes together and turned them upside down. "I came to drop off Shiloh's clothes, not to be invited to dinner."

"Yeah, but you're here and it's ready, so you might as well stay." He opened the gate to the deck and made room for Jeremy to come inside. "I've been meaning to talk to you about a problem I'm having with one of the greenhouses. A support beam is sagging and I was wondering if there was anything I could do to fix it myself."

"I'll stop by tomorrow and take a look." Jeremy hesitated at Andrew's invitation to come inside. "I'll be there as soon as I get Shiloh's clothes."

Andrew followed Jeremy to the truck. "I like her," he said.

Jeremy turned and frowned. "Who?"

"Shiloh's mother."

"I didn't know you'd met." An unreasoning flash of anger went through him. At times it seemed as if Melinda was taking over his life—and his friends. Even Shiloh's doctor had commented on how impressed she was with Melinda and how their biological connection was unmistakable. Even a stranger could pick them out in a crowd.

Oblivious to Jeremy's hostile feelings, Andrew went on, "Cheryl couldn't stop talking about how much she liked

Melinda, and I got to see why she felt that way when the three of them were playing a game. She was great with Bobby."

Jeremy's hand froze on the door handle. "Melinda's here?"

"Is that a problem?"

"No," Jeremy said, plainly annoyed. "It just seems like everywhere I go, she's there."

"What did you expect?"

Jeremy shook his head. "Of all the stupid things I've done in my life . . ."

"Cheryl told me that you're giving Melinda and Shiloh two more weeks to get to know each other and then you're sending Melinda packing."

Jeremy opened the back door and removed the hangers that held Shiloh's clothes. He handed them to Andrew and reached across the seat for a pillowcase filled with Shiloh's underwear, pajamas, bras, and bathrobe. "If you're going to tell me that's not enough time, don't bother. I've already heard it."

"Nice luggage," Andrew said, holding up the pillowcase. "Trying to impress Melinda?"

"Go back to the two weeks." He closed the door with his free hand.

"Face it, Jeremy. Whether she's here two weeks or two days, you've let the genie out of the bottle and there's no way in hell he's going back inside. For whatever reason, Melinda had to give up her daughter once. Whatever made you think she would do it a second time?"

"I'll deal with getting her to leave when I have to." They started toward the house. Jeremy looked at the pillowcase. Why hadn't he taken the time to get a suitcase out of the garage? Even his old gym bag would have looked better.

Andrew swung the bag up to ride over his shoulder. "I know you don't want to hear this, but you've already lost the battle. Unless you can come up with some compelling reason to keep them apart, something that Shiloh can accept, she's going to make your life a living hell from the day you send Melinda away until she turns twenty-one and goes after her."

"From now until she turns twenty-one? You think that might be a bit of an exaggeration?"

"There's too much at stake for Shiloh to back off and become your sweet little girl who thinks the sun rises and sets because you told it to."

Jeremy wanted to challenge Andrew, tell him that there were exceptions to every rule, but he couldn't. Not when the sinking feeling in the pit of his stomach told him Andrew was right.

"So what am I going to do?" Jeremy asked, wiping his feet on the rough mat outside the door.

"What you've always done. You'll find a way to get through all of this that will convince Shiloh you are exactly what she's always believed you are—the world's best father."

Andrew opened the door to a room filled with the warm light of energy-efficient bulbs and the sounds of triumphant laughter. Melinda and Cheryl had just lost a game of Clue to Bobby and he was not a gracious winner, demanding a high five acknowledgment from the losers. Melinda gave him a complicated fist bump that was as impressive as it was unexpected. He laughed and said he was going to text Shiloh that he really liked her new mom.

It was then that he looked up and saw Jeremy. He moved around the coffee table to give him a hug. "Mom said Shiloh is coming home tomorrow. *Finally*," he added. "Would it be all right if she went to my soccer game? It's a night game."

Jeremy glanced at Cheryl for confirmation. "Yeah, I don't see why not. If I can get off work in time how about if I come, too?"

"Really?" Bobby squealed, his voice in transition. He turned to look at Melinda. "Can you come? Dad takes us for ice cream after a night game."

"I'd love to."

Jeremy ignored the exchange. "It's been a long time since I went to one of your games," he said to Bobby. "Your dad tells me you're turning into a top-notch goalie and that you'll have recruiters knocking on your door one of these days."

"No I won't. Remember I'm going to Botswana. They don't play soccer over there. They play *football*. Which really isn't football, it's soccer." He threw his hands up in frustration.

Jeremy drew Bobby to him and rubbed his knuckle on top of his head. "I think you'll be able to fit in there, buddy," he said with a laugh. "And we don't have elephants or giraffes or zebras over here."

"Yes we do."

"Zoos don't count." Jeremy looked around. "Speaking of animals, what did you do with Coconut?"

"She spent the entire afternoon showing off for Heidi and has been sleeping since," Cheryl said. "Right now she's curled up on the bed in Shiloh's room."

Cheryl got up, letting out a groan as she worked out the kinks from sitting on the floor, and headed for the kitchen. "I hope you're all hungry. I made enough lasagna to last a week."

Andrew groaned. "Please be hungry. I'm good for three days tops. After that beans and hot dogs start to look good."

"You're in luck," Jeremy said. "I love lasagna and I'm starved." He glanced at Melinda.

"Me too," she said, sending back an innocent look. "My appetite is back big-time."

"I don't like lasagna," Bobby said.

Andrew laughed. "Since when?"

"Since you told me we're moving."

Cheryl rolled her eyes. "Wine, anyone?"

"Give me a minute to put Shiloh's clothes away," Jeremy said. He took the pillowcase from Andrew and made his way down the hall to the back bedroom. Everyone in the family referred to it as the blue room even though there had never been anything blue about it—no furniture, no paint, no curtains or blinds, nothing. Children who stayed at the cottage swore a soft blue light appeared if they were sad, and it made them feel better. The adults swore it was nothing more than wishful thinking. Not once did anyone question how wishful thinking could be passed from one child to another when the blue light was the only thing they had in common.

Jeremy put Shiloh's clothes away, opening and closing the closet door and pulling out all three drawers of the dresser. Coconut never moved. He flipped the light switch off and moved to leave when something drew him back. For several seconds he stood and stared, looking for movement that would indicate Coconut was still breathing. Just to be sure, he went to the bed and put his hand on her chest. She lifted her head and looked at him as if to say, "This better be important."

He ran his hand down her back. "I can see we need to have a talk about these Campbell women. Especially the four-legged variety."

AFTER DINNER, MELINDA and Cheryl took their half-finished wine to the back deck while Jeremy, Andrew, and Bobby cleaned the kitchen. The house rules for dinner at the Wellses was whoever cooked didn't clean. Since Melinda had helped with the salad, Cheryl insisted she'd squeaked through.

"He likes you," Cheryl said.

Assuming she was talking about Bobby, Melinda said, "I like him, too. He's the perfect best friend for Shiloh."

"Not Bobby—Jeremy." Cheryl put her elbows on the railing and stared into the fog before joining Melinda in the second chair. "Jeremy likes you."

"How can you tell?"

"The way he looks at you when he thinks no one will see him."

Melinda wanted to believe her, having Jeremy in her corner would go a long way to convincing him to rethink his list of restrictions. "I hope you're right."

"Really?" Cheryl said.

Melinda frowned. "How is being friends with . . . Oh, I hope you don't mean what I think you do. There is no way I want what's happening between me and Jeremy to go beyond friendship."

"Why?"

Melinda didn't want to think how awkward a relationship with Jeremy could be. "Right now the only person I care about is Shiloh. The last thing I want is Jeremy coming between us."

"I could be wrong," Cheryl said.

"But you don't think so."

She shrugged and smiled. "I call 'em like I see 'em."

This was the kind of conversation that led places Melinda really didn't want to go. She looked at her watch. "Heidi time."

"I hope I didn't scare you off."

"No—you gave me something to think about." She finished the splash of wine at the bottom of her glass. "This is really good."

"The winery is a client. Andrew supplies orchids for the guest cottages and they pay him in wine. It's a great arrangement, trading two wildly overpriced products to two people who normally can't afford either."

Melinda stood, but instead of moving toward the door, she leaned against the railing. "I thought Andrew supplied orchids to grocery stores."

"That's the commercial side of the business. The one that pays the bills."

"And the other side?"

"It's where the hybridization takes place. Andrew has a real gift for knowing which orchids will produce the best crosses. He's won several awards with his paphiopedilums."

"So Bobby isn't the only one leaving behind something he loves." Melinda cringed. *Damn it.* Would she never learn that not everything that popped into her head deserved a voice?

"I told Andrew I'd be content spending a summer with our daughter, but he got all wound up with what we could see and do if we stayed longer. Somehow the 'longer' turned into three years."

"I can see why you'd be torn. Three years is a long time."

"How do you handle being gone as much as you are?"

"It would be different if I had family or friends in Minneapolis, but there's no one." She worked to keep her tone upbeat, not wanting to sound pathetic. "I do have an apartment," she added. "It's nice, but it feels more like a fancy hotel room than a home."

"I know what you mean. I lived in Seattle for a while and my apartment had all the charm of a room in a museum of modern art." She waved her arm to encompass the house she lived in now. "Look at this. Can you imagine me being happy in that kind of place?"

"Honestly, I can't. Any more than I can imagine you living in Botswana."

"Have you been there?"

"Yes. I set up security systems for three banks in Gaborone, the capital. Randy had a crazy scheme for Wyndham and Parker to go international. It turned out to be more problem than profit so not only was it the first time he tried expanding, it was the last time."

"What was it like in Gaborone?"

"A large city with lots of shopping centers."

"Our daughter is in the northern region."

"Which is beautiful, especially during the rainy season, but it's isolated. There are no cities like Gaborone."

"No matter what I've done, I can't get Bobby excited about going. And now I'm beginning to wonder about Andrew."

"Here I go sticking my nose where it doesn't belong again, but is it possible Andrew's changed his mind about being gone such a long time but doesn't want to disappoint you?"

"With Andrew anything is possible. He's prone to do things impulsively, especially when I'm willing to go along with his ideas."

"I've never known anyone like that. The people I work with study every angle of every proposal until there isn't one drop of spontaneity left."

Cheryl drew her legs up and wrapped her arms around them. "Andrew's way of dealing with his best friend's death was to sail around the world. Solo. He didn't come home until he lost another best friend, this one the four-legged kind. That was when he decided he didn't want to live alone anymore and came looking for me."

"And he found you." Melinda basked in happy endings, tucking them away to bring out when it seemed her life was a constant uphill journey.

"That's a story for another time."

"Is it okay if I remind you?"

Cheryl looked at Melinda for what seemed like a long time. "Have you had so few happy endings in your life?"

That kind of intimacy made her too vulnerable. She got up and moved toward the door. "I just love great love stories."

"It's okay," Cheryl said softly. "I understand." She followed Melinda but before they went inside, she purposely gave her a hug meant to last a long, long time. "Heidi's waiting."

Basking in the glow of Cheryl's kindness, Melinda went inside, thanked Andrew for his hospitality and Bobby for the games they'd played, then turned to Jeremy. "I'll see you to-morrow."

"Give me a minute and I'll walk out with you," Jeremy said.

She glanced at Cheryl and saw the beginning of a smile twitching at the corner of her mouth.

"There were some things I wanted to go over with you at the hospital tomorrow," Jeremy added. "But there's no reason we couldn't get them out of the way tonight."

Jeremy and Andrew exchanged what passed for a hug between men, he kissed Cheryl on the cheek and thanked her again for what he insisted was the world's best lasagna, then leaned down to whisper something in Bobby's ear.

Bobby laughed and threw his arms around Jeremy's waist.

Melinda led Jeremy outside, surprised when he stopped in the middle of the driveway instead of following her to the house. "You're not coming over? You said you had something you wanted to talk to me about."

"It can wait. I have a bid for a kitchen remodel I promised I'd have to a client by tomorrow."

She nodded. "I'll see you in the morning, then."

He let out a pent-up sigh. "Actually, I was going to ask you not to come to the hospital. I'd like some time alone with Shiloh."

"Oh . . . okay. Of course."

"It's nothing personal."

"I didn't think it was." She looked down at the pathway and wondered how many people had used it in the past century. How many lives had changed? How many hearts had been broken? "That's it? There's nothing else you wanted to talk to me about?"

"Tess filed for financial disclosure papers this afternoon." The sentence spilled out of him like water escaping a sink with a plugged drain. "Brian said he thinks we should delay any request from her attorney as long as possible."

"Hoping she'll become desperate and willing to settle on your terms—as long as it's enough money to save her business," she finished for him.

"It's the best leverage I have to get her to give up her demand for shared custody. I keep going back to the belief that with her history, no judge in his right mind would let Tess anywhere near Shiloh. Then Brian reminds me about all the decisions that have come down in family courts that don't follow logic."

Why was he telling her about Tess? She found it hard to believe he wanted her opinion or that he would listen if she gave it. "What's the next step?"

"Hurry up and wait. In the meantime, Brian's drawing up divorce papers so they'll be ready when the time comes."

"What about visitation rights?" She waited for him to tell her she'd gone too far. When he didn't, she pushed harder. "One weekend a month? Every other holiday?"

Jeremy tilted his head back to look at the fog-shrouded pine tree on the far side of the house. Before he answered, he cleared his throat. "There's no way I can answer that without hurting you."

"I understand," she said.

"No you don't." He forced himself to look at her. As he'd expected, she was holding on by a thread. "For all the bad that's happened with Tess, it's easy to forget that in the beginning, there were good years. I don't know how many of those years Shiloh remembers, or if they hold any real meaning for her now, but I've decided she has the right to be a part of the decision-making process."

"You're talking about the time before Shiloh got sick."

"Yes."

There were pieces missing, big pieces. "Are you still in love with Tess?"

Jeremy's eyes grew wide in disbelief. "Love has nothing to do with how I feel about Tess." Before she could ask, he added, "Hate doesn't either. I decided a long time ago that hating her takes more energy than she deserves. I want her out of our lives but it's not up to me."

"So let me get this straight. Shiloh is old enough to decide whether she wants Tess to be a part of her life, but she's incapable of deciding whether she wants to see me?" She put her hand out in a familiar dismissive gesture when he started to say something. "Don't bother. I know the answer."

"I've known Tess over fifteen years and you less than a week. I might not like what I know, but there are no surprises where she's concerned. You, on the other hand, are a complete mystery."

"Hardly a mystery. You never would have let me come here if you hadn't done your research."

"I wasn't going to let you anywhere near Shiloh without finding out everything I could."

"Are we done? Have you told me everything you wanted to tell me?" She dug her key out of her pocket. "Heidi's waiting. And I'm tired."

He nodded and backed away from her. "See you tomorrow."

"Yeah . . . tomorrow." She went inside and closed the door, not looking back.

Jeremy waited until he saw the kitchen light come on before heading for his truck. For a long time he sat with his hands wrapped around the steering wheel, fighting an almost overwhelming urge to go back, to knock on the door, and when she answered tell her he was sorry—for so many things.

He was confused by feelings he didn't want and had never anticipated. On the surface it was easy to see why he would be drawn to Melinda. She was bright and stubborn and willing to slay dragons for a daughter she barely knew. His daughter.

He straightened his arms and pushed hard against the steering wheel. He'd given her two weeks. Fourteen more days. Less, if he behaved like the jerk she believed him to be and subtracted the time she'd already been there.

But Tess was the immediate problem. Melinda would come later. He hit his fist on the steering wheel and let out a derisive laugh. How many men could say they'd gotten rid of not just one, but two of their daughter's mothers in a matter of weeks.

Chapter Thirty-One

Melinda poured herself a cup of coffee and sat at the kitchen counter, an old-fashioned yellow tablet and her favorite mechanical pencil in front of her. She took a deep breath and called the number for the main office of Wyndham and Parker Security Systems. She went through the receptionist and Randy's assistant before reaching Randy himself.

"It's about goddamned time," Randy said. "Tell me you're ready to get to work on the New Mexico job."

"Yes—and no."

"What the hell is that supposed to mean?"

"What it always means when you give me a job like this." She'd spent the morning going over the information packet

Randy forwarded from the IT department at XON Imports. Of all the clients she'd worked with since starting at Wyndham and Parker, XON was the prime example of a company on the verge of imploding. Everything needed work, from sloppy encryption to using a cloud provider that didn't reveal which jurisdiction was storing their data.

"I'm going to set up a meeting with their IT for next week to see if telecommuting is even possible with this job." Melinda could almost hear the gears taking Randy through his thought process. She had a unique relationship with Randy, one that transcended the normal boss/employee position. He pushed, as he was doing now, while begrudgingly accepting there were times she would push back. Her infrequent displays of stubbornness and frustration were all right because she brought something to the job that employees with obligations couldn't—not only was she very, very good at her job, she was available and willing to spend months at a time away from home.

Bottom line, he was acutely aware that he needed her more than she needed the job.

"What are you saying? What do you mean if it's even possible?" His voice grew sharper and louder as panic set in. "Do you have any idea how important this job is to our company?"

Translation—how much money they would make. "Yeah, you've mentioned it a time or two."

"I want these people to have our full attention."

Heidi chose that exact moment to make Melinda aware

she expected her full attention. She climbed her regular route but rather than settling on Melinda's shoulder, she sat on the counter and stared at her. "I'll see what I can do."

"I knew I could count on you."

"Don't push me on this, Randy." She ran her hand down Heidi's back. Heidi arched in response and rumbled in satisfaction. "As a matter of fact, it would be a good idea for you to start thinking about who you want to take over if I decide not to take this on."

"That's not an option, Melinda. You either call XON and tell them you're headed for New Mexico to put together your team or you start looking for another job."

She waited just long enough to make him believe he'd won, and then said, "I'll arrange to move out of the apartment as soon as possible. Of course I'll take care of the rent until then."

He made a series of blustering sounds that sounded like a frustrated cartoon character surrounded by exploding stars. "You're not serious. Where would you go?"

"You're kidding. Are you really unaware how many job offers I get every month?" Heidi leaped to Melinda's shoulder and settled in. Melinda smiled. She owed this scrawny little kitten more than she would ever be able to repay.

"All right. You can have your two weeks. They're in a panic to get started but I'll convince them you're worth waiting for."

"That could be a major mistake, Randy. XON's security is such a mess they're one unencrypted laptop away from dealing with a major hacking problem." The line went silent. After several seconds Melinda heard a rapping sound as Randy rolled his fingertips over his glass-top desk.

"Give me a name—someone I can send to patch the leaks until you can get there."

"Fred Stephens," she said without hesitation.

"Who the hell is Fred Stephens?"

She wasn't surprised he didn't recognize the name. Randy focused on the people who made the most money for the company and Fred hadn't been there long enough to cover his salary. "He's the guy I found at the courthouse a couple of years ago."

"The one they caught hacking the personnel files at his school?"

"That's him," she said.

"You hired that kid?"

"I didn't hire him, you did. It was part of the plea deal we worked out with the district attorney."

"You want to tell me why I would do this?"

"Because the SOB he was after was a sexual predator who used his position with the women's soccer team to molest the players."

Again the line went silent for several seconds. "I'm assuming you ran this by legal?" he said.

Heidi turned and resettled, pressing her nose into Melinda's neck and kneading her collar, her claws piercing the material like fine needles. Time for a manicure. "Which part?"

"Don't be coy. I need to know if we're covered if he decides to play Good Samaritan again. I don't want some cocky kid destroying everything I've worked a lifetime to build."

"This particular cocky kid happens to be pushing thirty, is married, has two incredible daughters, lost both legs in Afghanistan, and has been working his way through school on the GI Bill."

"Okay. Plainly you've done your research. Fill him in on what we expect and—"

"Not going to happen, Randy. You need to meet Fred and decide for yourself how you feel about sending him to New Mexico."

"And if it doesn't work out?"

"Then you're on your own." If she gave him any reason to believe she could be maneuvered into taking over, he would jump on it.

Melinda glanced at the time on her phone. "You have an hour to get things set up with Fred. After that he'll be on the road for his daughter's soccer tournament."

Randy's frustrated sigh echoed through the phone. "How do you know these things?"

Melinda laughed. "Facebook."

"All right. I'll talk to him. But I don't want you to get it in your head that I'm happy about any of this."

"Wouldn't even cross my mind."

AT JEREMY'S REQUEST, Cheryl accompanied Melinda and Shiloh on their summer clothes shopping excursion. What started out awkwardly, with Melinda working to hide her disappointment that she wouldn't have Shiloh to herself, turned into something she'd almost forgotten existed—girl time, girl talk, girl secrets, and, most important, girl laughter.

Melinda wound up with far too many shorts and tank tops and sundresses and hats. For the first time in a long time she liked what she saw in the dressing room mirrors and basked in the positive comments from Shiloh and Cheryl.

Shiloh wandered through the racks holding high-fashion teen clothing, making no attempt to hide her look of longing. She tried on shorts and gauzy shirts, and beamed as she struck models' poses for Melinda and Cheryl. When she disappeared in the dressing room to try on the sundress with sexy cutout sides, Melinda turned to Cheryl and rolled her eyes at how eager Shiloh was to grow up.

Cheryl laughed and told her parenting through the teen years was not for the faint of heart.

They arrived back at the beach house at the same time the pizza delivery car arrived at the cottage. It was assumed Melinda would join them, but she begged off, saying she had work to do. In reality she had decided to walk the fine line of requests and rules Jeremy had given her, not wanting to give him any reason or opportunity to find fault.

She opened the trunk to retrieve Shiloh's packages, feeling a huge sense of accomplishment that they'd found clothes both she and her father would like.

Coconut gained her freedom when Andrew answered the door for the pizza delivery. A cloud of cheese and pepperoni brought her to an abrupt stop but wasn't enough to keep her from bolting across the pathway that separated the beach house from the cottage. She flung herself into Shiloh's arms. The wiggling and whining lasted until Coconut was convinced Shiloh hadn't come for a temporary visit.

"Pizza's getting cold," Bobby shouted.

Melinda handed Shiloh and Cheryl their bags and despite her disappointment at having them leave, gave them a smile as genuine and heartfelt as the time she'd been offered raw oysters by a client she wanted to impress. Despite throwing up almost before the oyster reached her stomach, she managed to convince him that her lack of culinary sophistication had nothing to do with her ability to set up a security system that would be next to impossible to hack.

Shiloh stopped and looked at Melinda. "What should I call you?"

Her heart in her throat, Melinda said, "Whatever you like."

"Okay." She caught a bag that had begun to slip. "What time should I come over tomorrow?"

"Whenever you want."

"I need an actual time. For my dad."

"Two?"

"So late?"

Melinda smiled. "Ten?"

"See you then."

After two trips from the car to the bedroom and a longing look at the cottage next door, Melinda stood back and stared at the new clothes she'd spread across the bed. Heidi climbed up to explore, taking in all the new smells while traveling from shirt to shorts to dresses with a mixture of curiosity and caution.

"Too much?"

Heidi arched her back and yawned before settling down on a cropped jean jacket.

"I expected a little more enthusiasm." She didn't need confirmation to know she'd gone overboard, especially on the short shorts and tank tops. And she didn't even want to count the number of sandals she'd wound up with. It was as if she'd had a moment of temporary insanity and managed to convince herself she was staying the entire summer, not just two weeks.

For all of her early bravado that no one and nothing could get her to leave, she'd been wrong. She'd gone from putting her own feelings first to the realization Shiloh was the only one who mattered. It was something Jeremy knew and lived with no matter the personal sacrifice.

Somehow, just in case she couldn't get Jeremy to change his mind about her leaving, Melinda had to find a way to go without hurting Shiloh more than she'd already been hurt.

She let out a sigh and sat on the edge of the bed, a gesture Heidi immediately took as an invitation. Treading less carefully this time, one of her claws caught on a bright orange silk chemise.

Melinda let out a squeal that scared Heidi and sent her clumsily running to the other side of the bed, dragging the chemise behind her. She tripped, and pulled out a thread, leaving a three-inch-long snag. Melinda caught her just before she tumbled to the floor.

"Oh, sweet little girl, I'm so sorry I scared you." She took her paw and worked the thread free. Heidi let out a tortured meow.

"Cut it out," Melinda gently chastised her. "You just need a manicure and we'll both be a lot happier."

She rubbed noses with Heidi before putting her on the floor and heading for the bathroom to get the kitten grooming kit. Heidi sat patiently through the nail clipping, curious but not fearful. Melinda put her on the bed and took the kit back to the bathroom. When she returned she found Heidi high-stepping through the shirts and pants, stopping to test each one by taking a few seconds to knead it before moving on.

Melinda laughed at Heidi's self-satisfied expression as she joined her on the bed. She was settled and purring when Melinda reached down to cup her hand over the kitten's baby Buddha midsection. "Don't take this the wrong way, but from the feel of it, you've packed on a pound or two. And somehow they've all landed right here."

Heidi stretched and did a wiggling shudder, plainly believing she'd been complimented.

"Can I tell you a secret?"

Almost as if she understood, Heidi rolled over, sat up, and stared at Melinda. "I can't be the noble mother who walks away for the good of her child. I did that once." A tear slipped from the corner of her eye. "I can't do it again." She took a deep breath and bit her lip. "I won't."

She'd traveled too far into this new world to go back. As much as she loved her job and reveled in her accomplishments, nothing could take the place of being with Shiloh.

And then, without preparation or planning or belief it could happen, there was Jeremy. She didn't want to like him. She didn't need to like him. But there he was in the most unexpected places. She found him when she'd looked in the dressing room mirrors and wondered if he would like the shorts or dresses or floppy straw hats she tried on. And she found him in sappy television commercials where the father sat on a sofa sharing a bowl of popcorn with his daughter, his wife staring at him adoringly.

Where she never found him was standing in her corner offering encouragement.

Chapter Thirty-Two

As Melinda had feared, the rest of the week passed with breathtakingly poignant speed. After several days, the only way to keep her sanity was to stop counting the minutes and hours and days as they rushed past and concentrate on living in the moment.

Cheryl and Bobby left to meet Andrew at the Disneyland Hotel Friday night. After he climbed into the car to leave, Bobby rolled down the window to say good-bye to Shiloh. "What do you want me to bring you?"

She shrugged. "Something from the Winnie-the-Pooh store."

"'Something'? That's not very helpful. And don't tell me to surprise you. My mom does that all the time and she never likes my surprises."

"A Christmas ornament."

He turned to Cheryl. "Got that, Mom?"

"I'll get you to the store but then you're on your own." She leaned forward so that she could see Shiloh. "Have fun with your mom."

"I will. My dad said I could show her the otters at Moss Landing as long as she got me home by ten."

Bobby stuck his hand out of the car for a fist bump. "Good job."

"What's that supposed to mean?" Cheryl asked.

He had the decency to give her a sheepish look. "I told her if she kept at him, her dad would give in eventually. He always does."

"You can't imagine how proud I am to know you two have figured out how to manipulate your parents."

"We aim to please," Bobby said with a grin.

TOO EXCITED TO sleep that night, Melinda went to an all-night grocery store and picked up the ingredients for oatmeal cookies. She knew it was a mistake to try to fit everything she wanted to share with Shiloh into a two-week visit, but she wanted to leave her with as many memories as she could manage. Cookies were in but spiced peaches were out. She'd checked at the grocery store and the peach variety her mother insisted was the most flavorful wouldn't be available for another month.

She put the groceries away and laid out the clothes she would wear for the otter excursion that evening, trying to

choose between zebra-print leggings and the more conservative navy blue hiking pants, both 100+ SPF sun protection.

"So, what do you think?" Melinda said as Heidi examined
the two shirts. Heidi ignored her and continued exploring,
tucking her head under the long-sleeved shirt and discovering she could make a tunnel. Within a minute, she'd popped
her head out the other side, immensely pleased with herself.

"Well, aren't you the clever one."

Heidi carefully examined her tunnel before she went inside again and rolled to her back. She had a sleeve artfully
wrapped around her neck when she came out again.

Melinda laughed. "It's a good thing you only get one fur
coat in your lifetime. I have a feeling there's a clothes fanatic
lurking inside that petite frame."

Tempted to join Heidi on the bed, Melinda checked the
time first. With a sigh, she headed for the kitchen. Truth be
told, she loved Heidi's little Buddha belly and the health and
energy that came with it.

For this one hour of this one day, Melinda was happier
than she'd been for a long, long time. It was how she would
live her life from then on. One day at a time, leaping from one
stone to the next in a creek filled to overflowing with happiness and promise. She might not have tomorrow, but she had
today. And a book filled with yesterday's memories.

Over the past week, Melinda and Shiloh's discussions had
covered everything from Shiloh's favorite teacher to bullying.
She learned that Bobby was teased about being the smallest kid in his class and that in fifth grade he had purposely

tripped a boy who was twice his size who had dunked another boy's head in a toilet. Shiloh agreed the tripping was deserved, but the broken arm complicated things.

This parenting business was hard. Doing it alone made it even more complicated. The more she saw, the more she appreciated the dedication Jeremy demonstrated as a father. And the more she begrudgingly admitted she liked him.

Melinda removed Heidi from her tunnel and put her on her shoulder. "Time to eat."

Shiloh loved the bottle-feeding portion of Heidi's diet and Heidi had no problem adapting to yet another substitute mother. Their initial meeting turned out to be the hands-down highlight of the first day they were all together. Two days later, Coconut joined them.

One afternoon, when fog rolled in almost as thick as the foam that topped the waves, the temperature dropped hard and fast. Melinda had Shiloh pick a book they had both read and could talk about over hot chocolate. They settled on *The Diary of Anne Frank*, focusing on whether history really did repeat itself, and if so, how and why it happened. It was a discussion Melinda had had with her father from the day he decided she was old enough to cope with reading about a tragedy that involved someone her own age.

Shiloh removed a second book and tucked it under her arm. "Just for fun," she said. "This is one my dad used to read to me." She laughed. "A long, long time ago."

Melinda held out her hand for Shiloh to show her. Not surprisingly, it was a book she didn't recognize—*Room on a*

Broom. Rarely did she and her father share beautifully illustrated, modern children's classics when she was growing up. Instead their reading was filled with stories by authors like Lewis and White and Dickens.

While Melinda set a fire they moved from favorite books to food, listing their top three. For Shiloh it was decorated cookies, curried shrimp, and garlic fries. Melinda settled on Cream of Wheat, crab cakes, and homemade German chocolate cake.

For movies Shiloh chose *The Sisterhood of the Traveling Pants*, *Whale Rider*, and *The Hunger Games*. Melinda said it was hard to pick second, but chose *Airplane!* because it was her father's all-time favorite and *The Princess Bride* because she'd watched it a half dozen times and could watch it another half dozen without getting bored. Last came *The Green Mile* but it could just as easily have come in first.

"Oh, wait," Melinda said. "Can't leave out *Up*. It's the only DVD I take with me when I'm going to be gone longer than a couple of weeks."

"I *love* that movie. So did my grandma."

Melinda smiled, refraining from reminding Shiloh she had another grandmother, one who would have loved *Up*— and who would have loved her granddaughter more than she could find words to tell her.

Melinda caught her breath as thoughts of all her mother would never experience filled her with a profound sadness and a startling anger. *See what you missed when you gave up so easily? Look at all you had to live for. Think what your granddaughter missed.*

"Your grandmother obviously knew her movies," Melinda said.

Heidi climbed on the sofa, stood in the middle and looked from Melinda to Shiloh and then back to Melinda again. Plainly confused, finally, gingerly, she made her way across the cushion toward Shiloh.

"Really, Heidi?" Melinda said in disbelief. "After all we've been through together?"

Shiloh grinned and reached for Heidi, creating a nest in her folded arms. "Coconut is so jealous. When I get home and she smells Heidi on me, she sits on her cushion in the corner and pouts."

"How long does it take her to get over it?"

Shiloh laughed. "As long as it takes for me to get a treat out of the kitchen and wave it under her nose."

Melinda asked Shiloh about her school, and Shiloh was politely curious about Melinda's job, asking all the right questions, even managing to pay attention to the answers.

"My dad said you were going to New Mexico when you leave here." It was a statement but came out more like a loaded question.

Melinda wasn't sure how to answer. If she told Shiloh that she didn't want to go or that she was doing everything she could to keep from going, what was she really saying? What if she succeeded and stayed in California? What did that mean?

"For a week or two," she said, hoping it would satisfy Shiloh. "Depending on how much work needs to be done and whether the encryption specialist who's there now thinks he needs my help."

"Are you his boss?"

"Not really. I don't want to be anyone's boss."

"Why?" Shiloh brought Heidi up to her face and kissed her nose. "Don't tell my dad you saw me do that."

Melinda laughed. "Your secret is safe. As far as being someone's boss, if I did that, I would have to work out of the home office in Minneapolis and I wouldn't get to travel near as much as I do now."

"Why do you like to travel?"

Shiloh was looking for an answer that had nothing to do with her questions. "Because my father never got to see any of the places he read about in his books and dreamed of seeing one day."

Melinda could see Shiloh thinking out loud. "So going to Alaska and all the other places is your way to tell him you love him and miss him?"

Melinda finally understood where Shiloh was headed. "Are you looking for a way to do something special to tell your grandmother you love her?"

"Maybe. I could be, I guess." She finally added, "I suppose it's possible. It bothers me that I didn't get to tell her good-bye. No one did, not even her friend Howard." Her lip trembled and tears pooled at the edge of her eyelashes. Heidi came on point at the outpouring of emotion. She stood and stared at Melinda, sending a silent plea for help in dealing with the abrupt change in her vivacious friend.

"It wasn't fair," Shiloh went on. "No one should die doing something they love."

Melinda could tell her there were worse ways to die, but it wasn't something she needed to hear. Not now. Maybe never. "Tell me about your grandmother. I think between us we can figure out a way she would have liked to be remembered." Shiloh leaned back into the corner of the couch, giving Heidi a platform where she could snuggle.

"She loved the ocean more than anyone I know. I probably shouldn't tell you this next part, but my dad said she was a hippie and that's why he doesn't know who his father is. She said it was okay because she only slept with men who came from a Nobel laureate gene pool."

Melinda blinked and her jaw dropped. What kind of mother told her son something like that? And what kind of father repeated it to his daughter? The more she thought about it, the funnier it became. "I can see why you loved your grandmother. She was someone my father would have called one of a kind. He believed people like that made life better just by knowing them."

But how did you share a life like that when it came to an end? "I'm going to have to think about this," Melinda said. "Give me a couple of days."

Shiloh laughed. "That's what me and my dad have been saying for months now. The best we've been able to come up with is a bench overlooking the beach where she found the baby seal."

"What about a plaque and an informational plate warning

people about rogue waves," Melinda added. "I think the story about what happened to your grandmother, how she was trying to save the baby elephant seal with its flipper caught in the fishing line, would be an important thing to add."

"Ohhhh . . . I like that." She shifted forward until she was sitting on the edge of the sofa and Heidi was left with nowhere to go. "I think my dad would, too."

Instead of looking for a new nesting site, Heidi leaped off the sofa and went to the front door where she sat with her head cocked and waited.

Melinda watched her, convinced she wasn't just waiting, she was waiting for something or someone special. "What's up, Heidi?" she prompted. Heidi ignored her.

"I'm not supposed to ask you this," Shiloh said to Melinda, "but will you be here for my birthday?"

Melinda made a face. How was she supposed to answer when she had no control over the question? She said the only thing she could. "I don't know."

"Why?"

"That's not fair, Shiloh." It was the first time Melinda had been even mildly cross with her.

"Why?"

"How am I supposed to answer that without it sounding like I'm blaming your dad for keeping us apart?"

"But that's what he's doing. He's the only one who doesn't want you here."

"It's complicated."

"Yeah, right. I get so sick of hearing that. It's what parents say when they can't come up with an answer that makes sense."

Oh my God, Melinda almost groaned aloud. One more example of how hard it is to be a parent. Should she blame her job? At least that way she could keep Jeremy from carrying all the weight for the decision. "I want to be here for your birthday but there are people depending on me that might keep me from doing what I want to do."

Heidi stood and engaged in an odd little cat dance, walking back and forth in front of the door. A second later, there was a summoning knock.

Chapter Thirty-Three

Jeremy rubbed the back of his neck and then rolled his shoulders as he waited for someone to answer his knock on the door. It wasn't that he was tired. Exhausted was a far better description for what he was feeling. Not physically. This was the mental kind. The kind generated by his manipulative wife and Shiloh's menacing mother.

The meeting Brian had arranged between Tess's attorney and Jeremy, the one that was scheduled to last an hour at the outside, wound up lasting almost four when Tess arrived with him to put on her "Oh, poor me" show.

Brian charged Jeremy a flat fee, Tess's lawyer charged by the hour, an amount he made clear he expected Jeremy to cover in the settlement.

Jeremy took it all in, listening without commenting, nodding when it was appropriate, and managing to keep from rolling his eyes when he wanted nothing more than to show his contempt.

Tess held her own until she said something that slid the final brick from the foundation that had supported their relationship. According to Tess, it didn't matter which judge was assigned to the case, there would never be one who believed Shiloh was worth all the fuss.

While her lawyer was slow on the uptake, failing to recognize the flash of fury that swept through Jeremy, Tess immediately recognized she had gone too far. With one simple sentence, she'd initiated a battle she would never win. Before her attorney could say something that would make things even worse, Tess frantically looked for a compromise.

It wasn't going to happen—not now, not ever.

MELINDA FIXED A smile when she saw Jeremy, opening the door with a flourish. "You're late," she said. "Mind you, I'm not complaining, just commenting."

Heidi stood on her hind legs and tried to climb up Jeremy's leg, almost succeeding. He picked her up and tucked her in the crook of his arm. She looked at him adoringly.

"How would you feel about me going with you to see the otters?" he asked. "We could take off now, if you don't mind."

"Of course I don't mind." She studied him through narrowed eyes. "What's up?"

"I've had a shitty day and can use some time away."

She turned to look at Shiloh. "What about you?"

She left the couch and did a skipping motion that left her with her arms around her father's waist and Heidi on her way to Jeremy's collar. "Thanks, Dad."

Melinda moved toward the bedroom to get her jacket then turned back. "Just to be sure I have this straight, you did mean we would all go . . . together."

"Yes."

Jeremy's heart melted a little at how excited she was about such a simple gesture. He was beginning to see and understand he wasn't the only one as lonely as he was alone.

THE LIGHT TRAFFIC put them at Moss Landing two hours before sunset, perfect timing with the fog lifting and the tide coming in. The state beach was one of Shiloh's favorite places to explore, a microcosm of marine birds and animals separated by a spit of sand. She and Jeremy usually came just after sunrise so it was a treat for Shiloh to be there to see the sun dip into remnants of fog.

As soon as they were parked, Shiloh got out of the car and ran toward the small bridge they had crossed on their way in. Melinda started to call out for her to be careful and watch for cars but Jeremy stopped her.

"I know it's hard, but you have to learn to back off. Kids need a sense of freedom. Especially Shiloh. I'm hoping if she has as much control over her day-to-day life as I can give her now, that we'll get through the rebellious stage without any lasting damage."

"It is hard," Melinda admitted. "I've just found her. I can't bear the thought of something happening that would take her away again."

"That's pretty much how I felt the first time the two of you went out alone."

Shiloh waved for them to hurry up. She ran back and grabbed Melinda's hand. "You have to see this. There are three really little baby otters sleeping on their mothers' stomachs. And there's another mother feeding an older baby. See how as soon as she cracks open the clam the baby comes in and takes the food?" She stopped and pointed toward the closer side of the culvert, not letting go of Melinda's hand. "Listen. Can you hear her breaking the shell? She does it with a rock."

Despite the sounds of traffic and barking seals, Melinda could hear the rapid tapping. "I do," she said.

Jeremy stayed with Melinda when Shiloh crossed the road again to watch the younger babies. "You're good with her," he said.

"You made it easy." She loved seeing Shiloh animated with excitement over the otters. "Feel free to tell me it's none of my business, but how is it going with Tess?"

"She's hoping I'll take pity on her despite knowing it's never going to happen. One thing you can say about Tess, she's not stupid. She knows she crossed a line and there's no way back."

"Does she have any options?"

"She could take on a partner but the terms wouldn't be in her favor."

"What about—?"

"There is no 'what about' at this point. I don't care what she does or how she does it, the only thing that matters is getting her to sign the divorce and custody papers. Once that happens, I'm done."

"Shiloh is okay with this? She knows Tess will be out of her life forever?"

"Tess was out of her life a long time ago. What's happening now is nothing more than the period at the end of a sentence."

Melinda stared at Shiloh wondering if it could really be that easy. Would there come a day of doubt when Shiloh wanted to see the woman who was her mother the first seven years of her life? There must have been a time when Tess and Shiloh laughed together at funny movies or Tess taught Shiloh how to set the table for a tea party picnic.

Shiloh looked up, grinned, and waved. "Come see what I found."

Jeremy slipped her hand in his as they crossed the road, the gesture as easy and natural as if it had always been that way. He let go as soon as they reached the other side and the moment of elation disappeared as quickly as it had arrived. First Shiloh and now Jeremy. How could something as simple as holding someone's hand carry such emotional weight?

"See the baby?" Shiloh said, taking the hand Jeremy no longer held.

"No," Melinda said. "Where am I looking?"

"Over there." She pointed with her free hand. "Next to the egret."

Melinda's gaze swept the surface. She squinted, wondering yet again if she was going to need glasses sooner than her doctor had told her. "Still don't see it."

Shiloh put her hands on Melinda's cheeks and turned her head toward the egret. "The thing that looks like a piece of wood floating next to the white bird with the long neck."

She caught her breath in surprise. "That's the baby? Out there all alone?"

"It's okay. The mom fluffs them up before she takes off and puts so much air in their fur that there's no way they can sink."

"How do you know these things?"

"My friend, Paul. He's a marine biologist. He and his mother used to take care of me when Tess left and I was sick."

Jeremy climbed down the embankment and stopped to wait for Shiloh and Melinda. "He's the only person I know who bought an iPad for information, not games. He's a walking, talking Wikipedia."

Melinda followed them down the slippery slope. "That's something my father would have done. He had an insatiable curiosity about anything and everything."

"Do you think he would have liked me?"

"He would have loved you. He used to tell me and my mother that he was the luckiest man in the world when it came to women. You would have fit right in." She caught her toe on a rock and almost fell, but managed to stay upright. Jeremy grinned. Shiloh frowned.

"Okay," Melinda said. "So now you know I'm not the

most graceful person you'll ever meet. As a matter of fact, some would say I'm clumsy." She saw Jeremy nodding in agreement. "Someone who was very, very mean," she added, grinning.

They had only another hour before it would be too dark to explore. Shiloh took advantage of every minute, timing the sunset on the ocean side of the dunes to show Melinda how the shorebirds pulled half-inch crabs from the hard-packed sand.

The sky yielded to a second sunset before Shiloh could be talked into leaving, and then only after Jeremy reminded her Melinda wasn't someone who should be wandering around after dark. They had reached the top of the dune when he removed a small flashlight from his keychain and handed it to Melinda.

"I should be annoyed," she said as she held up the light. "And I would be if I didn't think I needed this." She didn't, not really, but she liked the feeling of being taken care of.

Chapter Thirty-Four

Life went back to what passed for normal when Cheryl and Bobby came home from Disneyland. Andrew stayed behind to work out the final arrangements with the orchid grower in Santa Barbara who was buying his business. Several of the agreed-to conditions of sale were missing from the contract and Andrew refused to sign without them in place. The most important addition, a guarantee that several long-term employees keep their jobs or be given a generous severance package, was the one Andrew had the most trouble having reinstated.

The drive home should have been accompanied by the excitement of an anticipated celebration. Instead, a black cloud hovered overhead the entire three hundred miles.

Something about the sale wasn't right. He just hadn't figured out what it was.

JEREMY LIFTED THE restrictions on the time Shiloh could spend with Melinda and she took full advantage of it. When Bobby complained he felt left out, Cheryl and Jeremy agreed to let him stay with Shiloh and Melinda after lunch every day. In the beginning, Melinda resented the loss of her private time with Shiloh, but it didn't take long for her to understand the importance of Shiloh's friends, who were an integral part of her family.

When they baked oatmeal cookies, Melinda heard stories of how Shiloh and Bobby sneaked out of the house one night to sit on the gray log, curious to find out if anything happened at night that didn't happen in the daytime. Their reward for their adventure was the appearance of an enormous elephant seal. High tides carried it closer with every wave.

They were fearless in their approach, and eager to see the unbelievably large animal up close. Bobby insisted it was dead, Shiloh insisted it wasn't. Bobby moved in for a closer look. Standing less than an arm's distance away, he reached out to run his hand over one of the seal's battle-scarred shoulders. It was at this precise moment the seal raised his head and let out a bellow that vibrated through the sand and up their legs.

They both screamed, Bobby longer and louder than Shiloh, something he refused to admit later but Shiloh refused to let him forget.

Once the stories began they tumbled out and around like

acrobats in Cirque du Soleil. Melinda heard about the week Bobby spent reading *The Hunger Games* to Shiloh at the hospital when her hands were too swollen and painful to hold a book. Neither of them hesitated telling how they both cried when Rue died, and how frightened the nurse had been when she found them sobbing with grief.

Even though Bobby hated getting up early, he made an exception when Shiloh went into remission. Within weeks after she was released, they were back to their morning run, racing across the hard-packed sand, restoring muscle tone for Shiloh and strength for Bobby as he prepared for the upcoming soccer season.

The timer went off on the oven, summoning Melinda. It seemed like forever since she'd baked cookies or made a pie, not even a simple peach cobbler or apple turnover. What was the point when there was only her to eat whatever she made? Her mouth watered in anticipation.

Bobby reached for a cookie still so hot it burned his fingers. "You're really lucky," he said to Shiloh. "My mom never bakes anything."

"She made lasagna," Melinda said, defending her friend, albeit weakly. She loved whatever thought process had put her in the same category as Cheryl.

Bobby moved the cookie from hand to hand, breaking it in half and blowing on it. Unable to wait any longer, he broke off a smaller piece and popped it in his mouth, declaring it the best oatmeal cookie he'd ever had.

Melinda laughed. "First you tell me you've never had a

homemade oatmeal cookie and then you tell me this is the best one ever." She circled the island and ran her fingers through his hair in an affectionate gesture. "You need to make up your mind—which is it?"

"Best ever."

"Good answer," she told him.

A knock sounded on the front door. It opened before Melinda could get there.

"Oh my God," Jeremy said. "What is that smell?"

"Oatmeal cookies," Shiloh told him. "Your favorite."

"And how did that happen?"

Shiloh beamed. "I told Melinda. She made them especially for you."

He gave Melinda a questioning look. "Is that true?"

"They were a whole lot easier than decorated cookies." Why couldn't she just tell him the truth—that she wanted to do something special for him? Her heart sank when she saw his disappointment. "Most of all I was looking for a way to thank you for all you've done for me and Shiloh."

"You're welcome."

She lightened the mood with a self-mocking laugh. "You should probably taste one first."

He took a bite and let out a low moan of pleasure. "You're *very, very* welcome. There's only one way to make this cookie better."

"And what's that?" Melinda asked, playing along.

"A glass of milk."

Melinda smiled. "I can do that."

On impulse, she checked the date on the carton before she poured a glass. Three days. The milk and her two weeks were coming to an end. "You're early," she told Jeremy. "You weren't supposed to be here for another hour."

"We need to talk." He turned to Bobby. "Why don't you take your mom some cookies? There's something she wants to talk to you about, too."

"Can I go?" Shiloh asked.

Melinda was disappointed at Shiloh's eagerness to end their day together, but kept a smile in place.

"Don't take it personally," Jeremy said when they were gone. "That's not the way it was intended."

She was too raw to take it any other way. "What did you want to tell me?"

"It's over with Tess."

Her jaw dropped in surprise. "What happened?"

"Her lawyer found a buyer who was willing to negotiate a particularly lucrative employment contract. To sweeten the deal, he got them to offer a consulting agreement in exchange for a noncompetitive clause. Since all she really wanted from me was enough money to keep her business from failing, I became a moot point. Shiloh turned into a liability."

"So she's out of the picture . . ."

"Now and forever." Heidi stood on her hind legs and reached up to be held. He picked her up but she had no interest in snuggling, she wanted to find out what she was missing. He showed her the cookie and brought it close enough to sniff. She meowed as if he'd been trying to medicate her.

Jeremy glanced at Melinda with a look of shared frustration. "Don't take it—?"

"I know, don't take it personally."

Jeremy put Heidi on the stool. "I have a meeting with a client in Pacific Grove and I'm going to be late if I don't get out of here. I only stopped by to find out if you're going to be free tonight."

She sent him a puzzled look. Why wouldn't she be free? What did he think she was going to do? Pack up and leave without pleading her case one last time? "I don't understand."

He shifted from one foot to the other and back again. "A new restaurant opened a couple of months ago that I've been meaning to check out. I was thinking we could go together."

"Bobby and Shiloh were talking about getting fish and chips at Boehm's Seafood."

"I know."

He was asking her on a date? "What time?"

"Six thirty?"

"Do you want me to meet you there?"

"Why would I want you to do that?" he asked.

"Okay, I'll wait for you here." She watched him leave, wondering what was going on, but afraid to jinx their fledging effort at détente with too many questions. Instead she focused on deadheading the flowers along the walkway, using her thumbnail in place of clippers the way her mother had taught her.

She was halfway through one side when she looked up and saw Heidi standing in the doorway. The vet had warned Melinda about Heidi getting out, but she had absolutely no inter-est in taking even one step over the threshold.

Today it was the phone that had them both running in-side, Heidi for the sofa where she could burrow into a blanket, Melinda for the kitchen to answer the call of Vivaldi's *Four Seasons*. Five minutes later Melinda passionately wished she'd run in the opposite direction.

Chapter Thirty-Five

Melinda picked up Hwy 101 after leaving the beach house and headed north to Hwy 17. From there it was almost a direct route to the Mineta San José International Airport where she would catch a plane to Albuquerque, New Mexico, and what Randy Wyndham had described as a catastrophe of nuclear proportions. While he was prone to exaggeration, this time there was no doubt the panic was real and justified.

Three additional specialists were on their way from the home office, one to plug the security breach, one to look for the hacker who'd found a cyber door into the network, and one who was a recovery specialist who also worked to figure out why the network monitors hadn't communicated with the central server. Melinda was needed to make sure the pieces came together to create a whole and the company was up and operating again with minimal damage.

Cheryl had dropped Shiloh and Bobby off at the theater where they were meeting friends for a milk shake and fries before the movie started. Once they were inside with their phones in their pockets and on Silent, they would be impossible to reach without causing a scene at the theater.

Melinda called the agency that handled the travel arrangements for Wyndham and Parker, telling them it didn't matter what Randy had told them, she wanted the last direct flight to Albuquerque that night, not the first one. She would not leave California until she had a chance to tell her daughter where she was going and why. They arranged a flight that allowed her two hours and fifteen minutes to drive from Santa Cruz to the Mineta San José International Airport, arrange long-term parking, and go through prescreening. So what if it took a minor miracle to pull it off? Miracles weren't just for Christmas.

After trying and not reaching Shiloh, Melinda tried Jeremy. He didn't pick up either. She left a message saying how sorry she was to miss their dinner. And she was—more than she knew how to tell him. She considered saying something about rescheduling when she got back, but decided to let him take the lead, especially since he still hadn't told her whether or not she could stay.

She would stay, no matter what he said, but for Shiloh's sake she wanted it to be a peaceful transition. The thought brought a deep sigh. There were a hundred things she wanted where Jeremy and Shiloh were concerned. Little things like Shiloh teaching her what slang wouldn't make her sound ancient. And big things like the three of them becoming a real family, something Melinda was afraid to even contemplate.

She was in the middle of packing her carry-on when Cheryl rang the doorbell. "I came home as soon as I got your message," she said. "What's going on? Why do you have to leave?"

"There's a major meltdown at the company I was trying to handle through telecommuting." She'd instinctively known this wasn't a long-distance job but she'd so desperately wanted it to work that she'd convinced herself it would. "I have a minuscule window of opportunity to mitigate the damage."

Cheryl smiled. "You slipped into your business mode. Pretty impressive."

Melinda collapsed on the wingback chair and put her hands over her face. When she looked up again, she had tears in her eyes. "I don't want to go. My life is here now."

"Funny you should say that," Cheryl said. "Turns out I feel the same way. I don't want to move to Botswana either. I've never been there a week. Whatever made me think three years was a good idea?"

"So now what?" Melinda asked.

"We're going for six months."

"What about the nursery? I thought the sale was a done deal."

"Andrew discovered the buyer was already in negotiations

to tear down the greenhouses and sell the land. Which was in violation of the terms of the original contract so it was easy to have it set aside." She perched on the sofa arm and drew one leg up to cross it with the other. "Andrew was so happy when the whole thing fell apart that it finally got through to me he never wanted to sell."

"And Bobby?" Melinda asked.

"Couldn't be happier."

"What are you going to do with the house?"

She shrugged. "Either close it up the way they do the vacation homes on the cliff, or go with a renter."

"I'll take it," Melinda said without hesitation.

"It's yours. You can even stay in the blue room until we leave."

"Remind me about the blue room."

Cheryl tilted her head and gazed out the window, plainly trying to find a way to explain something that defied explanation. "There's magic in the blue room. Not the rabbit in the hat kind of magic, more the peace that comes with finding something precious that's been lost for a long, long time. I felt that way when Andrew and I found each other again."

"How long—?"

"A story for another time," Cheryl said. She glanced at her watch. "If I take off now, the movie should be over when I get there. I'll get back as fast as I can so you and Shiloh will have a chance to say good-bye."

"Are you sure you don't mind taking care of Heidi?" Heidi

raised her head at the sound of her name. She looked around, and seeing nothing, she put her head back down again and let out a contented sigh.

"Now that she's eating every three hours instead of two, she's easy. Besides, she's a great dog sitter for Coconut."

Melinda walked to the door with Cheryl giving her a long, loving hug. Why was it easier to hug a friend she'd had less than two weeks than it was her own daughter? "See you when you get back."

While she waited, Melinda finished packing and made a quick run to the pet store, buying enough supplies to last a month, while mentally refusing to believe they would be needed. It didn't matter that her normal assignment never lasted less than two months, she was convinced she would be back long before then.

With everything in place, including a conversation with Heidi reassuring her she wasn't being abandoned, Melinda took the last of the bags of litter out of her car and left them on the front porch of the cottage. She was on her way back to the beach house when she saw Cheryl's ancient green Volvo emerge from the eucalyptus grove and she moved to intercept them.

Shiloh had her door open before the car came to a complete stop. She ran into Melinda's arms. "Is my dad making you leave?" she said, her eyes red from crying. "I told him I don't want you to go. He promised he wouldn't make you."

Melinda took Shiloh's hand and led her into the house and out of the sun. At a loss for words, she brought Shiloh into her arms and rocked her gently, laying her cheek against the top of Shiloh's head, holding her the way she had held her own mother after her father's funeral.

Melinda put her hand under Shiloh's chin and tilted her head back until they locked gazes. "Your father had nothing to do with my leaving. It's my job. If I don't find a way to stop what's happening to one of my client's businesses, he's going to lose everything. He's counting on me and I can't let him down."

"My dad said you don't have to leave. He said he likes you." She could focus on only one thing and it had nothing to do with a company in New Mexico.

"I like him, too." Melinda smiled. "And I'm coming back. Nothing could keep me away."

"You can say that, but how do you know? All kinds of things could happen. My grandma said she was coming back. She promised."

"Oh, my sweet Shiloh." Melinda cupped her face with her hands and rained kisses on her forehead and cheeks. "I can see we should have talked about this a lot more than we did. What can I do to convince you that I'll be back as soon as I can?"

"Promise me."

"I can promise you a hundred times and you'll still have doubts." She had lived with broken promises, real and implied, her entire life.

"Take me with you," Shiloh said.

"I would if I could—in a heartbeat."

"But you can't because I'm sick and my dad wouldn't let you," she said in a singsong voice. She was angry and scared and Jeremy was an easy target.

"That's not fair, Shiloh. Your father has gone through hell this past month and the only reason is that he loves you. I've seen how he worries about you and how far he would go to protect you. If every kid had a father like him this would be a perfect world." She glanced at her watch. "We're going to finish this conversation when I get back. In the meantime, you're responsible for Heidi. Cheryl knows what to do and she will teach you everything you need to know."

"Really?" Shiloh said, her excitement overshadowing everything that had gone before. "Heidi's not going with you?"

Melinda closed her eyes and shook her head. Was Heidi a gift? Was finding her in the Dumpster an hour before trash pickup Daniel's way of telling Melinda it was time to move on with her life? No more grieving for what might have been, no more regrets.

Melinda put her chin on top of Shiloh's head and stared at Heidi. They locked gazes. There was no mistaking the understanding that passed between them. Melinda laughed. It was so like Daniel to have his message delivered by a half-starved, unfortunately unattractive kitten.

She'd read a dozen times in a dozen research papers that a cat can't smile. They were wrong.

Chapter Thirty-Six

Melinda missed Shiloh's birthday, but by working eighteen hours straight, over two weeks in a row, her team saved a business that employed seven hundred and fifty-eight people. That night Jeremy surprised her with a video showing Shiloh blowing out her candles and telling everyone that her wish had already come true. She got up, put her arms around Jeremy's neck, and thanked him for finding her mother.

"We're proud of you for what you do, Mom," she said with conviction. She blew a kiss at the camera.

The "Mom" left Melinda flushed and happy.

"Even if none of us understand what it is," Bobby chimed in.

"I do," Andrew protested.

Cheryl rolled her eyes. "No, you don't."

"One more voice to be heard from," Jeremy said. "And then we'll let you get back to work." He brought Heidi up to his phone. She spent a minute studying her reflection before she licked the screen.

"Eeeuw," Shiloh said. "Next thing you know she'll be sharing nose kisses." She laughed as if it was the funniest thing she'd ever said, came forward, and kissed Heidi's nose.

"Wait," Bobby demanded. "Don't hang up yet. Did you hear? We're not moving to Botswana."

"Yes we are, Bobby," Cheryl said. "But just for six months not three years."

She'd known since the day she left Santa Cruz but wanted to give Bobby the thrill of telling her himself. "That's great news, Bobby."

"I wish Shiloh could go, too."

"Maybe someday," Jeremy said.

"Why not now?"

"Cut it out, Bobby," Cheryl said.

Jeremy wiped the lens with his shirt and turned the phone in his direction. "In case Shiloh didn't tell you, for some unfathomable reason, Heidi has moved into the blue room at their house. Shiloh and I have tried taking her home every night but she was so unhappy we had to bring her back. When she's not whipping Coconut into shape, she's sitting on the windowsill watching the road."

"She's looking for you," Cheryl said. "I tried to convince

her it's only a matter of days now, but she's not interested in excuses."

As if on cue, Heidi looked into the camera and let out a plaintive cry. Jeremy gave everyone else a chance to say good-bye, too, and then went outside to film the sunset. "Don't worry about Heidi," he said softly. "She misses you—but then we all do."

There aren't enough words to express how much I miss all of you, Melinda said to the computer screen.

Jeremy went on. "I can't remember the last time I saw Shiloh this happy. You've made a huge difference in her life." He turned the phone in his direction and smiled. "And in mine."

The text ended with a final shot of the sunset with shouts of "Hurry home" coming from a chorus of voices.

A RIPPING SOUND filled the silence as Melinda ran the tape gun over the packing box she'd just filled. Box number six, the last of her belongings being shipped to California. Every-thing else, from kitchen appliances to lamps, was headed to a cat rescue thrift store in Minneapolis.

She sat back on her heels and reached for one of the ad-dress labels her assistant made for her. Two more days and she would be on her way to Kentucky. And then home to California.

First she had one last meeting with Randy and representa-tives from the firm's legal department to get through, a new employment contract to sign that gave her 5 percent of the company, 1 percent per year for five years, and full autonomy in the establishment of the new satellite office she would open in Palo Alto.

Then, finally, there was the "impromptu" party celebrating her team's success with XON. Somehow Melinda had managed to convince Randy that the bonus the company received from XON should be divided among the team members, her portion going to the people at the home office who had given up their weekends to help out. Reluctantly, fearing it would set a precedent, Randy agreed then basked in the glow of their appreciation.

Now that Randy no longer had to be told who Fred Stephens was or how important he was to the company, he was going to have a major meltdown when he discovered she'd asked Fred to join her in California, offering a housing stipend to cover the obscenely high real estate market in the Silicon Valley.

In the process of stacking the boxes she heard the elevator ding. The driver was early, but she was ready, as excited about starting her new life in California as if she were a landlocked oceanographer headed for the coast.

"Coming," she called as she flipped the lock. She opened the door and froze.

Jeremy stared at her for a long time before he said, "I'm not going to ask if it's okay, because I'll think of a reason it's not. I'm just going to do what I've wanted to do for a long time now." He cupped her face with his calloused hands and looked deeply into her eyes. "If you really don't want this to happen, tell me."

She touched her tongue to her lips in anticipation. The kiss was explosive, the fireworks rivaling those on the National Mall Fourth of July celebration. She wrapped her arms around his neck and came up on her toes. "I wouldn't mind if you did that again."

His answering smile was wonderfully intimate. "I have a feeling this is going to be—"

"Later," she said. "For now, just do it again."

He did.

Melinda closed her eyes and drifted into a world that beckoned with beautiful promise. After the sorrow and heartache that had gone before, she had found her way home again.

"I love you," she said. "From the first day in the hospital when I saw how much you loved Shiloh. It's okay if she comes first. I could never expect you to love me—"

"But I do. More than I know how to tell you." He kissed her again . . . and again.

It seemed a strange time for tears but that didn't stop them. One day she would tell Jeremy how he had healed her broken heart. She would take him to Kentucky and show him her parents' tree and Daniel's grave. It was the only way she knew how to express the loss she'd lived through every day before he and Shiloh came back into her life.

One story she would save for Shiloh. One that was tinged with a touch of magic that required a child's belief in such things. Melinda had finally come to understand the meaning of the tapestry her father told her the Fates had woven for her. The answer was there all along, tucked into gossamer folds of silver and brown and black. Six seemingly unconnected letters.

Her future.

JEREMY

About the author

Read on . . .

Insights,
Interviews
& More . . .

Meet Georgia Bockoven

John Bockoven

GEORGIA BOCKOVEN is an award-winning author who began writing fiction after a successful career as a freelance journalist and photographer. Her books have sold more than three million copies worldwide. The mother of two, she resides in Northern California with her husband, John. ∽

More from Georgia Bockoven

For more books by
Georgia Bockoven
check out

THE COTTAGE NEXT DOOR

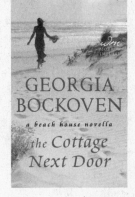

In this delightful novella, Georgia Bockoven brings readers back to the beloved beach house and the charming cottage next door . . .

What should have been the best day in Diana Wagnor's twenty-nine years easily turns into the worst when her job is downsized, she discovers her fiancé in bed with her best friend, and she watches her cherished grandmother's house burn to the ground.

Clearly it's time to start over and get out of Topeka, Kansas, where she's spent her whole life. But what should she do? And how can she ever trust herself in another relationship when her one indisputable skill seems to be picking the wrong man?

Diana finds her answers at the cottage next door to the beach house, with the help of a tall, sculptured, soft-spoken Californian, and a heart-shaped piece of sea glass. ▶

3

More from Georgia Bockoven *(continued)*

RETURN TO THE BEACH HOUSE

Over the course of one year, in a charming cottage by the sea, eight people will discover love and remembrance, reconciliation and reunion, beginnings and endings in this unforgettable sequel to Georgia Bockoven's The Beach House *and* Another Summer.

Alison arrives at the beach house in June to spend a month with her restless grandson before he leaves for his first year of college. More than a decade earlier, Alison lost her beloved husband, and has faced life alone ever since. Now she discovers a new life and a possible new love.

August brings together four college friends facing a milestone. During summer's final days, they share laughter, tears, and love—revealing long-held secrets and creating new and even more powerful bonds.

World-class wildlife photographer Matthew and award-winning war photographer Lindsey arrive at the beach house in January, each harboring the very real fear that it will mark the end of their decade-long love affair. Alone in the house's warm peace, they are forced to truly look at who they are and what they want, discovering surprising truths that will change their lives forever.

What's in the past is over and done with . . . or is it?

Sixteen years ago Carly Hargrove made a decision that would irrevocably alter her life. With little comprehension of the life-long consequences of her actions, she trades her own future happiness to protect the man she's loved since kindergarten, David Montgomery.

With an ocean separating them, Carly builds a life for herself without David. She's the mother of three, lives in a beautiful house, and is married to a man who comes home every night— even if most of those nights he drinks too much. What more could she want?

Her answer arrives on a cold fall day when David shows up at her door. In town for his father's funeral, he has come to see Carly one last time, hoping to rid himself of the anger that still consumes him.

Instead, he is drawn into a web of secrets that rekindles the fierce need he once felt to protect Carly. He becomes caught up in her life in a way he never could have imagined—a way that will bind him to her forever. ▶

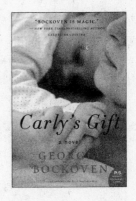

THINGS REMEMBERED

To face the future, a woman must let go of the past. . . .

Returning to her childhood home in the golden hills of Northern California means regret and pain for Karla Esterbrook. Yet she can't refuse when her ailing grandmother, Anna, asks Karla to help settle her affairs. After all, Anna raised Karla and her younger sisters after their parents' deaths twenty years earlier. But from the beginning a powerful clash of wills has separated Karla and her grandmother, leaving them both bitter and angry.

Little does Karla know that a very determined Anna will do everything in her power to bridge the chasm between them. But can the wounds of the past truly be healed? For Karla, opening her heart could lead to more hurt—or perhaps to reconciliation . . . and to a love the likes of which she has never known.

THE YEAR EVERYTHING CHANGED

As Jessie Patrick Reed's attorney, I'm writing to you on behalf of your father, Jessie Patrick Reed. I regret to inform you that Mr. Reed is dying. He has expressed a desire to see you. . . .

Elizabeth, even though sustained by a loving family, has suffered much from her father's seeming abandonment, and for years has protected herself with a deep-seated anger that she hides from everyone.

Ginger, in love with a married man, will be forced to reevaluate every relationship she's ever had and will reach stunning conclusions that will change her life forever.

Rachel learns of her father's existence the same day she finds out that her husband of ten years has had an affair. She will receive the understanding and support she needs to survive from an unlikely and surprising source.

Christine is a young filmmaker, barely out of college, who now must decide if her few precious memories of a man she believed to be long dead are enough to give him a second chance.

Four sisters who never knew the others existed will find strength, love, and answers in the most unexpected places in . . . *The Year Everything Changed.* ▶

More from Georgia Bockoven *(continued)*

ANOTHER SUMMER

Weaving together love and laughter, heartache and hope, promise and passion, Another Summer *returns to the world of the Beach House, with new stories entwined in a powerful emotional journey.*

A twentieth high school reunion reunites lovers who must learn to trust again. Teenagers from opposite worlds discover that having a chip on their shoulder only makes it harder to get through doors. An ambitious corporate attorney finds herself falling for the man she has vowed to destroy in the courtroom. A young family, reeling from a devastating loss, meets a mysterious older couple and a half-starved stray cat that will guide them back to each other.

None of these people will leave the beach house the same as they were before. . . .

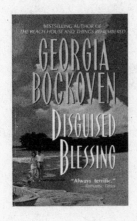

After years of being alone, Catherine Miller thinks she's finally found happiness. Engaged to an adoring, successful executive, she lives in a luxurious house, and her beautiful fifteen-year-old daughter, Linda, is on the brink of college and adulthood. Then, Catherine's rose-colored world is shattered. Her daughter is burned terribly in a freak accident, and just when Catherine needs him most, her fiancé abandons her. Now Catherine must call on every ounce of courage and strength she has to help her beloved daughter recover. Fortunately, she's got help in fire captain Rick Sawyer, an expert burn counselor. Ruggedly handsome, appealingly down-to-earth, Rick is like no man Catherine has ever met. But Catherine made the wrong choice before. How can she trust her emotions—especially when it's not just her heart at stake but her daughter's life, too?

In the tradition of Barbara Delinsky comes this poignant, moving story of the bonds of family, the strength of love, and the courage to dare. ▸

THE BEACH HOUSE

The beach house is a peaceful haven, a place to escape everyday problems. Here, three families find their feelings intensified and their lives transformed each summer.

When thirty-year-old Julia, mourning the death of her husband, decides to sell the Santa Cruz beach house they owned together, she sets in motion a final summer that will change the lives of all the families who rent it year after year. Teenaged Chris discovers the bittersweet joy of first love. Maggie and Joe, married sixty-five years, courageously face a separation that even their devotion cannot prevent. The married woman Peter yearns for suddenly comes within his reach. And Julia ultimately finds the strength to rebuild her life—something she once thought impossible.

With equal measures of heartbreak and happiness, bestselling author Georgia Bockoven's unforgettable novel tells of the beauty of life and the power of love, and speaks to every woman who has ever clung to a child or loved a man. ∽